FURY'S DEATH

By the Author

Fury's Bridge

Fury's Choice

Fury's Death

Visit us at www.boldstrokesbooks.com

FURY'S DEATH

by

Brey Willows

2018

FURY'S DEATH

ISBN 13: 978-1-63555-063-4

This Trade Paperback Original Is Published By
Bold Strokes Books, Inc.
P.O. Box 249
Valley Falls, NY 12185

First Edition: March 2018

Credits
Editor: Cindy Cresap
Production Design: Stacia Seaman
Cover Design by Sheri (graphicartist2020@hotmail.com)

Acknowledgments

Thanks so much to everyone involved in the creation of books at BSB. It's a road with a million starts and stops, and I appreciate every person who takes the time to make the book better. Thank you in particular to Rad and Sandy for taking a chance on this series, and to Cindy Cresap who always makes my work better and teaches me something new.

And as always, thanks to my wife, who never minds when we have to take a "research trip" at the drop of a hat. Rome was fabulous, love. Thanks for being my writing and travel buddy.

For Robyn, who keeps me writing and inspires me constantly.

Chapter One

Dani Morana knelt beside the bodies and gently closed their eyes. She could feel their souls waiting, confused by the sudden shift from life to death. In the distance were the sounds of crumbling concrete and the screams of those she'd likely be with soon. She rested her hands over their foreheads and called their souls to her. People thought the light they saw when they died was the road to the afterlife, but in fact, it was Dani's touch, lighting the way to her temporary care. Death waited for no one but stopped for everyone.

She felt the children's small souls leave the shells of their bodies, the glow of innocence dim but still present. They'd been killed instantly, which meant suffering and worry hadn't had time to darken their spirits. Their souls felt like winter silk in her hands, and she placed them carefully in her black bag. When she took them to the river where they'd cross into their afterlife, they'd regain some form, much like that they had in life. But for now, in transit, they could rest as the beautiful celestial elements they were.

She stood and brushed the dirt from her jeans as she looked around. In the distance, she saw all three of the fury sisters standing over a group of cowering, cowardly men. Dani knew they were the ones who had come into the newly built school and opened fire on the women and children trying to get an education. Alec's black mist and ebony snakes flowed from her arms to the man at her feet, while Tisera's snakes slid from her head and flew at the man below her, her red mist pushing into his ears and eyes.

And then there was Megara. Beautiful, irrepressible Meg. Whenever she was around, Dani couldn't take her eyes off her.

Especially as she was now, with her sunset red wings spread wide, her deep red hair flowing around her, her snakes crawling out of her feathers, and her mist flowing from her hands. Unlike her sisters' mists, Meg's wasn't just one color. It was like a bruised sunset allowed to flow from her palms, with grays, oranges, and pinks intertwining to create a mesmerizing effect.

When that beautiful multicolor mist enveloped the man at her feet, he began to scream. Pleading was clear in any language, but the three sisters were immune to it. Dani looked at the bodies around her and felt no sympathy for the men who had created such carnage, who had destroyed those who couldn't fight back rather than fight against those who were actually a threat.

"You done?" Alec stepped carefully over bodies and came to Dani's side.

"I've got them all, thanks. Though it sounds like there may end up being a few more soon." She nodded at the men writhing on the ground. "They won't do this again?"

Alec shook her head. "Not with what we've put in their heads. You know we each punish a different aspect. Because we could see into their minds, we knew who the leader was and who had followed. We punished accordingly, and until they take their own lives, they'll live with the daily horror of what they've done." Alec touched her arm lightly. "Still have trouble with it?"

Dani tilted her head in acknowledgment. "Sorry. It's just so awful. Death would be faster, and they wouldn't be around to do any more harm."

"That's the problem." Meg walked up, still letting her snakes slide back into place among her feathers. "These bastards don't deserve an easy death. They have to understand what they've done. Especially if they believe in some kind of reincarnation. If they come back, hopefully they'll have learned a lesson from this go-around."

Tis wrapped her arm around Meg's shoulders. "And if they don't come back, they'll have started learning a lesson that will hopefully continue in whatever afterlife they believe in." Tis rolled her neck to release tension. "Let's get out of here."

Dani opened the portal to her network of time roads and they got into her yellow Mustang convertible to make their way back to

California via the Deadlands. There were clusters of houses here and there, along with shops and bars. Dani loved the deep, profound stillness that enveloped her special territory that existed between time and space, the province of Death and those who worked for her. There was laughter and desire, fear and despair, just like there was anywhere else. But there was also a sense of respect and solemnity that pervaded all of Dani's world. People wouldn't fear Death quite as much if they knew she considered it an honor to carry their souls to the next stage of their journeys.

Time didn't exist in Dani's sector, and they were back at Afterlife, Inc. headquarters faster than anyone else would have been able to travel.

Alec grinned at her. "That's a definite benefit of traveling with you. I wish we had access to your mode of transport."

Tis shook out her wings. "Not me. No offense, Dani, but it's too dark in there. I feel like my wings would hit walls if I stretched them too wide."

"I like it. It feels sensual. Like people could be having really intense sex in every corner." Meg bumped Dani's hip with her own. "I bet you've had some crazy times in there."

Dani laughed and tried not to blush, but Meg always made her feel shy. "You'd be surprised."

They headed inside and went straight to Zed's office. *Zed and Kera's office.* Dani was still getting used to someone working not just for Zed, but almost as his boss. In her position as Death, she was used to change, perhaps more than any other person in the building. But gods and humans working together was a new one, and she was still wondering how it would turn out in the end.

Kera looked up when they walked in, and although she greeted them all, it was clear her attention was reserved for Tis, who quickly moved to her side and kissed her deeply. Their devotion to one another was moving and made a part of Dani ache.

"So? What was that all about?" Zed looked up from his paperwork and rolled his eyes at Kera and Tis, still kissing.

"Dumbasses, as usual." Meg flopped into a chair and closed her eyes. "Men thinking they could strengthen their cause by killing women and children."

"And their god?"

"Allah, technically. But when we looked into their minds, there wasn't a genuine religious component. They weren't zealots, just misogynists."

Kera broke off the kiss but kept her arm around Tis's waist. "Soul count?"

Dani rested her hand on her bag. "Sixty-two."

"Can you write up a report to Allah, please? Let him know who these guys were and the soul count involved. The more information he has at hand, the easier his job will be."

"Sure." Dani stood and put her bag on like a backpack. "I'm going to head out to deliver these. Need anything else?"

"Can you have your crew send through some reports of where they've gone and how many they've picked up by the end of the week? I'd like to get a sense of where we need to send the most help next, and body counts are a good indication."

"The gods can tell you that." Zed glared at Kera, and everyone in the office braced themselves.

Since the inception of combining Kera's company, GRADE, with Afterlife, she and Zed had had plenty of arguments, one of which had sent Kera's hair sizzling when Zed had let loose a lightning bolt. She'd thrown a chair at him in return, and fortunately, Tis and Alec had stepped in to demand a ceasefire. But overall, it seemed to be working. Gods were showing up where they were needed most and providing assistance with actual work. Farming was getting better, schools were being built, and to the extent they could, they were even helping with weather changes so areas depressed by drought were getting more regular, low-level bursts of rain. The planet did seem to be changing, slowly, for the better.

"They can tell me that a lot of people died. They can't always tell me why, or who did it, or exactly how many were killed, which means a change in the overall population." Kera glared back at him and swatted away Tis's feathers, which were wrapping around her more tightly. "Facts and numbers work better than general concepts, old man."

He stood, towering over them all. "What did you call me?"

Kera stepped into his personal space, craning her neck to look up at him.

"Okay. Well, I'm going to go now," Dani said. "I'll make sure my crew get those reports to you. Always nice to see you all." She backed toward the door and waved.

And just like that, the tension filling the room dissipated, and Kera and Zed began to laugh. "Don't take off on our account, Dani. This is just the way we do things." Zed clapped a hand on Kera's shoulder and smiled at Dani. "Death never has anything to fear anyway."

"She doesn't like confrontation." Meg yawned. "Big bad Death who only deals with people when they can't talk back."

Dani shrugged, embarrassed at how accurate Meg's assessment was. But then, she'd been friends with the fury sisters for centuries, and they knew her better than anyone. "Yeah. That's me. See you all later."

She headed down to her car, a pit in her stomach at the thought of Meg dismissing her so lightly. Although the one thing she loved about Meg was her forthrightness and the fact that she didn't play games, her directness could also be a pillow wrapped in barbed wire.

She fired up the Mustang, opened the portal to the road to the underworld, and floored it. She loved the wind in her hair and the feeling of home as she entered the area where she alone knew every in and out, every direction and need, of the world that was hers alone. The Mustang was her one concession to color in her usually gray-toned world. It felt extravagant, loud, and as though she could be someone more like that, and less like…well, herself.

She took the left fork into the Islamic sector. When she arrived at Allah's palace she grabbed her bag and headed to the basement. For centuries, Islamic belief held that heaven and hell were only places people would go once Judgment Day had happened. But Allah had been rebranding and altering his texts, as had all the major gods, and now he had an underworld waiting room as well, a kind of Limbo. Those who were worthy would, one day, ascend to heaven. Those who weren't, however, would immediately descend to hell, one based closely on the Christian version. He'd decided there wasn't much point in keeping the sinners around longer than necessary. Those waiting for heaven would stay here in the palace and surrounding lands. It was like the Catholics' purgatory but with nicer gardens and spicy food.

She took her bag to the sorting room, where several of Allah's angels were busy dividing souls. She handed it over, aware as ever when the person taking it from her made sure to avoid any contact. Even god's angels were wary of Death.

That chore done, she decided to head out onto the water. She stopped by her place, grabbed her board, threw on a wetsuit, and drove to Zuma. The waves this time of day were perfect, and she loved the way the sun glinted off the water. She parked the Mustang at the edge of the lot and pulled her Special T longboard from the back. The smooth wood was cool under her hands, and as always, she felt herself relax as she carried it out to the water, the sand cold under her feet. Winter swells were often best here, but she had this section to herself thanks to the frigid water. She dropped the board into the waves and slid in behind it. She grabbed the rails and pulled herself on. Though she'd never admit it to anyone, she'd always thought the anticipation of grabbing a perfect wave was even better than the anticipation of sex.

A few waves came toward her, too close together, and she executed some quick turtle rolls to bow under them. She was naturally cold, so the water temperature didn't bother her. The ocean called to her like nowhere else on earth. The vast array of life beneath her always took her breath away. She'd skied, she'd skydived, she'd bungee-jumped. Nothing compared to the power and serenity of surfing. Life below her, the tides surging to and fro under her board, the skill to ride the blue-green tunnels and even the power of the waves as they crashed down on her body…it was as perfectly alive as she could ever get. Though lately she'd been dealing with changes she wasn't prepared to think about, making life awkward in new ways.

As she paddled out in the dark water, she let her mind wander. She thought about Tis's comment about her domain feeling small and about Meg's joke about it being sensual. Any time Meg teased Dani about sex, she had no idea how to respond. Sure, she'd had plenty of sex in the Deadlands, as it had been called for ages. She'd had her share of relationships and enjoyed a goddess or two. But nothing ever lasted. Not a lot of people wanted to hang out with Death. Except the furies.

A perfect swell formed, and Dani turned to paddle. She moved fast, loving the way the board responded under her, the way she flew with the water. She popped up, put her back foot on the traction pad, and settled into stance. The waves were pulling hard right, and she focused ahead on the tunnel. As she swept through it, finally letting it collapse over her, she put everything else out of her mind. Right now, all she had to be was herself. No job, no friends, no crushes, no anomalies. Just Dani and the ocean, as one.

Chapter Two

Meg stretched her wings and stood on her tiptoes to stretch her legs as well. She looked at the various bodies in her bed and felt her clit twitch in response. After all the death and destruction of the mass shooting, she'd needed a release, the kind only a lot of sweaty, fun sex could provide. She'd called a few of her regular playmates, who hadn't hesitated to join her. Freya's long blond braids rested on Pan's dark, muscled stomach. Philotes and Hathor slept in one another's embrace, dark intertwined with light. It had been a good night, full of moans, laughter, and pleasure. Meg's body ached pleasantly from hours of exertion and sexual acrobatics.

She made her way to the kitchen after grabbing her robe and put on a pot of coffee. When everyone woke, they'd all have to get back to work, but for now, Meg enjoyed the feeling of having a full house of people who'd enjoyed sex the way Meg did, unreserved and without boundaries.

"That smells good." Pan came into the kitchen, his hooves echoing on the slate flooring.

Meg boosted herself on the counter and sipped from her mug. "Help yourself."

He poured himself a cup and made a sound of appreciation after his first sip. "This is one thing humans have gotten right."

Meg nodded but didn't say anything. The morning after was always special for her, a time when the closeness of the night before hadn't been washed away by the realities of the day yet.

They drank in companionable silence until Pan said, "You know I always love being included in your dirty get-togethers, Meg, but can I ask you something?"

She looked at him curiously.

"Don't you get tired of the parties? Of sex without strings?"

She scoffed. "You're one to talk, god of sex."

He grinned. "I wasn't saying *I* was tired of it. I'm a huge fucking fan. But you're not me. You're not a sex god at all, though you sure as hell act like one in the sack." He wiggled his eyebrows, and she laughed. "Seriously, though. Have you ever been in a long-term relationship, had someone to come home to?"

"I've had my share. Every couple of centuries I think I'll give monogamy a try and stick with someone for a while. But familiarity kills passion, don't you think? Seeing someone every day eventually means you get so comfortable with them you stop trying, and then before you know it, you've got pets you pay more attention to than one another, and you've forgotten what your lover actually looks like. Then you have to go through some big breakup and move your crap out of their place, and you spend ages thinking of them when you'd stopped thinking of them when they were right beside you. I'm all for drama, but that sort isn't what I'm interested in." She motioned toward the bedroom. "And besides, can you imagine limiting yourself to a single body for the rest of your existence? Think what you'd miss out on."

He laughed and tugged on a feather. "Spoken like a sex goddess. Maybe you could find someone who wouldn't mind enjoying these parties with you. Then you'd get the best of both worlds."

Meg poured another mug of coffee and handed it to Freya, who stumbled in with her eyes still mostly closed. "I've had that situation once or twice too. And it was crazy fun, but jealousy and insecurity aren't emotions reserved for humans. It still gets messy."

Freya opened one eye and looked at the two of them. "I say fuck until your legs give out, then switch positions and find someone else to jump in. Monogamy is for people who don't have imagination."

Pan laughed and stomped his hoof. "Well said, Nordic hot stuff. I was just saying Meg might want something more."

Freya pushed her chest out proudly. "How could she want more than this?"

Meg tweaked Freya's nipple. "Exactly what I'm saying."

Pan retrieved his shirt from the back of the couch and slid it on. "Okay, okay. I give in." He blew Meg a kiss and opened the front door. "I'd better get to work. Fuck like the goddesses you are."

He left, and Freya turned to Meg. "Let's go wake the other two. There's nothing like morning sex before returning to Valhalla to welcome dead warriors home."

Meg wrapped her legs around Freya's waist, and Freya carried her back to the bedroom. She pushed aside thoughts of Pan's words and focused on the soft bodies beside her.

❖

Meg flipped channels aimlessly, her attention wandering. Freya had been right—morning sex sent the day down just the right path, and Hathor and Philotes had been more than welcoming when Freya and Meg had slid in beside them.

Now, though, alone in the quiet of her home, she was drawn back to her conversation with Pan. What she'd said was true. She'd been in relationships before, and for a while, they'd been great. But when you lived for thousands of years, there was no denying it was hard to be with just one person. There was such variety out there. So many types of people, so many bodies, so many appetites and desires. Meg had tasted many and hated being told she couldn't do what she wanted to, when she wanted to do it.

The phone rang, and she jumped to grab it, glad for a distraction.

"Hey. Can you come down to the office? We need your fashion sense," Tis asked.

Meg smiled and skipped to her room to get dressed. "Tis, you know I can't resist a request like that. What's up?"

Tis sounded distracted. "You know how we discussed rebranding with everyone? The underworld gods were particularly interested, seeing as how they're the ones who have the most difficulty getting genuine followers. The courses Jesus is running are great, but a lot of people need more personal advice, and obviously, Jesus is busy running his own lines. Azrael's been bugging me for my opinion on stuff—"

"And you totally don't have the time for that. Not to mention you've got the fashion sense of a black crayon. No problem. I'll be there in ten."

Meg dressed quickly, her thoughts whirling. Ever since Alec had been designated as the one to work with the Bridge, and Tis had taken on the role of legal consultant at Afterlife, Meg had felt like the loose end sister. She knew she wasn't all that smart, and she wasn't exactly reliable. It was good to be seen as useful for a minute, even if it wasn't for saving the world.

She dressed in her favorite jeans and low-cut T-shirt and headed to the office. Living on the Afterlife campus meant she could easily walk to work, without the hassle of humans or having to drive. She took the stairs down to the basement level, where the underworld gods' offices started. Hades was on minus one, Azrael on minus two, and so on. Although they didn't have the large numbers of staff the other gods did, they still liked to have their own spaces, something Meg understood completely. She knocked on Azrael's door.

"Come in." Azrael looked up from his work and smiled when he saw her. "Excellent! Thanks for coming, Megara. You're looking stunning, as always." He kissed her cheek and squeezed her butt at the same time.

She shoved him away. "Always the groper. I can't believe no one has ripped your hands off yet. And why don't you come to my parties anymore?"

"Who has time to play when we're supposed to be out among the humans? And I'll have you know, plenty of people like my hands on them, thank you very much."

"Or they just don't want to chance offending you." She picked up a shirt folded neatly on the chair. "Is this what you're thinking?"

"I think so. Hell, I don't know. I like Tisera's idea about rebranding and rethinking what we offer the humans. I mean, now that the shiny gods can market themselves, it makes sense for us to do it as well. Who wants to follow a god that offers just death and misery, right? So I'm doing a full overhaul of Hell. Obviously, I still have to have the punishment element, I mean, that's my thing, right? But how cool would it be to offer more than that?"

Meg waved the shirt at him. "And you think horrible rugby shirts are the way to signal that?"

He shrugged. "Like I said, I don't know."

She thought for a second. "Show me around. Show me what changes you're making to Hell. That might give me some idea on where you stand."

He jumped up and opened the door. "Awesome. You'll be the first to see it."

They made their way down the hall, past offices full of demons and other creatures who were working on nightmare software and porn sites, easy ways to get to humans. When one office seemed to have lots of social media sites on screens, she looked at Az questioningly.

"Pride, greed, lust, envy, gluttony, wrath, and sloth. Social media sites work on every level of the seven deadly sins, all in one place. It's a fabulous way to watch humans come to our side without even knowing they're doing it." He opened the door at the end of the hallway marked "Staff Only."

The acrid scent of burning coal assaulted her instantly. "Geez, Az. I think you could start by containing that smell."

He sniffed and looked slightly offended. "I've always loved that smell."

"Yeah, well, if you want the fires of hell to be more welcoming, you're going to have to do away with the burning flesh candle scents."

He held up a finger, dashed back through the door to the offices, and quickly returned with a notepad and pen. "Okay. Let's go."

She laughed. "Seriously?"

He looked back at her, solemn. "Seriously. This isn't some minor thing, and I'm determined to do it right. You're the first person to come down here and give me the time of day. Yeah, I'm going to listen."

Meg realized just how out of the loop the underworld gods often were. And why they'd gotten out of hand sometimes. She took Az's arm. "Lead on."

They made their way down floor by floor, with Azrael showing her the changes he was making on each level, which were then divided again. "See, this is the second circle, reserved for sins of lust. I'm adding new furniture, some nicer lighting, and even giving it a fresh lick of paint. That will be for the ones whose lust sins aren't as bad as some of the others, who still get the whole fiery punishment business."

Meg stopped him and looked around. "But the nicer area is still a punishment area?"

He stared at her. "Well, yeah."

She scanned the area and thought of the world as it was. "Think about what Tis said. What if you offer more than punishment?" She motioned at the area being redone. "What if that section was for the believers who were basically good people, but because of the system setup couldn't go to heaven because they enjoyed this particular sin too much? Why punish them for enjoying themselves in this one area, when they didn't actually hurt anyone else?" She grinned and grabbed Az's butt the way he'd grabbed hers earlier. "Why not make this a destination for the humans who just really, really like sex? Let them enjoy that aspect of life down here. The fact that the rest of their existence will be all about sex will make it hellish, eventually. And you can still reserve the other section for people who have used sex as a weapon."

Azrael leaned on the railing and stared down at the construction area, thinking. "So, it's still a sin, and they still end up here. But now there's not as much fear attached, and the sin itself has degrees attached to it. But if someone wants to spend their eternity having all kinds of dirty sex, then they just might pray to come my way." He turned to her, and his excitement was palpable. "I love it." He grabbed her hand and pulled her to the elevator. "Let's do this with the other sections too!"

They made their way through each of the nine levels, discussing what the area was already used for, and how to alter it so that humans with that particular vice would actually want to go to hell to live in that section. Meg made suggestions about what to add, possible ways to market it, and even new ways to distinguish the area on a visual level. Az wrote as fast as he could, and before they left each section he made an appointment with the manager of that area to come see him to discuss the changes.

They got into the elevator to head back to the offices, and Az vibrated with excitement. "I feel like I've just had completely satisfying sex with a hundred people. I can't wait to get started." The elevator stopped at Limbo for someone to get on.

The door opened to show Dani waiting, looking as though she was considering the nature of the universe. Meg's breath caught as it always did when she saw her, though she made sure to never let it show.

"Meg. Az. This is a nice surprise." Dani got in and shook Az's hand.

Meg leaned over to kiss Dani's cheek and enjoyed the soft sweetness she always felt radiating off her. "What are you up to?"

"Dropping some souls off at Limbo receiving. What are you two doing?"

Az drew them both into an exuberant hug, and Meg nearly laughed out loud at how bewildered Dani looked.

"Meg has just helped me completely rethink my rebranding. This place is going to be heaving with people who actually *want* to come here. I can't wait."

"Wow. Hell as a religious destination. That's something." Dani smiled.

They walked back to Az's office, and Meg felt almost light-headed at how excited he was to implement some of her ideas.

He turned to her at the door. "You know, Meg, there are a lot of departments who could use your help. The shiny gods are all out helping their people farm and have babies and shit, and they're rebranding as they go. But the rest of us down here, we don't have that luxury. We have to do things differently, and the way you see things can really help."

Meg laughed. "Yeah, well, if they want my help, tell them to give me a call. In the meantime, get rid of those god-awful rugby shirts. Use your clothing to reflect each level and then sell it to those market bases."

Az wrote down what Meg said and then opened the door to his office. "Hate to use you and leave you, but you've given me a shit ton of things to do. Can I call you if I need more input?"

The god of Hell is asking permission to call me. That's a first. "Of course. Whenever."

She and Dani took the elevator back up to the Afterlife foyer, and Meg found herself wishing she had more time with her. The constantly present emotions that whirled inside her always calmed when Dani was around. There was also something different about Dani, some kind of energy thing, but she wasn't sure what it was and didn't want to bring it up until she knew what she was talking about.

"Want to grab lunch?" Dani asked, looking at her feet.

"I'm starving. Here or off campus?"

"You're always starving." She looked indecisive for a moment before she said, "What if we got Thai and took it back to my place?"

Meg tried not to let her surprise show. In all the centuries she'd known Dani, she'd never seen where she lived. The thought of getting to see something more personal about her made her pulse speed up. "Are you kidding? Yeah! Let's do it."

Dani led the way out to her Mustang, and Meg skipped along beside her, excited to be spending time with her, though she wasn't about to analyze why. Too many questions about life led to changes she wasn't about to make.

CHAPTER THREE

D is lit another match and let it burn to her fingertips before flinging it into the ocean below her balcony. Although she was greatly enjoying her time among the humans, she was finding gravity more irritating than she'd remembered it being. Her body was heavy and sluggish. Still, she'd put up with it for the trade-off of being in power once again. She was also growing fond of the body she was in. For a human flesh sack, it was nicely molded, with everything high and tight and bits and parts that gave a wealth of pleasure when touched the right way. It wasn't the birth of a universe, but it was nice.

"What are you thinking?"

She turned to look at her lover. His black hawk eyes watched her constantly, his pointed beak razor sharp. Horus was one of the true ancients, and although he and a few of the other Egyptian gods remained, they did so only because, like the Greek and Roman gods, there was so much statuary and continued research on them. Their powers, however, had faded greatly. Once, Chaos and the Egyptian gods had been close, but when times had changed and the furies had come to being, that relationship had died away like the dead stars she'd come to rule over. As soon as he'd come back to power and heard she was on earth once more, he'd made his way to her.

She crawled back into bed beside him and drew her nail down the center of his muscled stomach. "I always loved that the Egyptian gods understood my place on this strange little planet."

"Without disorder, there can be no order."

"You'd think the rest would understand that by now." She liked the way his beak shone in the dim light of the darkened room, like a deadly weapon she wanted to taste.

"What will you do next?"

Dis thought of the calls that had brought her back, the mental anguish many humans experienced when faced with their gods. Their blobby gray matter, surrounded by thick bone and prone to injury at the slightest provocation, just wasn't capable of being close to a deity of any kind. Even some who had started out strong had eventually turned to mush. And it was their confusion and mental destruction that had called Chaos to Earth. When she was the last person they understood, their very essences disintegrated, leaving nothing but cosmic strings in their heads and emptiness in their bodies. Their souls turned to dust, leaving nothing for Death to claim, no matter what religion they believed in.

"They've called me here, but it's not enough. It's an adapt or die situation right now. Those who can't handle it call to me. I give them a little nudge, and they do the most destructive, chaotic thing they can think of before they implode. It's good, but that will end when the weak are weeded out. I won't give the furies another chance to send me back to the void. The question is how to make the next stage of this era mine."

"Prey."

Dis looked at him, confused. "What do you mean?"

"When being chased, prey know nothing but fear. The weak are always on guard against the strong, knowing they'll be taken down at some point. Fear is what drives humans to call for you. Create fear among your prey, and they'll stampede to their deaths. Even the strong ones can be forced to kneel by fear."

She thought about it and knew he was right. "The weakest are already mine. I need to go after those who aren't quite as weak. Those who are unsure. If I can get them to spread doubt amongst themselves, which creates more fear, I'll have dominion over the universe and the humans." She leaned down and gave Horus a kiss on his beak. "I've missed you."

He wrapped his arms around her and flipped her on her back. "And I, you. When you have re-created this world in your image, we will step in to restore order. But until then, we will do all we can to help you bring the world to its knees."

Dis sighed and surrendered to the moment. *Bring the world to its knees. I like the sound of that.*

❖

Covertly, Dani watched as Meg wandered through the house picking up photos and looking at books. Her fingertips trailed along furniture and shelves, and Dani swallowed at the thought of her doing the same over Dani's body. She forced the thoughts from her head and started dishing up the food. "Glad you had the time to do this."

Meg came over and grabbed an eggroll. "Me too. What with the Humanity First stuff and the crap Dis is causing, it seems like we're almost back to the way things were before the gods came out."

Dani handed Meg her plate, and they sat at opposite ends of Dani's huge sofa. "I know it might feel that way, but I can tell you that the numbers don't back it up. War deaths are down by about ninety percent, and let me tell you, that's what has kept me and my crew busy since humans started walking on two legs."

"Really? I guess with everything else going on, I hadn't really noticed."

"Well, war isn't your purview anyway, is it? You take out some of the specific assholes, but you tend to leave politics and military alone. Right?" Dani hesitated, not wanting to sound too sure of herself and step on Meg's toes.

"For the most part, yeah." Meg slurped up a noodle, and they laughed when she got sauce on her nose. "Like the gods, there are areas we don't touch. I mean, melting someone's brain who was following orders in the military doesn't seem just. But going after the guys at the top who order shit done doesn't seem entirely just either, because they haven't pulled the trigger. Too messy."

Dani enjoyed the feeling of having Meg in her house while they ate silently together.

Finally, Meg said, "Why haven't I been here before? All of a sudden, I feel like I've been some kind of horrifically negligent friend. Like, when you invite someone out but they never accept, so you stop inviting them. Is that what happened?"

Dani shook her head. "Not at all." She stopped, trying to find the words to express herself. It had been years since she'd had a private conversation like this. "You're the first non-death person I've had here in a very, very long time."

"Why?" Meg ate without paying attention, her full focus on Dani.

Dani thought about it, glad that Meg seemed content to wait for an answer. "Have you ever tried to explain to a human what you are?"

"Duh. Of course I have. Way before Selene and Kera came into the picture, but they're the most recent."

"So you tell them what you do, right? Your job."

Meg tilted her head and looked thoughtful. "You mean as opposed to who I am as a person?"

"Exactly. Can you differentiate the two?"

Dani waited for Meg to answer. *Nice job. She's in the house for less than an hour, and you've skipped small talk and moved into existential philosophy. Jackass.* She looked up from her fried rice when Meg started to speak, her voice quiet.

"When you tell someone what you do, there's an assumption that's who you are, as well. And to be honest, I haven't put much thought into who I am for several centuries. I'm a fury. One of three. When I'm not delivering justice, I enjoy the hell out of life." She shrugged, looking sad. "At the moment, that's all I can think of." She motioned at Dani with her fork. "So? Explain your side of it."

"I'm Death, Meg. You're Justice. You're a powerful, terrifyingly beautiful fury. Your purpose is to make the world better. But me? I take. I never give. When I go to people, their time above ground is gone. When gods see me, they think of two things. I take away their followers, potentially causing the gods to weaken, and, even if they only worry about it a little bit, gods fade and die too. I remind them of that." Dani swallowed against a lump of emotion. "You and your sisters are the only ones willing to be near me, because you don't have followers, and you technically can't die. I can't tell you how grateful I've been for that over the years."

Meg scooted over on the couch and put her hand over Dani's, making Dani's skin warm and tingly. She hoped Meg didn't feel the strange new energy that had begun to surge through her, the one she felt even when Meg wasn't around.

"I had no idea. You've just always been there with us, part of what we do. I didn't realize it was so hard."

"That's why I never invited you guys to my place. The Deadlands are my home, and I love it here. But I never wanted you guys to see me the way other people do. I didn't want to lose your friendship."

Meg drew small circles on Dani's palm as she spoke. "Tis said the other day she didn't like it here. That's what you're talking about, isn't it?"

Meg's touch on her palm was driving her crazy, but nothing short of an apocalypse would make her pull away. "That's the gist of it, yeah. But I've been doing a lot of thinking, and if I want things to change, then I have to figure out how to change them. You said the other day that you liked it down here, so I thought maybe I could start with you."

Meg turned to straddle Dani's lap, and Dani had no idea where to put her hands, so she left them on the sofa. She knew Meg was a tactile person. She showed her emotions through touch, often reaching out to someone physically to make her point. Although it felt damn good to have her there, she didn't place any importance on it. Of course, that didn't mean desire didn't surge through her like a forest fire during a drought.

"I'm incredibly honored. Thank you for trusting me. And for the record, I really do like it down here. It feels like…well, it feels like you. Safe, solid."

Dani wasn't sure how she felt about that particular description, but having Meg on her lap was keeping her from thinking much at all.

Meg slid off her lap and went to the kitchen to grab a drink, and Dani instantly felt the loss of her warmth but also the return of her ability to think once again.

"You know, I don't remember what it was like before you. I feel like you've been around forever, but you haven't. I seem to remember an old guy who smelled funny and wasn't nearly as sociable as you."

Dani finished the last of her rice and piled the dishes on the table, as much to clean up as to give her hands something to do. "This isn't a forever position. Eventually, you get tired of living separate, and your term comes to an end. There's always a second, and third, in training to take over the head position when the time comes. I took the position not long before the three of you took up your duties, when old Aeron finally retired. Idona is my right hand, and my friend. She'll take over when I'm done."

Meg sat on the arm of the sofa. "Are you thinking of retiring soon? Does Death die? I've never even thought about it. Funny how you get wrapped up in your own work and you fail to notice the way other people's departments run. I hope you don't think I don't care."

She looked so concerned it made Dani's heart swell to think someone actually wanted to know more. "I'm not going to retire yet, but I do want to change some things, and I think now might be my chance. And no, Death doesn't die. In a way, we're a bit like the prefaders. As soon as we give up the post, we can choose what to do. We can go live among the humans, although they always feel a little weird around us, or we can retire to any one of the religious areas. Or we can stay here in the Deadlands."

Meg laughed so hard she snorted soda and started to cough. With her eyes watering she said, "Please tell me you've got a retirement community of old Deaths somewhere."

Dani grinned. "Two, actually. One is here in the Deadlands, down by Crater Lake. Nice place, lots of grass and golf. The other is in San Miguel de Allende, in Mexico. Gorgeous place with perfect weather, and the Mexicans have a different relationship with death than a lot of countries, so our retirees can relax there without the humans freaking out much."

"How long do most people stay in your post? I can't really remember anyone other than you and Mr. Smelly Grumpy Pants." Meg cleaned the soda off Dani's couch.

"It depends on how long you can take it. Most everyone does at least a hundred years, though there have been some who couldn't hack it and didn't make it that long. We serve as death crew for hundreds of years before we're even considered for a promotion, and that gets taken into account too. As far as I know, I'm the longest running Head of Death in history." Dani tried to keep the pride out of her voice, not wanting to sound vain, but she was proud of her long service record.

"That's amazing." Meg grinned. "I mean, we've been doing our jobs for thousands of years, but your record is even more impressive."

Dani laughed and threw a napkin at her. "You get to do lots of fun stuff too. That takes the edge off, doesn't it?"

Meg sighed. "Yeah, it does. That's part of why I'm damn determined to enjoy everything. We see enough of the ugly stuff. Alec has always dealt with it well, but I know Tis had a really hard time last year. In fact, she probably felt a lot of what you've just described. But since we were kids I knew I didn't want to take life so seriously." She flopped onto the couch and rested her chin on her fists. "We choose what we want out of life. I want it to be fun. I want sex, good food, friends, laughter, and anything else that makes me feel spectacular."

Dani watched as emotions Meg didn't voice flashed through her eyes. What she was saying was one thing, but she was feeling something else. Dani wouldn't pry, though. It wasn't her place.

"I guess it's kind of what you were saying about not being your job. Everything I do outside of work is *me*. The other stuff is just work. I've just never really sat down to differentiate the two." Meg grinned and raised her eyebrows. "I'm a fun-loving fury who takes out the bad guys as a day job, and then devours everything life has to give when I'm off. Maybe it's not much to other people, but it's enough for me."

Meg's phone buzzed, and she jumped up to answer it, leaving Dani to ponder what she'd said. There was more to Meg than most people knew, maybe even more than Meg herself knew. *If we spend enough time together, maybe I can get her to see how amazing she is.*

Meg hung up and grabbed a fortune cookie. "Work calls, Dark and Deadly. I'd better get back."

Dani grabbed her keys off the table, but Meg held up a hand to stop her. "No need to drive me. Just point me up the right road, and I'll fly. I'd like to see a bit more of your territory."

Disappointed in not being able to spend more time with Meg, but not wanting to push it, she set her keys down. "No problem. And if you ever want a personal tour, let me know. I'd love to show you around."

Dani opened the door and walked to the edge of the driveway with Meg. She waved her hand and a narrow road appeared to their right. "Fly straight up this road, and it'll take you to the back gate of Afterlife."

Meg turned and wrapped Dani in a strong hug, even draping her brilliant red wings around her. Stunned, she pulled Meg close and breathed in the spicy scent of her shampoo.

"Thank you for letting me in," Meg said quietly.

"Thank you for coming in." Dani reluctantly let her go and watched as Meg flapped her wings and lifted into the air.

"Selene is having a get-together this weekend. Come with me?"

Dani winced. "Are you sure?"

Meg rolled her eyes and flew higher. "If I wasn't sure I wouldn't have asked. I'll meet you at my place, and we'll go together." She did a little flip in the air, making Dani smile. "I'm off to be a worker bee." She waved and flew off down the road.

Dani shoved her hands in her pockets as she watched Meg fly off, like the most beautiful hummingbird ever created. *Did she mean go with her as a date? Am I meeting her at her place so we can go together, together? Or am I reading too much into it?* Though Meg's sexual exploits and adventurous nature were legendary at Afterlife, in three thousand years she'd never made a pass at Dani. *Surely that says it all.*

Regardless, the thought of their relationship, whatever realm that was in, taking a new direction was breathtakingly exciting. *Change is coming. I can feel it.*

CHAPTER FOUR

Meg circled the little farmstead in Northern California, taking note of the long grapevines and small wine tasting center behind the main house. She loved this area, but the smell of death clouded her senses, and she shifted to her most primal self.

The call from work had been to check out a possible mass death scene. But as with more and more work calls lately, the details had been vague. She scanned the location but didn't see anything unusual outside. She dropped lower, still circling, and then caught the scent of something other than death. Fear tinged with desperation and confusion underpinned the rest, something she usually felt only in war-torn areas. She hissed and landed outside the main house. She could feel it emanating from inside like a sound wave crashing against her. She opened the front door. Her feathers tingled, and her snakes hissed softly.

The living room was gorgeous, with floor to ceiling windows that let in the sunlight California offered plenty of. Now, however, that light only served to illuminate the fifteen bodies lying in the middle of the room, their bare feet forming a perfect circle and their arms crossed over their chests. Next to each of them sat an empty cup.

Meg searched, but there didn't seem to be anyone left alive. She lowered her wings, confused. The furies were only called out when there was someone to punish. Mass death scenes like this weren't all that uncommon in history, but if the leader of the group didn't chicken out, then there wasn't anyone to take the blame. There was no reason for her to be here, yet…something definitely wasn't right. She walked around the bodies, careful not to disturb any, and looked out the big windows at the back.

Instantly, her wings were up and her snakes at attention. Her fangs extended, and she nearly pushed the windowpane from the frame to get outside.

Dis stood in the clearing by the grapevines, staring back at her. Horus, the Egyptian god of war, stood beside her, his bird eyes intense and unblinking. Dis waved and plucked a grape from the vine. She popped it in her mouth and made a show of enjoying it.

Meg opened the back door and flew to within a few feet of them. "What have you done?"

"What I do. Their confusion called to me, and I came and had a chat with them. They were already lost. I just moved them along a little. No point in them hanging around, is there?" She plucked another grape.

"Why was I called?" Meg needed to keep her temper in check, something she'd never been good at. But Dis was the oldest being in form, and there was no telling what kind of powers she had. The last thing Meg wanted was to become space dust. The fact that Horus was looking solid and way too glowy was interesting and something she'd be sure to share with Afterlife.

"Well, I suppose because someone *was* behind these silly beings' departure. The fact that it's me, and there's nothing you can do about that, makes the situation quite humorous, really."

"You can't go around killing humans." Meg wasn't sure that was true but felt it should be said.

"Of course not. What would be the fun in that? No, the fun comes from getting them to do it themselves. All I have to do is nudge the fear, heighten the confusion within them, and they'll do all kinds of things of their own volition. When the gods began to walk among the humans, they sowed the seeds of doubt and the kind of awe humans aren't equipped to deal with. I water those seeds and see what happens next. Exciting, isn't it?"

Horus, silent the whole time, held out his hand to Meg. "With a fury beside us, we could change the world. Destroy it and rebuild it as something far greater."

Meg flapped her wings hard, blowing wind at them. "Not a chance, beakface. Destroying humans isn't what we're here to do."

He shook his head and lowered his outstretched hand. "Not true, vengeful one. You destroy those who hurt others for no reason. In this age, that's all humans are doing. Hurting one another, from their rulers to their neighbors. They must be taken in hand, controlled. They must be taught respect and fear so that we can restore them to their rightful place beneath the gods. Only then will they function peacefully once more."

Meg laughed. "Have you forgotten that you need them more than they need you? Haven't you only just come back?" The lack of expression on his hawk face was disconcerting. She hated not being able to tell what someone was feeling.

"Even more reason to remind them of what we are. Make sure they'll never forget again. You see what they've become without true belief. They're despicable, spiteful creatures. They created us so they'd have someone to trust in, someone to guide them. And that's what we'll do, once we cleanse the earth of those too weak to live." Horus tilted his head, his beakface expression unreadable.

Dis sighed dramatically and took his hand. "I'm bored now, and I can feel others calling to me. Lovely to see you, as always."

And just like that, they were gone. No tunnels, no wings. Just gone. They left an invisible void where they'd been, as though the air itself had been wounded. Meg lowered her wings and relaxed slightly. *I really hate that woman. And he creeps me out.*

She moved back toward the house, unsure what to do next. Should she head back to the office and report? What should she do with the bodies? Just when she decided she'd head back to headquarters to talk to Zed and Kera, a portal opened a few feet away, and one of the death crew stepped out into the late afternoon sunshine.

Meg vaguely remembered seeing this one before, but when their paths crossed with anyone from Dani's team, everyone was usually embroiled in whatever was going on at the scene, and they rarely had time to talk. It seemed surreal to see one of the crew in a setting so serene. Meg waved and the woman came over.

"Hey there. I'm Idona." She reached out to shake Meg's hand.

Dani's next in line. "Nice to meet you. I'm Meg." Idona's laugh was deep and throaty, just the kind that turned Meg on.

"Believe me, everyone knows who the furies are. Nice to meet you in person, though. Dani has told me a lot about you."

Meg's stomach flipped slightly at the thought of Dani talking about her. "I'm sure most of it's true." She grinned and looked Idona over. She was sexy in that afterlife unreal kind of way. Her pale skin glowed, and her light blue, nearly white eyes were captivating. *Like Dani's.* Her long, thick black hair hung to her waist. *I wonder if she and Dani have ever—*

Idona cleared her throat slightly, and Meg smiled at being caught perusing. The tiny flare of jealousy caught her by surprise, and she quickly squelched it.

"So, what do we have here? The dispatch info didn't have a lot."

Meg came back to the moment and grimaced. "It's not a good one, and I think we'll find more like it as time goes on. Come on." They walked into the house.

Idona frowned and walked around the circle of bodies. "No souls." She stopped and knelt beside a young woman. She held her hand over the girl's forehead for a long moment, and Meg was fascinated when she saw a faint shimmer beneath Idona's hand, which got stronger as Idona slowly pulled her hand away. She cupped the light with her other hand and gently pulled it all the way out. She held it carefully and glanced at Meg. "Can you unhook my bag from my shoulder?"

Meg undid the clasp holding the cross-body satchel in place and slid the bag forward under Idona's hands. She'd never really watched a soul being taken before, and the moment felt incredibly special.

Idona gently placed it in the bag and zipped it closed. "I'm surprised one survived. The rest have dissolved. She must have been a fighter."

"If she were a fighter, she wouldn't have been in this group at all." Meg was having trouble wrapping her mind around what Dis was able to do.

"Nah. Humans exist at many levels of ability to cope. This one was probably just below the threshold. They're wonderfully complex, these evolved apes. The problem is that she didn't know what she believed in anymore, so we'll have trouble placing her soul." She scanned the bodies one last time before turning back to Meg. "I'm done here, and Dani and I have plans to hit the waves this afternoon. You good?"

She and Meg walked back outside, and Meg was grateful for the feeling of the sun on her face, warming the cold feeling of despair from inside. The information about Dani liking the water was new too. *What kind of friend have I been?* "I'm good. I'll phone the office and have dispatch call the local police to come deal with the bodies."

"Cool. See you around." She waved and entered her portal, which quickly closed behind her.

Meg was left alone in the clearing. She thought about what Horus had said and about Idona's comment about complexity. She wasn't a deep thinker like her sisters and felt overwhelmed by the multiple issues of the situation. Tension made her shoulders ache. *The best way to work out stress is through multiple orgasms.* She jumped onto a fence post and stretched her wings, letting the warmth of the sun hug her. She'd file her report and then call a few friends for some relaxation time.

Kera placed a pin on the world map posted on the wall behind her desk. It marked the location Meg had just been to, and it joined a number of other pins all over the map, which were there to track situations they thought were caused entirely by the appearance of Dis. Chaos was wreaking small sections of havoc everywhere.

Zed leaned back in his chair and stroked his beard. "Horus's offer is interesting. Asking a fury to join them is asking you to change the essence of who you are. You'd have to actively hunt people rather than punishing them after the fact." He leaned forward and looked at Meg intently. "Are you tempted at all?"

Kera stopped what she was doing and faced Meg, obviously interested in the answer.

"Seriously? I mean, really? Do you think this is the first time in three thousand years someone has tried to use a fury for their own schemes? And have any of us ever turned away from what we were born to do?" Meg's temper flared at the very idea she'd be so easily used. One of her snakes slid from her feathers and moved like a red river across the conference table toward Zed. "Have you forgotten that we've had an absurd amount of crazy-ass bosses in our lifetimes, including you, all of whom had their own agendas? We still did exactly what we were born to do, just at different headquarters. And you have the nerve to ask—"

He zapped the table near the snake's head, and it reared back. "Megara, it doesn't hurt to ask."

Kera kept her eye on the snake on the table, its head still pulled back as though to strike. "The unasked questions are the ones that can get you killed in the field. Well, not you, obviously. But those of us who are a little more breakable."

Meg calmed and held out her hand. Her snake returned to her, slithering up her arm and over her shoulder, back to its place in her feathers. "Fine. No, I'm not tempted. She's a whack job, and he's a weirdo."

Zed frowned at her. "Meg, this is serious. The Egyptian gods are older than we are. If they're coming back to power thanks to their believers returning to the old ways, we might have to make room for them here. And I don't think they'll take kindly to having to answer to a Greek god and a human."

Meg noticed he didn't mention handing over power as an option. "I don't think you'll need to worry about that. They don't want a place here. They never have, even when they lost most of their powers. They want to tear it all down and rebuild."

Zed and Kera were quiet for a moment. Finally, Kera said, "You know, from a distance, they've got a point."

Meg ruffled her feathers, and Kera held up her hand to stop her.

"Not Dis. I mean, chaos is part of life, but what she's doing is just dickish. But think about it from Horus's point of view. He's an old god who watches the world being turned upside down, and there's nothing he can do about it. Then, when the gods start to regain their powers, things get even more out of kilter. Gods are working in the fields with humans. A giant chunk of the population doesn't want anything to do with the gods at all and openly defy them. Humans hurt one another all the time, which is why you and your sisters have full-time jobs." She shrugged. "Before I came on board, the gods were fading out completely, and humanity was a mess. Now that the gods are helping out, things are getting a little better. I don't agree with him, but you can see his logic."

"I guess. Whatever. I'm going home to get drunk. I've had enough today."

Kera laughed. "Will you be at Selene's this weekend?"

Meg stretched and then pulled open the office door. "Of course. I'm bringing Dani."

Zed nodded. "I'm glad to hear it. She could use some fun in her life. I've always liked her."

"Did you know there are retirement areas for old deaths?"

Kera scoffed, and Zed laughed. "Of course. I play chess with a few of them occasionally. I like the place in Mexico. Nice golf too."

Meg tried to picture Zeus, most powerful of all the Greek gods, playing golf, but the image eluded her. "That's too bizarre for me. See you later."

She left the building and walked back to her place. Once inside, she poured herself a big glass of wine and shed her clothes. She loved being naked, her wings free and the air on her skin. She picked up the phone but hesitated. Sex was always good, but at that moment, she couldn't think of anyone she actually wanted to be with. An image of Dani crossed her mind. Her tall, lithe form, her crystal-clear eyes and short, thick hair…she was gorgeous. But Meg wouldn't go there.

Dani was kind. Sweet, gentle, honest. She seemed…fragile. Though Meg had lusted after her often through the years, she'd never made a move on her. To be with Dani would mean being open and honest, since she deserved nothing less. And Meg felt pretty sure Dani was a monogamous type, which was way outside Meg's comfort zone. No, Dani was the kind of woman you didn't sleep with, just in case it became something too real. But as Meg stared at the phone, she couldn't stop thinking about her. She tossed the phone on the couch and took her wine to the bedroom.

Just because I won't sleep with her doesn't mean I can't think *about sleeping with her.* She pulled her purple vibrator from the drawer and crawled beneath her cool sheets, ignoring the feeling of loneliness creeping through her.

CHAPTER FIVE

After a good session on killer waves, Dani and Idona strolled along the streets of the Deadlands. Though time didn't exist where they were, Dani was always aware of time passing outside her territory. The tides, sunsets, and sunrises were as much a part of her as her skin. That meant she was extra aware of the weekend get-together at Selene's getting closer. Anticipation and worry warred for first position in her thoughts.

"What do you want me to do?"

Dani looked at Idona, startled out of her thoughts. "Sorry. I was miles away."

"Clearly. I was asking what you want me to do with the soul from the winery."

"Agnostics are always a tough one. Usually, they believe in some element of one religion or another that makes them placeable. But you say this one isn't leaning anywhere?"

Idona kicked a pebble and sent it skittering down the long, empty street. "Nope. She so desperately wanted to believe in something that it saved her soul from Dis. But she wasn't pulled toward any one system."

The problem weighed heavily. This wasn't the first soul they'd had this issue with, and Dani knew deep down it wasn't going to be the last. She likened it to the American grocery stores. With extreme choice, a buyer became paralyzed by the number of options, and, overwhelmed, left with nothing at all. But they still had the desire for something.

"I suppose we'll have to place her in Limbo until we figure something else out. Or maybe, once she's there, she can decide where she wants to go. But then, I suppose the head of that department will have to determine whether she's allowed in, given that she didn't believe in them when she was alive." She shook her head. "This job used to be really straightforward."

"Speaking of complicated situations, I ran into Megara Graves at the winery scene."

Dani gave Idona a warning glance. "Oh?"

"Don't look at me like that. I'm not afraid of you, even if you are looking like a firefly lately, which we need to talk about. And Meg was looking as hot as she usually does. In fact, I thought she was going to throw me down and have her way with me right there and then." Idona jumped away from Dani's shove before she could connect. "Hey, if you're not going to make a move, there's no reason for me not to."

Dani's stomach churned at the thought of Idona in Meg's bed. "You mean aside from the fact that you're my closest friend. There are rules about that kind of thing."

Idona laughed and clasped Dani's shoulder. "You know I'm messing with you. I'd never go there, no matter how hot she is or how wild her reputation is. Not to mention, I'm having way too much fun with those twins from sector seven. But I think lusting after someone for centuries is the saddest thing *ever*. In all of history, *you* are the saddest thing in it."

This time Dani managed to shove her. "I hardly think my love life ranks up there with world wars and starvation. But thanks for the confidence."

"Any time. By the way, why are we walking the streets?"

"As the next in line for my position, I wanted to talk to you about something serious."

Idona stopped walking and stared at her. "Hell's bells. Are you retiring? Do I finally get to move up in the world? Is that why you look like you swallowed a lightbulb?"

Dani winced. "Nope, sorry. I know you've waited longer than any other second in command, but I'm not ready yet." Idona sighed, and Dani pulled her in for a quick hug. "But I want to talk to you about some changes I want to make. And the whole nuclear glowing thing is something for another day."

"You know, if I could kill you off and finally take your job, I totally would. But since you have to legit step down, I guess I'll just roll along beside you. What's on your mind?"

Idona's smile was genuine, and Dani was glad she wasn't actually upset. "Have you heard about the rebranding the underworld deities are doing?"

"Not just the underworld ones, I think. Isn't everyone suddenly interested in marketing themselves?"

"They are, but the underworld gods have to do it on a different level, because they're not out among the people as often as the others. It got me thinking about our territory. Maybe we need to do some sprucing up too."

"Okay…what do mean?"

Dani shrugged. "I'm not entirely sure, really. I mean, I love the Deadlands. I love the quiet monotones. But maybe just because I like it doesn't mean that's the way the entire territory should be." She turned right toward the park. "Doesn't it ever bother you how frightened people are of dying? What if we could do something to make them less afraid? Be more visible and less, well, less terrifying, I guess." Dani wished it weren't so hard to explain herself sometimes.

"I get what you mean. It would be nice if every living thing on the planet wasn't afraid of us, but as for our territory, it's not like anyone stays here. We're not a destination, we're just the highway. Hardly anyone even sees this place except for staff and the occasional guest." They stopped and sat on a bench by the lake. "Why bother to change the territory when we're all happy with it?"

Dani didn't have an answer. Maybe Idona was right. Maybe the territory itself wasn't a problem. "So, is the answer that we change our image? Give the concept of death a makeover?"

Idona raised her eyebrows and stared out over the water for a minute before she answered. "Maybe. The thing is, though, death is a big part of what makes humans appreciate life. The very fact that it will end is what makes it precious. If they stop fearing death, won't that make life a little less valuable?"

Dani hadn't considered that aspect, and the enthusiasm she'd been building for a bit of a change waned considerably. "You're right. It was a stupid idea."

Idona put her hand over Dani's. "No, it's not a stupid idea. I like where you're headed, I just think it needs some fleshing out to make it work."

Dani squeezed Idona's hand. "I'll think about it some more before I decide to do anything. Thanks for being a sounding board."

"Hey, I have myself to think of, you know. A thousand years from now, hopefully I'll be running this place. I don't want you messing it up before that." She grinned.

They took a meandering walk back to Dani's place, touching on various topics but staying away from the deep stuff. She and Idona had been lovers briefly a few hundred years ago but found they were better suited as friends. The transition had been easy, and as Dani walked next to her now, she wondered if she'd be better off trying to have a relationship with someone from her own territory, someone who understood the nature of what they did. She'd been with some of the underworld staff, many of whom understood the nature of death better than their above ground counterparts. Still, those dalliances weren't meant for the long term either.

When they got back to Dani's house, Idona touched her arm. "You know I don't care when you retire. But I do care about *you*. Happiness isn't something that falls into our laps, Dani. Sometimes you have to go out, grab it by its neck, and drag it home. Do what you have to do to feel alive again, okay?"

Dani gave her a tight hug. "Thanks. I'll figure it out."

They made plans to hit the sunrise waves at Zuma the next day, and she watched Idona walk away before going inside. *Happiness doesn't fall into your lap.* She thought of Meg straddling her during their meal the other night. *Maybe sometimes it does.*

"Who are you?"

Dis looked at the small human man, his eyes wide and his hands visibly trembling as he knelt at her feet. The small community of snake handlers in the Midwest had been chanting and praying as they played with their venomous vipers when Dis had arrived. Horus was back in Egypt making appearances among his followers. He didn't want to show up in public too often, as he felt the mystery of the gods needed to be kept alive. But he wanted them to know he was back as well, and it seemed to be working. His powers were growing every day as the Egyptians returned to the old religion. Which meant Dis was traveling on her own, and she loved the freedom of it. She'd found this little sect and decided to have some fun. She'd walked among them, touching them as she went, sowing the seeds of doubt about what they were doing, and in worship of whom. The snakes, sensing that fear, began to lash out. She'd felt as powerful as a newborn star as the people fell around her, thinking their god had forsaken them or that they'd been wrong and their god didn't exist after all. Their minds quickly disintegrated into chaotic strings, just as their bodies were eaten away by snake venom.

She felt amazing. "Who do you think I am?"

"Satan? Or one of his demons?"

His faith was strong; she had to give him that. She crouched down in front of him and held his chin tightly. "Look into my eyes and tell me what you see."

When he whimpered and sagged, his mind unable to cope with the vision of the universe she held in her eyes, she let him drop to the ground. She looked around, satisfied when she saw most of them were dead or dying. She went outside and looked over the long, bland grasslands. This was the fourth small gathering she'd been to this week, and although she was chipping away at the humans, causing the kind of discord she loved, it still felt like it wasn't enough. Moving among the small groups of believers in order to dismantle their faith was good, but it was too slow. She'd been away far too long to move by human standards. And the longer she moved among them, the more she understood why she'd been called back. The level of disruption they lived in every day was fascinating. That they managed to exist at all was amazing.

She only needed to think about the nearby café she'd passed earlier and then she was there. When she entered, the waitress dropped a stack of dishes, someone knocked over a cup of coffee, and a fat man started to choke on his food. It was all normal when she was around humans, and she ignored them as she moved to the counter and ordered a bottle of water and a Danish. She didn't understand how humans continued to drink milk so long after being weaned. The drink they made of coffee beans mixed with milk was bitter and disgusting. She liked their bread products, though.

She watched the television as she nibbled on her pastry. The news station played nothing but the horrors happening around the world, and she found she quite liked it. An idea began to form as she watched disaster after disaster, and she wished Horus were there to listen to her work it out. When they showed a land conflict of some kind in the Middle East, things began to fall into place. *War and disease. Places where people pray. Places I can create doubt on a larger scale.* She thought of the place she'd just seen on the news and found herself on a street covered in rubble. Bullets flew around her, pinging into already burned-out cars, the acrid smell of cordite and fear thick in the smoky air. She went into the nearest building and found several families huddled together. They were praying.

She smiled, deciding not to let them see her. Sometimes it worked even better if the doubts came from nowhere rather than a specific person they could then blame. She waved her hand over them and felt the doubts begin to take hold, like a parasitic vine entering its host. They began to doubt anyone was listening. They began to believe they were going to die. They started weeping, wailing. One of the fathers, enraged by his feeling of hopelessness, jumped up, grabbed a gun off the nearby table, and ran out into the street, firing at anything and everything.

She watched, mildly amused, and kept walking through the war zone toward the ones with the most guns. Again, she dropped the seeds of doubt and discord among them and watched them flourish. They turned on one another, on themselves, on their gods. Hope died with them on the dusty roads.

In minutes, she'd been able to do more than she had by visiting all the small communities. It occurred to her that it wasn't only those areas where there were few believers gathered together that were weak. Their naturally violent nature left humans open to fear and insecurity. Their refusal to care for the poor and marginalized meant those communities, too, were ripe for her visit. All she had to do was show up, and she'd tear them down en masse.

She passed an enigmatic road sign that said, "What is your endgame?" by some company named after the goddess of victory. She considered the question and decided she didn't actually have one. She was Chaos. She did what she did because that's who she was. She didn't want to rule over the silly humans; that would be as dull as a black hole. Horus wanted humanity brought back into line so the gods could rule over them the way he felt they were supposed to. But Dis didn't care about that, either. The gods could live on or fade away; it made no difference to her. They were, after all, simply paradoxical manifestations of the human need for solace on an unstable planet. When she'd affected all she could, when humanity had, indeed, been brought to its knees, she'd probably move on. She'd go back to the beautiful vastness of the universe and check in on the other planets, who for the most part were far beyond this planet ruled by evolved apes.

And before she left, she'd take at least one of the fury sisters with her.

CHAPTER SIX

What in the seven hells is going on?" Zed stared at the map on the office wall.

Kera looked at everyone around the table. "Thoughts?"

Dani tried not to let the despondency she felt show. "I can give you numbers, but I think you'll find it's worse than that. Some of the dead still have their souls intact, but when we take them, they're like moth-eaten cloth. Some of the souls are gone, much like we've been seeing in Dis-hit territories." She looked around. "But worse, there are plenty of humans who survive in these zones."

"How is that worse?" Tis asked.

"Because they're different. If one of you went with me and saw into them, I think you'd see it more clearly. I can feel it. It's like something inside them has been coated with darkness. Even if they continue to have faith, it's tainted. They're hurting, full of doubts and insecurity. They're scared, and it's making them act out. In a way, that's worse than death, because although they have a semblance of faith left, they'll keep doing things that put their souls in mortal danger."

Zed slammed his hand on the table, making everyone jump. "Are the underworld gods in on this?"

No one answered. Dani noticed that Meg looked preoccupied as she doodled on a notepad in front of her.

"If they're not, they should be." Selene looked contemplative, as she always did. "This is going to get them a lot of influx."

Kera pressed the intercom button. "Get Hades and Azrael up here, now."

Meg looked up from her doodling. "That's not a great way to deal with the underworld gods. It could get your rather adorable human ass fried." She looked at Tis. "No offense."

Tis grinned and blew her a kiss. "None taken. You're right."

"She keeps doing things I tell her will get her killed, but she doesn't pay attention. It won't be my fault when she finally pushes someone to turn her into clay." Zed noisily sucked on a piece of candy and nodded knowingly.

Kera shrugged and pushed the intercom button again. "Tell them I said please."

While they waited, Dani leaned over to Meg. "Hey. You okay?"

Meg touched Dani's hand. "Just a lot on my mind. You?"

"Same. I'm looking forward to Selene's party, if that's still on?"

Dani loved the feel of Meg's hand over her own.

"For sure. Hopefully, we can set work aside and just have a good time."

Dani could feel that Meg's energy was low, and it also seemed tinged with sadness. "You know if you want to talk, I'm always here."

Meg looked at her for a long moment, as though searching for something. She finally smiled slightly and kissed Dani's cheek. "Thank you. I might take you up on that."

The door opened and both Hades and Azrael came in, neither looking happy. When Azrael saw Meg, though, he seemed to brighten. He took the seat next to her and rested his hand on her back, making Dani twinge slightly with jealousy. She knew the furies had worked for Azrael for quite a while, and they had a strong connection, but the familiar touch still bothered her. She forced herself to focus.

Kera quickly explained the situation, and it was clear from their expressions that neither of the top underworld gods had any idea what she was talking about.

Azrael steepled his fingers under his chin and stared at the map. "Yeah, it seems like a good thing for us, on the surface. But the people who come to us aren't going to arrive because of their intrinsic natures or because they've done something truly egregious. They're going to come to us because they've been infected. That's not the same, and I take issue with punishing people in my domain who don't really belong there." He smiled and looked at Meg. "But then, in my new plans, maybe I can accommodate them in a new way."

Meg nodded, finally looking interested in the conversation. "True.

It doesn't make up for them being there, but it makes it a little less unfair."

Zed turned to Hades. "And you, brother?"

Hades waved dismissively. "Souls come to me because they believe in us, and they're dead. Olympus isn't an option, and I'm going to get them no matter what. Like Az says, it's where they end up that's the issue. But these days I'm allowing far more movement for those who don't belong in punishment realms. They'll be fine in my areas." He indicated the Asian areas on the maps. "But the Eastern religions might have some issues in this area. Souls are weighed against feathers in some of theirs, so they may face greater complications."

"I think you might need to call a meeting." Tis was taking notes, scribbling and crossing out, adding more. "See if you can come up with a collective idea on how to deal with what's going on."

Dani raised her hand to talk. "I'd like to be at that meeting, if I may? I'm facing an interesting issue I've never seen before. Souls who believe, like agnostics, but don't actually follow any particular faith. They only believe because they know for a fact the gods exist, but they don't want to follow a religion. True atheists simply return to dust, but these souls linger like the ones who believe. I don't know what to do with them."

Everyone was quiet as they took that in, and Dani knew they too hadn't considered the possibility of people believing, but not in a particular faith.

"We'll let you know as soon as it's scheduled." Azrael stood. "If you don't mind, I'll go start gathering folks now." Hades stood, and they both left, already discussing who would do what.

Zed turned back to the others in the room. "What do we do next?"

Kera turned to Tis. "Do you think this is Dis's work?"

"I don't see how it could be anything but. The question is why? I mean, she's Chaos, but surely she must want something out of all this?"

It was Zed's turn to press the intercom. "Can you please ask Clotho if she'd be willing to come to my office for a moment?" He rolled his eyes as he did his best to be politic.

"You're thinking if there's something she wants, maybe we can bypass all this shit and just give it to her?" Kera played with a rubber band, twisting it around her fingers.

"Exactly. Maybe we can make it less messy."

Meg leaned back in her chair. "She said she was here for as long as it took humans to settle into the idea of having the gods around. Don't we have to wait for that?"

The door opened, and Clotho came in, her expensive suit setting off her regal air. "While that's true, Megara, she seems to have taken it upon herself to further develop the humans' innate fight-or-flight responses. The level of confusion that brought her here is no longer enough to interest her. She wants to see how far she can push."

No one was surprised that Clotho answered a question asked before she'd come into the room. She was a Fate, and nothing was beyond her.

"How do we stop her from being an extra level of psycho?" Kera asked.

"Find a way to help the humans. That's always the answer, isn't it?" Clotho smiled enigmatically. "If you can get to them first, bolster their belief not only in their gods but in themselves, perhaps you can slow her down."

"And if we can't?"

"Then she runs riot over the world. Humans die by the thousands, and those left standing are the strong. She weeds out the weak and leaves behind those she couldn't get to. Gods lose believers by the score, and those humans left have either unshakable faith or no faith at all." She gave Zed a short nod. "Next time, come to my office." She left, clearly done with answering questions.

"I think that's the most direct she's ever been," Dani said, impressed with the level of forthrightness.

"That's what worries me," Zed said. "If she's willing to answer that clearly, there's either something we're missing, or they can't take a chance on leaving anything too unclear this time."

"So they know that batshit-crazy asteroid is out of control. Excellent." Kera shot the rubber band at him, and he batted it away.

Tis pinched the bridge of her nose. "Okay, everyone. I think we all need some time to process. Let's think about what we know and come up with a list of questions. At the same time, let's think of ways we can bolster faith and self-esteem." She sighed and gave them a weary smile. "It just gets easier, doesn't it?"

Meg stood and grabbed Dani's hand. "I need a drink."

Dani was happy to go anywhere with Meg, whatever she needed.

Selene stood and stretched, and Dani noticed how tired she looked. *Even the humans who are strong are having trouble keeping up.* Would they need to worry about Selene's and Kera's states of mind? She focused on the conversation, unable to think of an immediate answer.

"Let's meet up at my place at seven. Meg, you bring the alcohol. We'll handle the food." Selene leaned into Alec, who draped her wing around her protectively.

Meg dragged Dani out the door, and Dani waved at the others over her shoulder. The energy of the room had become oppressive as everyone mulled over their own concerns about the future. It would be good to relax away from the office with people she considered friends.

She followed Meg to the small convenience store on the office campus, where Meg bought enough alcohol to get an entire army drunk and paid to have it brought to her place. She followed Meg to her house, bemused by Meg's lack of conversation and total focus on her task. When they got inside and closed the door, Meg surprised Dani by falling against her and wrapping her arms around her.

"This day sucked." Meg's voice was muffled against Dani's sweatshirt.

She stroked Meg's hair, hoping Meg wouldn't notice that her hand trembled slightly. "Yeah. It seems like a lot of days suck right now."

Meg looked up at Dani. "I'm really glad you're here. Thanks for coming with me tonight."

Dani smiled. "Well, I had to move a lot of things around on my social calendar, but I guess you're worth it." *Am I flirting? Am I any good at it?*

Meg pinched her and smiled, some of the tension leaving her body. "You guess? That means I have to work harder."

Yes! I must be okay at it. "You do that. Play your cards right, and you can have all my time."

Meg's expression faltered slightly, and she pulled away.

And...fail.

"I'm going to hop in the shower before we head to Selene's. Do you want—" She bit her lip and blushed. "I mean, do you want to hang out while I get ready?"

Do I want what? What were you going to say? Dani desperately wanted to ask but wasn't sure she wanted to know. "Thanks, but I'll head home and get changed. I'll be back here about six thirty, if that's okay?"

Meg nodded, once again looking distracted. "Perfect. See you soon." She disappeared into the bedroom, leaving Dani to let herself out.

Dani opened a portal road and decided to walk home. She wanted the air and space to think. Meg was distracted, her energy off. *Was she going to ask me to shower with her?* Was it reflexive, just something she'd normally do with people? *But not something she'd do with me.* The thought left her deflated. Still, she was going to get to spend time with all her favorite people, and that was something.

CHAPTER SEVEN

Meg stood under the hot water, relishing the feeling of it sliding through her feathers and over her skin. *What was I thinking?* She'd very nearly asked Dani into the shower with her. Part of the request was habit. She loved showering with people. The way soap made bodies slide together, the hot water steaming up the room and giving the moment a sense of sensuality, made for great passion. But as she stood under the water, alone, she knew she'd made the right decision.

Dani wasn't a casual play partner, and taking it beyond friendship would surely create tension Meg didn't want with someone she felt safe with. Sex could complicate things if everyone wasn't on the same page, and she knew instinctively she and Dani weren't even reading the same book. Sex with gods was often simple. The nature of their existence meant damn near everything was temporary, so no one tended to put a lot of stock in "forever." But there were some, like her sisters, who found solace and comfort in coming home to a special person every day.

It wasn't something Meg had ever wanted for herself. Despite what she'd said to Pan, however, part of her wondered what it might be like. She shook her head and splashed water against the shower wall. *Don't be stupid. You can have that kind of friendship with someone and still have sex with anyone you want. That's the best of both worlds.* She knew that; so why did she feel out of sorts about it?

She finished her shower, feeling edgy and disgruntled. And when she went to choose her outfit, she ended up flinging clothes all over the place in a tantrum. She didn't want to look seductive and give Dani the wrong impression, especially after she'd nearly slipped up. But she also didn't want to look like some muted version of herself. Finally, she closed her eyes and stopped to calm down. *Who am I?* It was a good question, and she decided that today she *did* feel like a muted version of herself. She grabbed her favorite comfortable jeans and a loose gray tank top with a wing design over the breasts. She added heeled black sandals and looked in the mirror. *Still me.*

She shook out her hair and noticed how long it had gotten. Over the years she'd had it in every color and length imaginable. For the last several years she'd worn it natural, letting the thick waves set off her natural red. *Maybe it's time for a change.* Like her sisters, she didn't age, and she didn't need to worry about wrinkles or age spots or middle-age spread, thank the gods. Still, she liked having the ability to change her style at a whim. She'd often felt bad for Tis, whose snakes were part of her hair, meaning it had stayed the same since she was a child. With her own snakes tucked safely away in her feathers, she could go wild with her look whenever she wanted to.

She opened the door when she heard Dani knock and was struck by how sexy she looked. She didn't seem to have a spare ounce of fat on her body. Her eyes were like crystal with the mists of time hidden in them. Her shaggy dark hair sometimes fell in front of her eyes, hiding her expression, as it did now. She was a perfect package of androgyny, something that had always appealed to Meg's desire to have it all. In her black skinny jeans and black T-shirt with red Chinese symbols on it, she looked delicious.

"Hey. I'm not too early, am I?"

Meg gave her clit a mental order to back down. "Nope. All ready to go. What's that?" She pointed at the foil-covered tray in Dani's hands.

Dani blushed. "I like to bake. I thought I'd make some brownies."

"Well, aren't you the most adorable Death baker in the world." Meg grabbed her car keys and purse. "Let's go."

"Do you want to take your way or mine?"

Meg popped open the trunk to make sure all the alcohol was there before closing it and getting in the driver's seat. She laughed when she noticed Dani hunch slightly so her head didn't brush against the roof. "I forget how tall you are sometimes." She lowered the convertible top, and Dani looked far more comfortable. "Let's take your way, and you can give me a tour as we go."

Meg backed out of the driveway, and Dani opened a portal. "I'm not sure what you know and what you don't."

Meg thought for a moment, wondering if she should admit to not knowing, or at least not remembering, much about Dani's world.

"It's okay, you know…to not remember stuff. I don't remember everything about what you do or where you come from either."

Meg glared at her. "Are you in my head? That's not cool."

Dani held up her hands placatingly. "No! I wouldn't do that. I just…well, I can read you pretty well, you know? After all these years, I've learned what your expressions mean. Not that you've ever hidden them very well."

As quickly as she'd gotten pissed off, she was calm again. "Sorry. Of course you wouldn't do that." She squeezed Dani's hand and quickly let go, though the desire to hold on to it was strong. There was also a strange new energy around Dani that Meg could feel every time she touched her, but since Dani hadn't said anything yet, she didn't bring it up. "I have an idea. Let's pretend we don't know one another at all. Like this is the first time we've met, and we're doing that super awkward getting-to-know-you thing."

Dani laughed. "Weird, but okay. Where do I start?"

Meg motioned around them. "What did you think about the first day you took over as Head Death?"

"That was a long time ago. Let's see…I remember feeling small. I'd been the second in command for ages, and in training for a long time before that. But the moment I knew it was all up to me, I felt like a speck in the universe, and I wasn't sure I was up to it." She looked at Meg. "Did you always know what you were going to be?"

Meg smiled at the memory of her childhood. "Not at first. We were just normal kids. I mean, we were kids with wings and pet snakes who lived as part of our bodies, granted, but still. We played, and tested our wings, and fought. It was only when we got older that our mother sat us down and explained why we'd been brought into the world. It was a head fuck, I can tell you that. One day we're messing with geese in the sky, the next we're in charge of punishing humanity when they're naughty. I think I get what you mean about feeling too small for the job."

Dani pointed to a large building on the left. "Sorry to interrupt.

You said you wanted to know about the area. That's the centrifugal fork. It has a door that leads to each of the primary religion's main offices."

"I thought you just waved your hands and created roads where you wanted to go?"

"Not exactly. The road network is constantly changing. As the head of the department, I'm in charge of creating new links to the places where needed and removing any roads that are no longer necessary. Once a road is created, like the one you took to Afterlife the other day, it will always be available, but it might not always be visible. It's only if we're certain we won't need a road any longer that we remove it from the network." Dani looked proud as she motioned around them. "You can't see them, but there are thousands of roads available to most everywhere on earth, anywhere the Sundo might have to go harvest a soul."

"So why the shiny building?"

"Right. It made more sense to have a direct link to the big religions. We take the roads to where we're picking up souls. Then we can come back here, go straight to the fork, and right to the department we need. It takes away some of the hassle. Plus, if any of the department heads want to come talk to us, they can use the fork to get here."

Meg looked at Dani, surprised. "The department heads come to you?"

She looked a little embarrassed. "Sometimes. When they've got questions about numbers or rituals. My crew has a wealth of information from being among people when they die."

"But you're like us, right? You're in charge of a specific area, and there are people like you doing the same job somewhere else?" Meg had no idea she knew so little about the realm between, and the new knowledge was like going on a treasure hunt.

"Not exactly, no. I *am* Death. There's no one above me. I've got department managers all over the world, and they run their own sections and crews. But they all report back to me."

Meg thought about what that meant. The concept was staggering. "That's…that makes you responsible for every human being on the planet. All seven-odd billion of them."

Dani nodded, looking serious. "That's me."

"Christ on a stick. And I thought I was overworked. Now I feel like a whiny child." She said it lightly, but it was true. Dani managed to be humble and kind, when she probably had more right to ego and power trips than any other god in existence.

"Well, I have a lot of help. It's not like I do it all myself. I used to do a lot more, but I've got better at recruiting Sundo to help."

"How do you find your death minions? And why do you call them Sundo? And what about the animals? Do you deal with those too?" Meg wasn't paying any attention to where she was going. She turned right, then left, then went forward for a while. She passed housing tracts of lots of similar houses and went down streets with more individual cabins.

"Sundo is an ancient word for death, and all the death workers are referred to as Sundo. Keeps it simple. And they find me, generally. Some of them are the children of parents who have been on crew. Some are low-level employees from other religious departments who want a change of scenery or who just like to travel. It's a great way to see the world. And no, I don't deal in animals. Their souls don't believe in an afterlife, so they're like atheists. Their energy simply returns to the planet." She paused, thinking about it. "Unless they're from a religion that believes in reincarnation, and the soul of that animal was once human. Then crew from that religion deal with that animal's soul, returning it to the afterlife center it came from so it can continue on its journey." She laughed lightly. "I've never really explained it before. It's all pretty strategic."

"You sound like an ad for some kind of travel-military crossbreed." They drove down a tree-lined street with enormous houses. "Who lives here?"

"Managers for this region, mostly. We have pay scales a lot like the human world. There aren't any poor here, but crew can rise through the ranks and get better pay grades. Obviously, it takes a little longer in a realm without true time."

"You have your own money?"

Dani reached into her jeans pocket and pulled out a coin. It was a silver hexagonal piece with a skull on one side and a boat on the other. "Death and crossing." She put it in Meg's glovebox and then tapped the clock on the dashboard. "As much as I love this, we should probably get to Selene's."

"Shit. I wasn't paying attention. Which way?"

Dani opened a portal ahead. "Head that way. It will let us out at the base of the mountain she lives on."

Meg floored it. She liked being fashionably late to a big gathering, but when it was a small one, it felt rude. "Why not just open it into her driveway?"

"Because I can't always be sure what's changed in a small location. I can let us out onto a main road because it's not likely to have changed much, and I can tell where the big movement is. But I could bring us out into Selene's driveway only to find someone standing right where we come out. The same can happen when it comes to weather. Her area floods and gets snow, so it's better to give some leeway in case that kind of thing happens."

Meg loved listening to Dani talk. She was quietly certain, intelligent but simply spoken. Conversation with her was easy and interesting. It was sexy too, but she shoved that thought away. "Makes sense." She came out of the portal onto Highway 15 and turned left off the off-ramp into the San Gabriel Mountains. The winding path up Lone Pine Canyon was covered with flowering yuccas, their white blooms like suspended spring snow against the desert scrub. Within minutes, they were driving through the pine forest, and it felt like the regular world was far below. She navigated the narrow roads to Selene's, wondering what Dani was thinking. But all the information Dani had given her made her feel a little less-than. All these years, she'd just been Dani, Death personified. She was their quiet, unassuming friend that other people couldn't always handle being around. But she was much more than that, and Meg wondered how she'd missed it all these years.

Alec's Hummer was parked on the street outside Selene's cabin, and Tis's SUV was in the driveway. Meg parked behind the SUV, but before she got out, Dani stopped her.

"Thanks."

Meg frowned, confused. "For what?"

"For listening. For wanting to know. For asking questions." Dani shrugged and gave her a shy smile. "It's really nice to have someone interested."

Dani's vulnerability and gentleness made Meg's heart ache. She leaned across and kissed her cheek. "I fully intend to do it more often."

She opened her door and grinned. "But for now, I want to eat and get drunk, and not necessarily in that order."

Dani laughed and followed Meg to the front door.

Alec opened it before Meg knocked and pulled her into a tight hug. "About time. We're dying of dehydration in here." She took Meg's keys and headed to her car. "I'll grab the drinks. Go on in."

There were hugs and teasing all around when they went in, and Meg was glad to see Dani seemed relaxed. She'd always loved Selene's cozy cabin in the woods and was glad she and Alec had decided to keep it as a getaway home. The smell of spicy food hit her, and her stomach growled in response. "Oh my gods, that smells amazing. Please tell me it's nearly ready."

Kera tasted something out of a pot and nodded. "Just about."

Dani set her foil-topped pan on the counter. "For later."

Kera peeked under the foil. "That's awesome. Brownies from Death. No one believes me when I tell these stories."

Dani blushed and took the proffered beer from Kera, and Meg smiled at how gorgeous and mellow she looked. She looked away when Tis tugged on her hair.

"You look like you've got something, or someone, very specific on your mind." Tis tilted her head toward Dani and gave her a mischievous grin.

"I've got a lot on my mind, thank you very much. The first thing being why I don't already have alcohol sliding down my throat." She knew her tone was sharper than she intended, but she couldn't help it. Apparently, Dani had become a sore spot.

"Spoken like someone in proper denial." Tis poured her a glass of wine and handed it to her. "But I'll stay out of it for now."

Kera started serving dinner, and they settled into various couches and chairs around the living room. Meg found she was slightly disappointed when Dani sat across the room rather than next to her, but she drowned the feeling in merlot.

Conversation was easy and flowing, and Kera's cooking was delicious. As if by pact, everyone avoided talking about work, and Meg was light-headed with relief for the respite. She had to force herself not to stare at Dani, but that meant she was focused on the others, and as the night went on, that didn't help either.

Tis sat curled up on the couch next to Kera, whose arm rested along Tis's shoulders, holding her close. Selene reclined between Alec's legs as they relaxed in front of the fire. They were all so happy, so in love. *So not alone.* In her wine-soaked state of mind, emotions she'd never felt, or at least never acknowledged, began to well up inside her. This wasn't one of her parties, where it was a free-for-all of sex, drugs, and alcohol fueled competitions of power. This was... real. It was deeper. It had meaning. *I want meaning too. I want real.* She wanted to cry, but instead, she set her wine glass down and crawled across the room, unable to stand since the earth was spinning faster than usual. She made it to Dani and drew her knees to her chest as she rested her head on Dani's thigh. When Dani began to stroke her hair, she sighed contentedly. *Just for tonight.*

CHAPTER EIGHT

D is stared out the window at the Pacific Ocean, glittering as it swept into and away from Santa Monica Pier. *They think it's so big. They have no idea how small they are.* They were microbes compared to other planets with life, but for them, living their short lives on the blue planet, it was everything. *Such strange complexity for so little time. They fill every moment and spend more time worrying about things than actually doing them. So easy to manipulate.*

"Lunch?" Clotho emerged from her office and gave Dis a perfunctory nod.

"Why?"

"Because it's an interesting social aspect of life. And it's often tasty." Lachesis closed the door to her office, where graphs and charts covered the walls.

"But it's just so…human. Surely to rule over them you don't need to behave like them."

"There are advantages to living among them instead of beyond them. Food is one of them. But feel free to go to your own home if you don't want to join us." Clotho waved toward the door at the end of the hall that led to Dis's domain in the cosmos.

She sighed. "Fine." She followed them down a maze of stairwells and hallways until they emerged in a comfortable room with deep chairs and luxurious table setups. She could hear the cacophony of others dining but couldn't see them.

Lachesis twitched a heavy curtain aside, allowing Dis to see they were on a balcony of sorts above the regular café area. "When much of your job affects beings with big egos and a lot to lose, you're not usually welcome company. As I'm sure you know."

Dis was well aware she was generally disliked by the few she'd met since she'd come back. Some of the older gods remembered her from times long past and weren't big fans either. "No, I don't imagine you are."

Lachesis dropped the curtain, and they sat down. "Atropos won't be joining us. All your little tricks have knotted the threads, and she's trying to figure out whose lives you cut shorter than they should have been." She shook her finger at Dis like she was a naughty child. "No one but us should be cutting threads."

Dis shrugged, unconcerned. "I didn't cut them. I just mixed things up a little. You had to know when I came back there would be issues for the three of you."

The server dropped a jug of water and then tripped over the chair behind her. Clotho threw a bread roll at Dis. "Rein it in, at least while you're here."

Dis sighed and pulled her power more tightly to her. The server visibly relaxed and managed to put the soup bowls on the table without spilling any.

"That's true. We calculated for the basic level of disruption you cause." Clotho sipped at her soup, not bothering to look up. "What we didn't plan on was you actively meddling in human lives and making things worse than they need to be."

Dis tried the soup and found it pleasant enough. "They've overrun the planet. It's not as though losing some will do any lasting damage. Dust to dust and all that."

Clotho set her spoon down and leaned forward. Dis felt the ancient woman's power like a blanket pressed against her face, smothering her.

"Don't forget who we are, Chaos. You are unquestionably powerful, but you have your limitations. Stop pushing, or we'll send you back."

They ate the rest of their meal, though Dis's anger radiated through her like a supernova about to explode. *How dare they threaten me? Who do they think they are? Little godlings who are only here because humans exist. I'm beyond time. Beyond space. Beyond them.* The soup tasted like bile in her mouth now, and she shoved it away. *If they think*

I've been pushing before, they're about to see what I can really do. Let them try to send me back. She'd been content to play, to see what levels she could get away with. Now she wanted to burn the world and all the beings with it to the ground. When the two old women got up to head back to their office, she made sure she was behind them. She pulled open the curtain and looked down at the array of gods and creatures beneath her, all there to serve humanity. *Let's make you figures of power again, shall we?* She waved her hand over them, letting her special brand of disorder fall like star dust. She let the curtain fall and followed the old women back upstairs. *Let's see how you handle this, little godlings.*

The woman made it onto the fury's punishment list when she'd killed her children. All seven of them lay in a long, creepy row in the living room. Meg stepped into the room and winced. *Well, that's messed up.* Their mother sat in a recliner, sipping a mug of something, staring at them as though they were a mildly interesting TV program. Meg had seen it before. Parents and children had been killing one another since they'd started developing family units. But scenes like this one always made her want a shower after.

She opened her wings and allowed her fangs to extend. She appeared in front of the woman and stared down at her.

Instead of the usual screaming and pleading, though, the woman simply looked at her over the rim of her mug, much like she'd been looking at her children.

"Do you want to know why?"

"Because you were tired of doing laundry? Or having to cook enormous meals?" Meg hardly ever spoke to the people she was going to deliver to, but something about this situation called for more than the usual response.

The woman smiled slightly and looked back at the children. "Because the world has gone crazy. The gods are here, but they've brought terrible evil with them. And that evil is going to grow and consume everything it can. I couldn't let them live in a world that's going to die, so I sent them to Heaven." She set down her mug and looked at Meg. "I don't regret it. Do what you will."

For the first time in centuries, Meg hesitated. *This is why I don't talk to them beforehand.* She opened her hands and let her mist come. It slid over the woman's skin, into her eyes and ears, and then into her mouth when she gasped.

Meg pulled it back and turned away when the woman curled into a ball and started to weep. Startled, she nearly tripped over a little body on the rug when she saw Dani in the doorway. In her ceremonial cloak and holding her enormous scythe, she really was the sexiest thing Meg had ever seen. She was also emanating power, something Meg had never seen before. *Or maybe I'm just more aware of her than I've ever been.*

"Hey."

"Hey. Another fun day in paradise." Meg tried to sound light-hearted, but she had a feeling Dani would see through it. "All yours."

Dani touched her arm as she tried to walk past. "Is everything okay? I haven't seen you much since the party."

Meg moved to put some physical distance between them. Being close to Dani was too hard. It made her think of the party at Selene's and how lonely she'd felt that night, and every night since. "Totally fine. Just busy with work, you know? And Az is keeping me busy with the Hell makeover." The truth was far more irritating than that. She wanted to be around Dani. She missed her friendship and how calm she felt around her. And she missed her sisters. But all of them served to make her feel out of place and out of sorts. She wanted something she knew she didn't actually want, and she couldn't figure out why she thought she wanted it. It was something more than the loose, relaxed life she'd built for herself. But instead of trying to figure it out, she did what she'd always done when things got too heavy. She drowned her thoughts in alcohol, fed them drugs, and fucked them away. It had always worked before.

But now, standing in front of Dani, she knew that strategy wasn't working this time. At other work scenes, she'd tried to get in and out before Dani or her Sundo got there so she wouldn't have to have the conversation she was having now. She hated lying but couldn't bring herself to say anything more.

"Maybe we could grab coffee later?" Dani looked at the bodies on the floor and pulled off her snazzy backpack.

"Maybe. I mean, I'm a little busy right now. Can I call you and let you know?" Meg walked backward down the drive, as desperate to get away as she was to ask Dani to spend time with her. Dani looked so downcast she nearly gave in.

"Sure. Yeah. Whenever." Dani turned to her task.

Meg closed her eyes against the tears that were threatening. She knew she was doing the right thing. The weird feelings of jealousy and loneliness would pass as long as she didn't give them room to grow. Being on her own for a while would be a good thing.

She repeated the phrase constantly as she flew back to Santa Monica. Before she got back to the office she saw the King's Head pub and thought of Fin. Suddenly curious, she landed at the pub and went inside. Sure enough, Fin, a pre-fader Celtic god, sat in the back with a half-empty glass of Guinness and a book in front of him. She went to the bar and ordered him another, as well as a Sex on the Beach for herself. She took them to the table and said, "Any time for an old friend?"

Fin looked up and smiled. "Red wings! Slap my ass and call me sugar tits. It's been ages. Sit, sit." He gulped down the last of his beer and slid the other one forward. "I hadn't seen Alec in a month of monkey's arses, and now I get to see you too." He flicked some foam from his beer at her cleavage. "You're looking well, lass."

She laughed and threw the paper umbrella from her drink at him. "You're looking human." She made a face at the book on the table. "Crossword puzzles? Really?"

He held his heart as though in pain. "Ay, you insult a man after buying him a drink. Just like the old days. I happen to like crosswords. And this one is put out by one of the Muses, you know. Look. Right out of the Afterlife press room." He pushed it away and tapped his glass to hers. "Anyway, what brings you to my table?"

Meg sipped her drink and shrugged. "I have no idea. I was headed home and suddenly wanted to see you."

His eyes narrowed slightly as he looked at her for a moment. "These days, there's little likelihood of coincidence, my love. Tell me what's going on in your life."

"You know me, Fin. Fucking and drinking and good food. That's my story." It sounded as hollow as it felt.

"Nah, love. That's what you like people to think. And you've gotten so good at gettin' them to think it, you've gone and believed it yourself." He smiled at the waitress who set another two drinks in front of them. "But you're more than that. Tell old Fin what's the matter."

Unexpectedly, Meg started to cry. "I don't know. I like my life. I *love* my life. I mean, do you know what it's like to have sex with a Viking goddess and a centaur at the same time?" He looked impressed, and she kept going. "Right? I mean, who gets to do that? I do. I do whatever I want outside of my job, whenever I want to do it, wherever it can be done." She blew her nose on a cocktail napkin. "Why isn't that enough anymore?"

Fin sat quietly for a few minutes. "You've got to do your own growing, no matter how tall your father was."

Meg stared at him, baffled. "What? What the hell does that mean? I don't have a father. I mean, not one I can go and chat with."

"It's a saying we have in Ireland. No matter what, you have to become your own person. Not your sisters, not your friends. Just you, and you have to do it on your own."

"When did you start sounding like the Fates?" He winked at her and blushed, and Meg started to laugh. "You're doing one of the Fates? I'm both intrigued and repulsed."

"You sleep with man-horses. Don't tell me you're repulsed by old folks having sex." He grinned. "And the older the fiddle, the sweeter the tune, Red."

She'd think about that later. "I feel lost. And I don't think there's any reason to feel lost. And that's stupid. I hate feeling stupid." She sucked on a piece of pineapple and tried to quell the tears.

"Well, girlie, I can tell you this much. Dig deeper. If you're determined to drown yourself, no sense in playing in shallow water. Be the person you think you are to the full extent of it. Then you'll really know if that's you, or if you're playing at being you. Maybe you'll figure out you're someone else."

Meg closed her eyes and puzzled over what he was saying. "Be me. Or not me." She opened her eyes again and shook her head. "Thanks. Very helpful."

He laughed. "It will be, if you give yourself time to think about it."

She laughed with him, feeling a little better. "Okay, I'll think about it later. For now, tell me which Fate you're doing and what she's like in bed."

He started talking and Meg let herself be drawn into the conversation. The serious soul-searching would wait. Right now, sitting across from an old friend, she was where she needed to be.

❖

Dani stood on Meg's porch, debating the wisdom of knocking. Although she and Meg's sisters had tried to reach her, she'd been refusing to talk to any of them. But that didn't mean she'd been alone. They'd heard about the excessively wild sex and alcohol-fueled parties she'd been throwing almost constantly, though it seemed clear none of them were invited.

When it had been time to leave Selene's place after the dinner party weeks ago, Dani had carried Meg out to her car. Meg had been weepy, talking incoherently about how her sisters had everything and she had nothing, and how they were teacher's pets. Although they'd looked confused, her sisters hadn't responded. Presumably, Meg got like this from time to time. When she'd gotten back to Meg's place, she'd carried her inside and laid her in bed. When Meg had pulled her in for a kiss and locked her legs around Dani's waist, it had taken all her willpower to gently disengage herself. As much as she wanted what Meg had offered, she didn't want it when she was too drunk to even walk, let alone know who was in her bed. Meg had told her to leave and turned away, and Dani had let herself out, hoping everything would be fine in the morning.

But it hadn't been. Instead, Meg seemed to have gone on a bender. Her parties had always been known for their decadence, but rumor was they'd taken on new levels of hedonistic pleasure. Dani didn't want to think about the bed partners Meg probably had every night. Meg wasn't ever going to be defined by who she slept with; for her, a body was a body, and they were all interesting in their own ways. Dani wasn't bothered by that; people were people, and over the centuries, Dani had enjoyed plenty of variety herself. What Dani couldn't stop thinking about, though, was the desperate feeling of longing filling Meg's energy when she'd brought her home. She knew deep-seated emotions like that could turn destructive if not dealt with. And it certainly didn't seem like Meg was dealing with them. But whenever they ended up at a work scene together, Meg did what she needed to do and left quickly. Not only was she avoiding Dani, but it was obvious she was avoiding her sisters too. At the mass shooting two days ago, Meg had arrived late and left as soon as they were finished. After she'd left, Tis had asked Dani if she knew what was going on, and the hurt in her eyes was unmistakable. Unfortunately, Dani didn't have any answers either. She'd been spending a lot of time out on the water with Idona, and she knew Idona was tired of her hypothesizing about Meg's state of mind. Yesterday, she'd threatened to knock Dani out with her own surfboard and drown her if she didn't do something about it.

The problem was that Dani wasn't sure how to approach it. She wasn't Meg's girlfriend. Plus, Meg had always been wild, and who was Dani to quell that? But after talking to her sisters, she knew this wasn't "normal" Meg. This was something different, and Dani felt compelled to step in. She raised her hand to knock, but before she could, she heard Meg's voice from inside.

"If you make me get up to answer the door and you don't have coffee in your hands, I'll send my snakes to haunt your dreams every night."

Dani's tension eased a little. She let herself in and glanced around the house. Bottles, cans, and remnants of food littered the tables and floor. Meg lay facedown on the couch, one wing draped over the back and one trailing on the carpet. Dani couldn't figure out what was off until Meg shifted slightly. *Her hair.* Instead of the beautiful thick mane that hung down her back, it was now a messy, tangled bob with blond streaks. She made her way around the mess on the floor to Meg's side, where she wafted the cinnamon latte under her nose.

"Oh gods. Give me." Meg slowly turned over and groaned. She held her head for a second before reaching blindly for the cup Dani pressed into her hand. She sipped, and Dani stayed quiet until she'd opened her eyes.

"Morning."

"Is it?" Meg looked around her place and winced. "Yeah, that looks like morning."

"Want some help cleaning up?"

Meg struggled into a sitting position and rubbed her eyes. "You're kidding, right? You don't think I clean this up?" She sipped her latte and finally looked at Dani. "Thank you for this, by the way."

"No problem." Dani tried not to stare at Meg's extremely apparent cleavage above the sheer top when she stood to stretch.

"I reek. I'm going to shower."

Dani nodded, forcing that image from her mind. "Breakfast when you're done? I've got something I'd like to talk to you about."

Meg yawned. "Sure. Sounds good. If the cleaner comes, let him in, will you?" She went into the other room, already stripping off her clothes.

Dani sighed and tried to slow her racing pulse. Short hair or long, hungover or sober, Meg was still the most beautiful woman she'd ever known. She didn't know what was driving Meg to extremes, but she hoped she had an idea that could help. Someone knocked, and Dani went to let the cleaner in.

He looked around the room and shook his head. "Good thing she pays me well." He focused on Dani and stilled.

Dani nodded, unwilling to engage in conversation with someone who might pee themselves if she got too close. Instead, she left him to it and went into the kitchen, where she started piling bottles and cans on the counter, since she had nothing else to do.

Meg came out sooner than Dani expected, dressed but looking less energetic than usual. "You mentioned breakfast?"

Dani jiggled her car keys. "Have you been to Wild Thyme in Pasadena?"

"Not one I know. Let's go."

Meg waved to the cleaner and said thanks before they headed out to Dani's car. He simply grunted in reply and mumbled something about life being too long for some people.

"I thought we'd take real streets today, if that's okay? It's a beautiful day."

Meg nodded but didn't say anything. She closed her eyes and tilted her face to the sun.

Dani respected her unvoiced request for quiet and headed down the 110 to Pasadena. When they pulled into the parking lot, she gently touched Meg's leg to wake her. "Hey. We're here."

Meg looked around groggily and sniffed the air. "Yes!"

She jumped out of the car, and Dani followed her into the little breakfast café that really did smell amazing.

"Dani! It's been ages! Come on in. Your favorite booth is free." Carlos, the owner and a longtime acquaintance, ushered her in warmly.

"Thanks much, Carlos. This is my friend, Meg."

His smile faltered slightly. "Megara Graves. It's been a very long time indeed." He brightened again. "I seem to remember you truly enjoy food. Let me get you some coffee."

Meg looked up from where she was nearly drooling over the coffee cake on the counter. "Sorry, have we met?"

"A very long time ago, red one. Too long to revisit." He motioned them toward the booth and disappeared into the back.

Dani and Meg headed to the booth and sat down. "I take it he's one of ours?" Meg said, looking thoughtful.

"Pre-fader, kind of. Centeotl, the Aztec god of maize. Most of his people died off of disease brought by travelers, and the rest were decimated by war. Several of the Aztec war gods got out of control and refused to stop pushing against the other tribes. When humans didn't kill each other off fast enough—"

"The primary god started killing off humans directly. It'll be a wonder if he doesn't poison my food." Meg looked at the menu, but it was clear she wasn't seeing it. "Maybe we should go."

"What happened?" Dani asked softly. This wasn't what she'd intended, but it could work to her advantage if she didn't push too hard.

"The fury sisters killed a god." Carlos put their coffee down on the table, and his smile was sad. "They were the most terrifying, magnificent women we'd ever seen. But by the time we saw them, it was too late. Tezcatlipoca had turned everything to darkness. Night was all we had, and war was everywhere. He began destroying the humans in our care, heedless of which side they were on. Essentially, he went mad." He took a deep breath. "And so, Megara and her sisters stood before him, condemned him to death, and when the dust settled, he was gone." He picked up their menus and put them in their hands. "This is far too heavy for breakfast conversation. Ancient history belongs where it dies."

He walked away to help other customers, and Dani looked at Meg in awe. "You can kill gods?"

"We can, as a trio. Not any one of us individually. That's why Tis was a good choice for the legal stuff. She's fucking scary on her own, but when the three of us come at someone, they don't have a chance." Meg shrugged, looking sad. "We punish those who hurt others, and if the one doing the hurting on that kind of scale is a god, we have to step in. It's one of the powers given to us as defenders of humans, but we've only had to use it once."

"Good to know. I'll make sure I don't get on your bad side." Dani smiled, hoping to break the tension, and when Meg smiled back, she moved on. "The banana pecan waffles are incredible. So are the biscuits and gravy."

Carlos came back over, and Meg ordered both of Dani's recommendations. Dani ordered her favorite, a spinach and cheese omelet.

Meg looked at Dani over her coffee cup. "You said you had something you wanted to talk to me about?"

Dani started to speak, but Meg interrupted her.

"Wait. If it's to tell me off about anything, don't."

Dani held up her hands. "You just told me you can off a god. I'm not about to take you to task for anything, ever."

Meg smiled, and this time it reached her eyes. "Okay. Go ahead."

"Remember that day you helped Azrael figure out how to start rebranding? I've decided I want to do something similar, but I have no idea where to start."

Meg looked surprised. "Why would you want to rebrand? You're not a destination."

"True. But what are any believers, in pretty much any religion, afraid of?" Dani pointed at herself.

"But fear of death is what makes human life meaningful, isn't it?"

"But should it? Shouldn't life be meaningful for what the humans bring to it, rather than for the fear of what comes after?" Dani didn't fully understand her desire herself, but she knew it was important.

"Hmm. So, you think that by reducing the fear of death, people can focus on doing good for the sake of it, rather than because of their fear of death or the afterlife?"

Dani played with a napkin, trying to order her thoughts. "I don't know. Maybe? There has to be a way to reduce people's fear of death."

She laughed softly. "You said I sounded like a travel ad once. Maybe that's the route to take."

Carlos came over and set numerous plates of hot food on the table. "Enjoy."

Meg made appreciative noises over the food, and Dani knew better than to try to talk to her when she was engaged with eating. She tucked into her own food and remembered why she loved the place. When half of Meg's food was gone, she finally looked up. "I think you've got something there."

Dani lifted her napkin to her face, embarrassed.

"No, silly. With the travel thing." She chewed, looking thoughtful. "I mean, you're kind of a...a limo service. For dead people. They die. You pick them up and take them somewhere else, where they'll spend the next portion of whatever eternity they believe in."

Dani laughed. "Right."

"That in itself isn't scary, but you get the blame for it. What they're afraid of is what comes after you, right?"

"Not entirely. I think they're also afraid of what they're leaving behind. All the experiences they haven't had, the people they love, the regrets. All that comes into play too."

Meg finished off her biscuits and gravy and licked her fingers before returning to her waffle. "That makes sense. We have to think of a way to show them that what they're leaving behind is...well, not your fault. It's theirs. We have to get them to see you as an exciting travel guide rather than the final dissolution of lives. Easy."

She laughed, and Dani watched with fascination as she licked maple syrup from her lips. *What I wouldn't give to be that syrup.* "Do you think it's possible?"

"It's totally possible. I mean, if Satan can do it, you can, right? We'll just have to work out the logistics."

Dani smiled at Carlos as he refilled their coffee cups and left. He always seemed to know when conversation was wanted and when it wasn't. *Perhaps that's the old god in him.* "Here's the thing, though." She shook her head when Meg offered her a bite of waffle. "I don't want gaudy. Moving souls is a huge responsibility, and I don't want it to feel like less of an honor than it is. If it means negating that in any way, then I'd rather not do it."

Meg pushed her empty plates away and sighed contentedly. "Obviously. You think I don't know you well enough to know you'd hate having a neon emblazoned Hummer blaring rap music to pick up souls in? Although it would be hilarious to see you in a Hawaiian shirt."

"Never going to happen. Where do you put all the food you eat?"

"I have no idea. I've always loved food, and I'm eternally grateful I can't get fat."

Carlos came over and stacked the plates. "I knew you'd enjoy that."

Meg touched his hand, and he stopped to look at her. "It was wonderful, thank you. And thanks for not asking me to leave."

He covered her hand with his, and Dani saw the old god light in his eyes, something the ancients never seemed to lose.

"You did what was necessary, red one. When it comes down to it, that's what we all do when the time comes." He leaned closer. "But we have to be strong enough to see exactly what is necessary." He let go of her hand, and the moment lightened. "Can I get you anything else?"

Meg was looking at him thoughtfully, so Dani answered. "I think we're good. Just the bill, please."

He shook his head. "No bill today, gorgeous. When old friends come by, it's a celebration, not business." He put his hand over his heart. "Just promise to come back."

Meg smiled. "Are you kidding? I want to try everything on the menu."

"And I'll be happy to cook it for you." He gathered the plates and said over his shoulder as he walked away, "See you soon."

Dani followed Meg out into the sunshine. "Thanks for coming with me. Sorry it got a bit weird."

"Who knew pre-faders were everywhere, right?" Meg got in the car and turned the radio on.

They drove in silence back toward Afterlife. Dani could practically feel the whirlwind of thoughts in Meg's head but wasn't sure if she had the right to ask. *If you're really a friend, then you should.* "What're you thinking about?"

Meg sighed heavily. "So many things I don't know where one thought ends and the next begins."

"Anything I can help with?"

Meg was quiet for so long Dani wasn't sure she was going to answer.

"Honestly? You coming over today was probably exactly what I needed, even if I felt like hell when you came in. I feel lost. Like there's this hole inside me, and no matter what I put in it, it just drops straight through, leaving the hole just a little bit bigger."

She sounded so sad Dani ached to put her arms around her. She settled for reaching over and holding her hand. "Maybe you're trying to fill the hole with the wrong things."

Meg grinned slightly. "It sounds dirty when you say it."

Dani felt herself flush. "Definitely not what I meant."

Meg rested her head against the seat and closed her eyes. "I know what you meant. I just need to figure out what I want, I guess."

Dani's heart raced slightly at the thought, but she quickly stopped it. *Don't be an ass.* "Your sisters are worried about you. So am I."

Meg squeezed Dani's hand and let it go. Dani pulled it back reluctantly.

"I know. Thanks. It's like Carlos said, right? We do what's necessary, eventually."

Dani pulled into the Afterlife campus and went to Meg's. Once in the driveway, she decided to say what needed to be said. "You know the story Carlos told about you and your sisters dealing with an out-of-control god?"

Meg turned to look at her. "Yeah?"

"Who deals with an out-of-control fury?" Dani said it softly, a gentle question rather than a judgment, and hoped Meg would take it that way.

Meg's shoulders slumped and tears welled in her eyes. "I don't know," she whispered.

"Maybe we should fix things before we find out?" Dani gently wiped away a tear sliding down Meg's cheek.

"Probably a good idea." Meg got out of the car and paused. "Thank you again for breakfast. And for being a true friend." She looked away, staring into the distance. "I have a lot to think about. Can I call you tomorrow?"

"Call me whenever you want to. Even if you just want someone to sit with. I'm here, okay?" Dani really didn't want to leave, but she also needed to respect Meg's desire to be alone.

"Thanks, Dani. Really." Meg turned and headed into her house. Dani pulled away. She needed to focus on work for a while. She could only hope Meg would be okay on her own. *I'm worrying about a fury. Like she needs someone like me looking after her.* She tried to quell the unease she felt and headed back to work.

CHAPTER NINE

Meg stared out the window at the other houses on campus. She'd chosen to live on the Afterlife grounds because she liked being surrounded with others of her kind, but now it felt claustrophobic. She had a horde of people over every night. Most she knew, some she didn't. The past two weeks since Selene's dinner were a blur. She remembered making a pass at Dani. She also remembered Dani turning her down and the horrible disappointment she'd felt at her refusal. The self-reprisals and desire to feel wanted had fired her desire to party even harder than usual. And she did. She had a vague sense of naked bodies in her bed, various sizes and colors, but didn't remember much else. She wasn't even sure she'd been in bed with them or had just watched from the sidelines. What she did know was that Dani was never far from her thoughts, particularly when she was in the throes of an orgasm. Beautiful Death had become the primary figure in her fantasies.

And then there she was, coffee in hand, gently pulling Meg from her self-destructive tornado and back into the world. Meg wasn't fooled by Dani's request for help, though she didn't doubt that there was truth to it. Dani was too honest to outright fib. She picked up the phone but realized with dismal clarity that there was no one to call. The people she'd surrounded herself with weren't friends or confidants. Dani and her sisters were her only truly close friends, and she certainly couldn't talk to Dani about her issues with Dani.

She hit number two on her speed dial. "Why didn't you come check on me?" she said when Tis answered the phone.

"Because you were wallowing, and when you're wallowing, it's best to leave you alone with your filthy mind and dirty orgies. It's when you stop being insane that we worry about you most."

"Fair enough. Are you free?"

"Sorry, Sis. I'm on my way to a meeting at the office. But I bet Kera would love a reason to escape. Would she do?"

Meg thought about it. She hadn't had any alone time with Kera, but her reputation prior to Tis suggested she might understand what Meg was going through. "Yeah, actually, she might."

"Excellent. I'll tell her to pop by your place in about half an hour. And, Meg?"

"What, pale face?"

"We love you. If we thought you were in real trouble, we would have come. You know that, right?"

"Of course I do. Thanks for giving me space." The heavy hand of disillusionment pressing on Meg's soul began to ease off. *I'm so fucking lucky to have sisters.*

"Anytime, fang face. See you later."

"Wait. One more thing. I went to a case the other day. Another weird one, not that that's anything new these days. I wish we could get sexy cases, you know? Like people fucking each other to death in bizarre ways, or—"

"Meg, honey, I have a meeting to get to."

"Right, sorry. It was this mom who had killed her kids. But she wasn't one of our usual, you know? She did it because of the confusion caused by the cosmic shithead herself. She couldn't live with the world being what it is. She said 'what's coming,' and that was creepy, but whatever. I thought you should know. We're heading to cases that aren't our thing. I don't know if you want to create some kind of super squad to deal with the headfucks caused by our nightmarish friend."

Meg blinked back tears, something she thought she'd long ago given up, but something that snuck up on her regularly these days. "It was really sad. I hated having to do anything about it."

Tis sighed. "Thanks. That's exactly the kind of thing we need to keep tabs on. I'll let Kera know, and if you come across more, send the info our way."

"Will do, pale face. Love you."

Meg hung up feeling better than she had in weeks. *You just have to do what's necessary.* She rolled her eyes. *As if I know what that is.*

❖

"I had no idea furies could have so many issues. I thought you'd have those all worked out by now." Kera peeled the label from her bottle. "I think you should get nasty. Full out down and dirty. It will either get her out of your system, or you'll want more. Either way, it's a win."

"And if I get her out of my system and it ruins our friendship?" They'd been talking for hours, and Meg had finally admitted to her overwhelming attraction to Dani, which no amount of hedonism was helping cure. She also told her about her desire to be more than a party fury but that she had no clue where to begin.

"Yeah, that would be shit. Don't do it. Ignore me."

Meg threw a wadded-up candy wrapper at her. "Thanks. That's helpful."

Kera threw the wrapper back at her. "Meg, you're hot. You're also slightly crazy, which makes you even hotter. Scarier too. You could have, and if reputation serves, you *have* had, anyone you want. But you don't want just anyone. You want one of the few people in existence more powerful than you. Which is cool, I get that. Power is sexy. And Dani has that whole too-sexy-for-life thing going on. Like a Calvin Klein ad, but with Death instead of some crack-skinny supermodel." She nodded as though wise. "The question is, does she want you?"

Meg groaned. "Pretty sure she doesn't."

"What makes you say that?"

Meg closed her eyes, unable to look at Kera and admit it. "I made a pass at her after Selene's party. She turned me down flat."

Kera started laughing and had to set her beer down so she didn't spill it. "The night you couldn't even stand upright on your own? When you fell asleep mid-conversation and answered the question someone asked you ten minutes earlier when you woke up?"

"Gods. Was I that gone?"

Kera picked her beer up and settled back on the couch. "If you have to ask, that's your answer. Have you ever tried to have sex when you're that wasted? I can tell you from experience, it's not pretty. It's not sexy. Hell, it's not even good. It's all fumbling and alcohol burps. I wouldn't base your perception of her interest in you on that night."

Meg was crazy glad Tis had suggested Kera. *Maybe she knew this was more of what I needed. Thank the gods for my sisters.* "So you think I should try again?"

"If you're this worked up over her, yeah. But do it when you've still got verbal capability and don't smell like the bottom of a box of wine." Kera's expression turned serious. "But really, yeah, you have to be prepared for it to go tits up. You could go for it, and it could be a teenage-fumbling-in-the-dark disaster. And then you could end up not talking for a while. I say a while, because in your world, *never* doesn't seem like a real thing. Especially when you have to work together. Shit, that's another thing, isn't it? You have to see each other for work a lot." She popped the top on another beer. "Yeah, it could be a fuckfest all right."

"You know, I really like you, but you're absolutely no help at all." Meg smiled and tapped her beer bottle to Kera's.

"I'm shit at helping with matters of the heart. Tis would have told you that, if you'd told her that part." She pointed at Meg. "But I can totally help with the other part. That's something I'm good at."

"I don't think Tis would go for a threesome." Meg grinned, knowing full well it wasn't what Kera meant.

"Ew. No offense, but the sister thing never did it for me. And Tis keeps me well sated. Not to mention I'd never piss off someone who can *poof* me into the kind of meat-puddle I saw when that bastard kidnapped me." She made a *poof* motion with one hand and took a long swig of beer. "I mean the bit where you're at loose ends. That, I totally understand."

"You do? Because I don't. I'm a fury. I do what furies do. And I have fun. Why doesn't that feel like enough anymore?" Meg got up and rummaged through her cupboards. "Want some popcorn?"

"By the gods, woman. Do you ever stop eating?"

"It makes me feel better."

"Yeah, well, remember those of us who can gain weight, would you? Bring it over. I like extra salt."

The tension Meg had been holding in her shoulders had dissolved rapidly once she'd started talking to Kera. It had been a little weird and awkward at first, but after the first beer, they'd settled into conversation like old friends. It was strange, talking to someone she wasn't related to, didn't want to sleep with, and who didn't want anything from her, either. *An actual friend. Who knew?*

She brought over the bowl of popcorn and set a pair of fresh beers on the table. "So, you were saying you understand the other problem of my life, even though I don't?"

"Recap it for me so I'm sure I have all the facts." Kera popped a big handful of popcorn in her mouth.

"Okay. Well, I'm bored, I guess. Alec is Miss 'I saved the world and fell in love with the Bridge,' and Tis is Miss 'Keep-it-legal-or-I'll-kill-you-all.' And they've got you and Selene, who are all-powerful humans changing the world in big ways. I, on the other hand, throw amazing parties and get too drunk to have sex."

"Do you like being a fury?" Kera asked.

"That's like asking you if you like being human or female."

"No, it's not. I can't change being human, but I could change being female if it wasn't how I identified."

"Well, I can't change being a fury any more than you could change being human." Feeling petulant all of a sudden, Meg stuck her tongue out at Kera.

Kera laughed. "Crazy. Okay. We'll use fury as a job title instead of a state of being, the way I'm a badass boss who tells gods what to do. Do you still like going out and giving the bad guys the brain melting they deserve?" Kera held up her hand. "Wait. Don't answer right away. Think about it."

Meg stopped her initial answer and really did think about it. Instead of going with the answer she expected, she looked into her heart. "Yes. I still love what I do. I still believe in it too. But the world is more complicated now. It used to be really black and white, mostly. Now there are all kinds of deep questions and issues. I feel like I want to be more than just a fury. Like there's something more for me out there."

"Exactly what I thought you'd say." Kera pushed the popcorn bowl at Meg. "Take this away from me. I can't stop eating it."

"You're supposed to eat food when it's there." Meg ate a handful and then picked the fallen ones off her shirt.

"What do you enjoy doing? Aside from having copious amounts of sex with a lot of people and drinking like a whale? Both of which I applaud heartily, may I add."

"Helping people?"

"Is that a question? Because I don't know the answer."

"Jackass. I like helping people. Like when Azrael asked for help redesigning hell."

"Keep going." Kera motioned with her beer, some spilling out.

"I feel like you're a shrink. A really bad, drunk one."

"I'm the best there is, at pretty much everything except being tactful, humble, or immortal. Keep going."

"Fine. I like the logistics of helping people. Thinking of ways around their problems. I like turning things upside down and looking at them in a new light."

Kera tipped her bottle at Meg. "Exactly."

"Exactly what?" Meg threw a handful of popcorn at Kera.

"Design and logistics. There's a whole building full of gods behind me who don't know their ass from a mirror. And yet they want to reinvent themselves, even though they haven't the faintest clue on how to do that, because they don't really know who they are to other people. What do you think, Sherlock?"

"Interior design. That's your answer?"

Kera shrugged. "I don't have any answers. I'm here because my terrifying girlfriend said her sister needed someone to talk to." She grinned to show she was kidding. "But I'm fucking good at business, and I've always said you have to do what you enjoy in order to be happy or good at it. You're already a fury, and it's not like that doesn't keep you fairly busy. Maybe helping the gods with their redesigns and images would give you something interesting to focus on until you figure out who you want to be when you grow up. Because apparently, three thousand years isn't enough, which I have to say, is pretty fucking disheartening for my puny mortal self." She stood up and swayed. "I need to pee. You'd think I'd have learned by now not to try keeping up with a fury when they're drinking." She staggered off to the bathroom.

Meg stared at the condensation on her bottle, thinking about what Kera had said. The more she thought about the possibilities, the more excited she became. First Azrael's place, then the Deadlands, which would give her more time with Dani. There were six major religious zones, all of them broken down into further sectors. From Afterlife, Meg could help every sector. She didn't need to wait for them to come to her, either. There was no reason she couldn't go talk to the department heads and get actively involved. Kera came out of the bathroom looking extremely unsteady and an unnaturally green shade for a human. Meg jumped off the couch and gave her a huge hug. "Tis is going to kill me for getting you drunk, but I don't care. You're the best jackass shrink I know."

"Thanks, I think. Wake me when Tis gets here." Kera flopped onto the sofa and promptly passed out.

Meg grabbed her notepad and started sketching the portions of the Deadlands she could remember. *Time to make some changes.*

CHAPTER TEN

D ani leaned back to avoid the glass pitcher that flew through the air and crashed into the wall beyond her.

"I told you, it's not enough!" Iblis slammed his hand against the table, leaving a dent in the wood. His dark skin glistened with sweat, and his little fangs were extended. "We want to be included in all decisions, not eat the scraps of the ones you've already made."

A few of the other underworld gods nodded their agreement though Azrael and Hades both looked thoughtful rather than angry.

"And I told you, that's not how it works. That isn't how it's worked for centuries. Why are you adamant about changing it now?" Zed remained standing, his shining form a visual reminder of his power.

"Because *everything* has changed. The world isn't the same. We deserve the same respect. We demand it!" Iblis looked around the table for support and frowned when at least two people didn't seem to agree with him. He pointed at Azrael. "Aren't you tired of being told what to do? Of your cloud god making the decisions?"

"We follow the books we wrote together with the other gods. Yes, we're rewriting them for clarity. And yes, we have to tread carefully when it comes to understanding the changes happening among the humans—"

"Tread carefully? We're GODS. For perhaps the first time in our existences, we have the chance to be more than what the humans created. We can be who we want to be, and let them see that side of us. Once they see it, they believe it, and then it becomes part of their vision of us, which only makes us stronger."

Freya tapped the table for attention. "Perhaps the horned one is right. Now we can show the humans just how amazing we are." She stroked the tiger beside her, who sat with its head on her lap, snoring as usual.

Iblis winced slightly. The last person he really wanted to agree with him was a woman, even if she was a goddess.

"Aren't you doing just that, with your new marketing campaigns?" Dani said from her place against the wall. She'd worked with every god in the room throughout time and wasn't afraid of any of them. Little did they know how much she hated conflict.

Azrael nodded. "I am. With Meg's help, I'm redesigning my territory and my image at the same time. I'm changing the way the humans think of me, regardless of which bureaucratic meeting I sit in on."

Osiris shook his head. "That's not the point. We can make all the marketing changes we want. But if decisions on the way the gods behave are being made without us at the table, we remain less than. Our voices aren't heard." He looked at Zed. "And that is no longer acceptable."

The room was silent, everyone looking at Zed. He stared back at them, clearly at a loss.

Dani finally spoke up. "Perhaps Zed can discuss it with the others and get back to you?"

He looked at Dani gratefully. "That's exactly what I'll do. I can't make a decision without speaking to the rest of the council. We'll convene and discuss your concerns."

Yama stood and the others did as well. "I believe I speak for all of us when I say they are not *concerns*, Zeus. They are demands which must be met." He left the room calmly, Iblis, Osiris, and Freya following. Azrael and Hades lingered.

"And you two? Where do you stand?"

Dani watched as the two of them seemed to struggle to say what they wanted to. Something seemed off, as though they were confused.

Hades held out his hand. "I can't explain. Feel."

Though he looked confused, Zed took his brother's hand. He held it for only a moment before pulling away with a thunderous growl. He nodded at Dani, who took Az's hand and shuddered when she felt the black strings of confusion suffusing his being.

She let go and wiped her hand on her jeans. "Dis. Only she could have left that kind of stain."

Azrael sighed and rubbed his temples. "Of course. All of a sudden, nothing made sense. I was pissed off all the time. I even torched an entire sitting area because the color reminded me of a demon who worked for me once. I didn't even really like her..." He drifted off, staring blankly beyond them.

Dani touched his shoulder, and he jerked back to awareness. He motioned almost helplessly.

"Yes. She's brought her poison into our home." Hades sparked with electricity, blue and white flashes appearing on his clothing like lightning bugs on speed. "I too have been beyond reason. The difference is that Az and I knew something wasn't right, even if we weren't in complete control. The others are being manipulated and don't even know it."

"Would it matter if they did?" Dani asked softly.

"What do you mean? No god wants someone controlling him." Zed sat down behind his desk, looking weary.

"No, of course not. But I have a feeling that the ideas in their heads were already there in some form, even if they were deeply buried. Even gods can be manipulated. Dis feeds on the chaos and doubt *already* within people. She can't really do anything to those who know who and what they are." Dani looked outside at the office cubicles buzzing with busy workers. "All she needed to do was drop the seeds of doubt over them and let them take root."

Azrael sighed and leaned against the table. He gave Zed an apologetic smile. "And there are plenty of people who would agree with them. You know some of what they say makes sense."

Zed nodded, his eyes closed and his head back. "Yes. I can see they have a point. And I really will raise it with the council. It may take some time to get everyone together, given how busy everyone is in their own areas, but I'll make it happen."

Hades looked at Dani. "No offense, dark one, but why were you here tonight? You're rarely at these meetings." His eyes narrowed as he focused on her. "Though it looks like you may have a place at our table soon enough."

Dani tried to deflect the conversation she wasn't ready to have and handed him a notebook. "I wanted to talk to the underworld gods about the number of lost souls arriving. I'm seeing an unexpected rise in people who believe, because they can't do otherwise in the face of gods walking the planet, but who don't subscribe to any particular religion. They're quite literally souls with nowhere to go."

Hades flipped through the notebook, and Azrael read over his shoulder.

Az looked up. "What was it you wanted to ask us?"

Dani shrugged and shoved her hands in her pockets. "I'm not sure, really. We're trying to figure out what to do with them. They're dead, so really, they should go *somewhere*. And it affects your numbers too. Some of their souls are heavy and dark, and if they believed, they'd be in some kind of hell for sure. Some are light, like cotton candy, and want peace. But I have no idea where to take them." She paused, thinking about the events of the evening. "And it doesn't seem to me it's a topic that can be discussed without you. This affects all the gods, but most especially the underworld gods who deal with death."

Hades and Azrael both smiled at her. "Well played, dark one." Hades closed the book. "Can I take this? I'll call a meeting with the others and discuss it. Let's see if anyone has any ideas. If we come up with anything, we'll let you know."

Dani felt like she could breathe a little easier, knowing she didn't have to solve this problem on her own. "That would be great, Hades. Thank you."

Zed stood and put one hand on Hades's shoulder and one on Azrael's shoulder. "In the meantime, fight Dis's seeds. Chaos among the humans is one thing. Chaos among the gods is another. We're going to need all the sane people we can get now."

Azrael stretched and smiled. "It's weird. Acknowledging it and talking about it out loud seems to have taken away some of its power. We'll keep talking to each other, and we'll try to tell the other gods what's taken place. Hopefully, their irritation at being manipulated will calm their sense of righteousness."

Dani opened the door for them as they turned to leave. "Remember you're always welcome in the Deadlands if you need a place to get away."

Hades nodded, back to his remote self, but Az kissed her cheek.

"You're a gem among pebbles, beautiful. Don't think we didn't notice you skirting your own situation. Remember that you've got friends too."

They left, and Dani pondered what he'd said. She looked at Zed, who shrugged. "Who knows? He's always liked his vague metaphors. I think he secretly wishes he was born a Fate instead." He motioned her to a seat and took one across from her. "Any thoughts on what to do next?"

Dani considered. "I think you need to let Tisera know right away. This has serious implications with regard to the company's constitution. And if Dis is meddling with the gods, who knows how bad this could get."

He sighed. "It was a lot easier when we were answering emails and eating donuts all day."

Dani laughed. "True. At least no one is fading now, though."

"No, they're not. And now that the gods have shown their faces so the masses know what they look like, they're getting even clearer. Stronger too. They're acting like...like..."

"Gods?" Dani smiled gently. "No shore pounded by waves is left unchanged. Still the water flows, and still the shore remains. Both are changed, but both are still there."

He smiled back at her and held her hand in his. "I forget how long you've been around. Between you and the fury sisters, we'll make it through this."

Dani's heart swelled, and she looked away so he wouldn't see the tears in her eyes. For the first time in her existence, someone believed she offered hope rather than just darkness. And to be counted among the women she respected was more than she could have asked.

The moment passed, and he stood. "Guess I'd better start calling the troops. Thank you for coming. And I'll take your question about the lost souls to our council as well. You're right, it's something that affects us all."

He turned toward his desk, and she turned to go.

"Dani?"

She stopped halfway out the door.

"You're not alone. We all respect you too much to ask, but when you're ready to talk about what's going on with you, find someone to talk to."

She swallowed against the irrational fear of being found out. "I don't know what you mean, Zed."

He shook his head. "You're glowing like a pre-fader coming back to power, Dani. Humans like Kera and Selene may not see it yet, but the rest of us do." He opened a bag of candy and popped a few in his mouth. "Like I said, when you're ready." He turned back to his work.

Dani left, her pulse racing and her stomach churning. *How do I talk about things I don't even understand yet?* It was confusing to know other people could see it taking place, and she had no real way to hide it from her own kind. *Maybe I need to hide away like Meg.* The thought was depressing. She'd only just begun putting herself out there more. *He said when I'm ready. So, I wait until I'm ready.* She pulled out her phone and called Idona.

"I really need some board time. You in?"

"Can't, sorry. I'm overseeing a new batch outside Moscow. Backwoods church. An outsider came in and shot the place up with an automatic. Alec has already been here for the shooter, but we've got forty souls to pick up."

Dani could easily picture the scene. "Faith based?"

"Alec says kind of. The people praying were all fine, and we'll make sure they get processed. The shooter was pissed off about his wife and kid dying of poisoned water, said god didn't help."

"So there were health problems?" The gods couldn't do anything about science-based issues, something the human population couldn't be told about. It would destroy their belief and lessen any hope they might have, a necessity if they were to continue as a species.

"Yeah, major." Idona hesitated. "Thing is, though, maybe the god could have helped clean up the water?"

Dani picked at the cuticle on her thumbnail, trying to think it through. "I don't know. I think it depends on how much poison there was. If it became a science thing, where it would be impossible to clean it up without chemical intervention or something, they couldn't have helped. But maybe there's a way to get the gods thinking about issues like poisoned water and working around them, rather than tackling them head-on." She was at a loss, and with everything going on, she had a feeling it wouldn't be a welcome question. Still, she had to raise it. "I'll let Kera know, and I'll let her bring it up with Zed and the council. We'll just keep doing our jobs."

"Got it, thanks. I'll give you a shout when I'm back."

Dani headed home, grabbed her board, and headed to San Diego for the late afternoon waves. She paddled farther out than she needed to, but she wanted space from the other surfers. She caught wave after wave and let the blue-black water carry and swallow her, spit her out, and carry her again. The Pacific was dark, cold water, but the waves were perfect, and the chilly opaqueness mirrored the feeling in her soul.

By the time she made it back to shore she was centered again. *I can do this. Whatever this is. Whatever I can feel coming, I'll be ready. Somehow.* She thought of Zed's reminder that she wasn't alone, and of the women at Afterlife she'd become close to. And Meg. Always, there was Meg. If there was one being in the world Dani would always keep going for, it was Meg.

CHAPTER ELEVEN

Chants filled the air, voices raised together in disharmony. Placards reading things like *Anti-Theists for a New World* and *Send the gods back to their clouds* were held aloft like beacons of poorly inked truth. Humanity First's national billboard campaign had many of the same slogans, encouraging people to think for themselves and to consider the price of religion rather than some reward in the afterlife. *The Bible taken literally is a horror novel* was one of Dis's favorites.

She watched as Angie Hitchens, the latest in a line of leaders of Humanity First since Frey Falconi's death, stood on a platform outside Afterlife, Inc. and motioned her rabid followers to silence.

"Thank you for coming. As you know, we're here because the religious landscape has changed. While we were formed on the basis of atheism, we have now moved into anti-theism territory instead. Though we can no longer say gods don't exist, we can still maintain that religion is the foundation of a disease eating away at all of humanity."

The crowd roared their approval, and Dis noticed a few Afterlife staff at the windows above, watching the protest below. *How does it feel to watch people protest your existence?* She nearly laughed at the thought. No one liked chaos in their lives, but she never took it personally. But then, her ego wasn't tied up with having followers, either. She loved the deep sense of discord heavy in the air around her, focused on every being in the building. The anger, frustration, and disappointment of the protesters caressed her skin like an old lover.

"Belief in the gods creates false hope. Have they given us the cure for cancer? No. Fifteen hundred people a day are still dying. Have they provided the most desperate with a way out? No. Three billion people in the world are still living in absolute poverty. Have they stopped wars? No. Granted, the deaths from religious conflicts have slowed dramatically, that's true." The crowd didn't seem to like her backing down at all, and there was a rumble of anger. "Wait. Hear me out. Even though religious wars have decreased, the desire for land, for resources, for money…all of those things are still causing problems all over the world. To date, there are more than fifty mass conflicts surrounding those issues, all of which are killing both those who fight and those on the sidelines. Isn't religion supposed to temper those desires, those so-called sins? What are the gods waiting for? Who are they really for?"

The crowd responded with a resounding battle cry. "Themselves!"

She nodded. "Themselves." She motioned to the building behind her. "And this is where they sit on their thrones, letting their believers down with every sobbing prayer not answered."

Dis loved the woman onstage. She *wanted* her. She wanted to possess her, body and mind. The fact that the gods inside sat on office chairs in front of computers like many of the people in the crowd did every day would have made a poor battle cry, and the fact that this woman chose her words carefully made Dis want her all the more.

The crowd screamed their approval, and a bottle shattered against the front doors of the building. The resulting roar from the guardian, Cerberus, silenced them for a moment before they roared back as one.

"We will not be silenced. We will not be ignored. We will continue to bang on their doors and protest their inhumanity until they either prove their worth or leave us in peace." She raised her fists in the air. "We will resist!"

The noise from the crowd was deafening, and Dis felt the emotions running through them. It was fascinating, the way a single focal point could dampen the confusion and funnel the communal rage. Jesus had done much the same his first time around. People had flocked to his gentle voice and simple ideology. Of course, while the outcome for him hadn't been stellar, it had skyrocketed the number of followers, and his father had been happy. He was doing it again, and his following was strong. But with a group like Humanity First challenging everything the gods stood for, confusion and entitlement were spreading among humans like theological rabies.

Angie left the stage and was instantly surrounded by bodyguards who ushered her past her adoring fans and into an armored car. *She has her own zealots. Interesting.* Dis could use that to sow her own brand of fun, but at the moment, she wanted to talk to her first.

She thought of the car and Angie inside it and was transported onto the backseat beside her.

"What the serious fuck?" Angie jumped and pressed herself against the window.

Dis smiled. "Sorry, I know that's probably unnerving. But I just had to tell you how fantastic you were at the rally, and I didn't feel like waiting."

Angie glared at her. "And you are?"

"I've gone by many names throughout time. At the moment, some call me Dis. Others, Chaos. Nice to meet you." Dis held out her hand, wondering if Angie had the courage to take it.

She hesitated for only a moment before accepting. "I won't say it's nice to meet you. I dislike being taken by surprise, and if you haven't noticed, the gods are kind of on my shit list."

Dis let go of her hand. She'd read Angie's emotions, her thoughts, her fears. She was one of the strong ones. She believed wholeheartedly in what she was preaching. There was no doubt, no reserve of adolescent religious guilt or remorse. Not only was she not confused, she had a clear desire for one outcome: the eradication of religion.

"Yes. I figured that out. And it's exactly the reason I'd like to have a special conversation with you."

❖

The building shook with Zed's thunder. Dani, Meg, Tisera, Alec, Selene, and Kera kept their distance as Zed gesticulated and flung lightning bolts haphazardly through the room.

"Is this what it comes to? The ungrateful bastards. Sons of clay-bitten slime. How dare they?"

Tis stepped forward in her full form, wings outstretched in front of the two humans in their party. "Zed. Stop. Your tantrum won't get us anywhere."

He turned on her, his hand raised as if to throw. She narrowed her eyes at him and hissed, and he instantly backed down. He lowered his hand and slumped against the wall. Dani felt the whole group relax slightly. When Zed moved back to his desk, the others cautiously made their way to the conference table.

Tis folded her wings but stayed in form. Alec and Meg were in their natural states as well, ready to jump in front of Selene and Kera if necessary. Zed was no match for the fury sisters when they came together, and he knew it. *If he stops to pay attention.* Dani sat beside Meg and nearly laughed at Meg's expression. Never one to shrink from drama, the situation clearly had her engaged. She looked like a kid trying to figure out what ride to take first at the county fair.

"So, legal council? What do we do?"

Tis doodled on the legal pad in front of her. "I haven't the faintest idea. The gods are contracted to Afterlife. But that was based on the collective. There's nothing in our constitution that says they can never leave the company. Once we all came together, it seemed like a given. Plus, everyone has played by the rules we set in place for centuries."

"It's that fucking whack-job you let in from outer space. Nothing's been right since she got here." Kera pointed out the window, presumably at the sky.

Selene shook her head. "While it's true it's gotten worse since she got here, and the issues with the gods are undeniably her fault, given what Dani and Zed have told us about the underworld gods, the confusion and unease were what called her back in the first place. We couldn't have predicted the reaction of the human population." She bit her lip. "When I suggested the gods make themselves known, I had no idea it could have this kind of psychological backlash."

"I agree with Kera. Can't we shove the whack-job back to where she came from? I mean, it's right upstairs." Meg grinned at Kera, who nodded back.

"The Fates have said she can't leave until the situation here is settled. They wouldn't allow us to send her back." Tis gave Kera a warning look.

Alec tapped the table. "So, let's look at the crisis of the moment. Several of the underworld gods have decided to go back to their own countries of origin. They're leaving Afterlife altogether, which means they're no longer bound by any of the codes set in place. Right?"

Tis nodded. "Right. And when a few of the lesser-known gods heard the underworld gods were leaving, they decided it was their chance to strike out on their own as well. They're hoping that by being in their territory full-time and no longer bound by Afterlife rules, they can develop more followers and gain status."

"And the ramifications?" Zed opened a candy bar and stuffed half into his mouth.

Dani had noticed several of the gods developing new coping strategies. *Stressed gods. That doesn't seem like a good thing.* Zed had always loved food, but he'd turned to chocolate for true stress eating. One of the Eastern gods had started snapping a rubber band on his wrist all the time, and she'd seen one of the old Roman gods surreptitiously drinking from a flask.

"We can no longer keep an eye on them. They have the right to behave as they see fit, though as furies we still have jurisdiction should they step too far out of line."

"Like by killing humans." Meg said it so softly they all turned to look at her. "The Aztecs."

There was a second or two of silence before Alec said, "I'd forgotten about that."

Kera looked at them in turn. "Want to share, vague terrors?"

Tis sighed. "If the gods begin actively killing their followers, we can step in. One of the old Aztec gods did just that, and we dealt with him."

Kera looked contemplative. "While the knowledge that you can kill off a god should probably make me wet myself, it's actually kind of a turn-on. Not to mention, it could be important information if this all goes to hell."

Meg laughed and choked on her soda. Dani patted her back until she stopped coughing, and she was surprised when Meg leaned into her slightly as they continued to listen.

"Before we came together here, we were often at each other's throats. Denying one another's existence, damning our own followers when they looked to another religion, getting involved in human affairs. It was messy." Zed opened a package of individually wrapped chocolates and started popping them in his mouth a few at a time.

"It could cause a strange type of human migration. People associated with particular religions could make their way back to the home of that belief system, if they know the god is actually staying among them. Even if they're not originally from those areas." Selene looked at Tis. "Wouldn't that make the need for Afterlife redundant? If followers were once again mostly in specific territories?"

"In a way, it would. But the human world is complex now, especially with Dis messing things up. I don't think it would be that simple."

Kera stood and looked at the enormous world map on the wall. "So, what's the plan?"

Meg shrugged. "Plan for what? Technically, no one has done anything wrong. And as far as we know, no one is planning on doing anything crazy. There's nothing to plan for, at the moment."

Dani thought everyone had a point, but none of them actually knew anything for certain. "When the Olympic and the Egyptian gods walked among humans, they disguised themselves, well aware that seeing them as they were would kill them. But today, we expected the humans to be fine with it. Maybe we've become less self-aware too." She looked around the table at the people she considered her closest friends. "I can tell you this. In the Deadlands, we can feel the tides changing. Something is coming, and it's like we're getting prepared for it without even knowing what it is yet."

They all stared at her until Kera said, "Well, that's not at all terrifying. Nothing like an omen from Death to give you the warm fuzzies." She winked at Dani to show she was at least partially kidding. "But if that's the case, then maybe we need to discuss some kind of contingency plan. If this, then that, kind of thing."

Meg's stomach growled loud enough for the room to hear it.

"You're like a never-ending pit of sex and food." Zed threw a piece of candy at her.

"Some of us like our pleasure in piles of yay rather than little sips of yum." Meg popped the chocolate in her mouth but continued talking as she chewed. "If we're going to create contingency plans for things that may or may not happen, can I be excused? I have a serious case of the boredoms."

"It affects you too, you know." Selene looked at Meg calmly, and as always, there was no judgment present.

"Believe me, I know. I've been out in the field. I've seen what Ms. Black Hole is up to firsthand. But I'm going to waste away of serious starvation, and the intense let's-work-shit-out thing is your field, not mine." She stood and blew her sisters a kiss. "And you know damn well I'll be right beside you when the watery poo shoots from on high." Tis smiled affectionately at her. "We know. Go feed that beast in your belly. We'll get you up to speed when we've worked some things through. If, that is, we can even figure out what to work through in the first place." She looked at Dani. "You know you're welcome to stay, but you don't have to for this bit. Maybe you could take charge of feeding our ravenous sister?"

Dani felt herself blush and quickly stood beside Meg. "I know what a tyrant she becomes when she's hungry. That's bad news for anything living. I'll take the mission seriously." She mock saluted and grunted slightly when Meg punched her in the shoulder.

"Perfect timing. I've been thinking about your redesign." She took Dani's hand and tugged her from the room. "Love you all. See ya."

They headed down the back stairs to the courtyard and across to Meg's place. Dani desperately hoped Meg wouldn't notice she hadn't let go of her hand. She loved the way it felt in her own. So warm, so alive. Dani's nature was to be cold and dark. She loved the way Meg's presence felt like sunshine piercing a storm. When Meg let go to open her front door, Dani instantly missed the connection.

She went straight to the kitchen. "I went shopping. Sit. I'll cook and tell you my design ideas at the same time."

Dani sat on the indicated bar stool and waited. She could always tell when Meg's mind was busy, and it definitely was at the moment. She seemed to move without thinking, grabbing things from the fridge and cupboard and throwing them onto the countertop.

"Oh! Wait." She darted from the room and came back with a folder. "Here. Start looking."

The folder had DEADLANDS REMAKE scrawled across the front, with a faded photo of Dani looking out over water beneath it. "Where on earth did you find this?"

Meg glanced over her shoulder to see what Dani was looking at. She turned back around. "I found it in a collection of old photos I was going through the other day. I can't remember where it was taken. Can you?"

As though I could forget. It was the summer the four of them had spent nearly a month together at a lake in Bulgaria. They'd made it a base of operations and lounged in the sun or played in the water when they weren't out on a job. It was the first summer she'd been able to spend real time getting to know Meg, and her life hadn't been the same since. "No, I don't recall."

"Well, I liked it and decided it was totally how I picture you in your territory. All thinky and pondery."

Not exactly sexy thoughts, then. "Yeah, I guess it's a serious place."

Meg spun around with a massive knife in her hand. She shook it at Dani. "Ah, but that's the thing. It doesn't have to be, does it?"

When Dani went to respond about the honor of taking souls, Meg waved the knife to stop her.

"Yeah, I know. Honor, duty, gray. I get it. But if you want to do a true remake and really rebrand your department, you have to take some chances. You've got to allow it to be something new."

She went back to chopping, and Dani opened the folder. Sketches of various sections of her territory were color coded with words like "shops" and "spa" and… "tourist information."

Meg shifted so she could see Dani and keep cooking. "Here's my thought. First of all, we're dealing with the issue of people being afraid of dying, right? Humans naturally want to live for as long as they can. Except the ones who don't, but we'll get to them. So, humans get to the point of death and get all freaked out. Right?"

Dani nodded, content to let Meg spell things out.

"What if we created a marketing campaign that showed them how totally *not* scary leaving with you is? I mean, we'd have to take into account the whole not-living anymore thing, sure. But if coming with you is an inevitability, which, clearly it is, then let's make it something exciting." She popped a piece of carrot in her mouth and motioned at the book. "Page ten."

Dani flipped to the designated page and blinked. Sketches of posters with her in her ceremonial garb and scythe were joined with a photo of her yellow mustang and a background of the Deadlands that looked slightly more like Las Vegas. The coin she'd put in Meg's glove box was represented too. "Um."

Meg leaned across the counter and studied the sketch. "I know, right? Over-the-top. But why not? If we can rebrand you as a kind of travel operator, someone who is happy to take people from this place to that one, and it's not all gloom and despair, you'll have changed the way they see you. We'll make your money a collector's item. People used to have to pay to cross the river, right? We'll use that. Humans understand money."

She dumped a ton of vegetables in a huge pot and kept moving. She stayed quiet, and Dani knew she was giving her time to process. *She knows me well.* She flipped through the other pages. There were lots of parks and green spaces. A few spas. A golf course.

"Can I ask a question?"

"Well yeah, obviously."

Dani tapped on the spa and golf course. "I get the marketing thing, to decrease fear. But people don't stay in my realm long enough to use these things. They rarely even come out of my soulpack. Why put them in if no one is there to use them?"

Meg speared a sugar snap pea with the knife and held it out for Dani. When she went to take it off the knife, Meg pulled it away and shook her head before holding it out again. Dani swallowed against the flutter of eroticism and ate it off the tip of the knife. Meg nodded approvingly before going back to what she was doing.

"Here's the thing. Your territory is beautiful. Your people seem to be happy. But why not give them a little something to take the pressure off? I mean, it's not like their jobs are about unicorns peeing rainbows, is it?"

Dani raised her eyebrows and smiled.

"Okay, you know what I mean. But here's the other thing." She wiped her hands and came around the countertop. "You said you've had an influx of souls you don't know what to do with, right?"

Dani nodded. "More by the day."

"Why not make yourself a receiving area and allow them to stay with you if they want to?"

Dani stared at her, unable to take in what she was saying. "Sorry, what?"

"It's the time to do it. Make death itself a destination. Make it a place where the lost souls can hang out. It's not like you don't have the room, right?"

"Well, no, but…"

"Wait. These souls are lost. And you feel really protective of them. Why not give them a place to stay?" She turned to a page in the book with LIBRARY scrawled across the top. "They could stay with you, if they wanted to. Or they could take the time to read up on the other religions, and if there's one that suits them, away from all the stuff going on in the living world, then they can apply to enter that religion's realms."

Dani was overwhelmed by the idea, and questions flew through her mind too quickly for her to grasp them properly. Meg smiled and placed a noisy kiss on her cheek before she went back to cooking.

"I won't take offense that you look like you're going to be ill. We don't have to talk about it any more today. Just think about it."

Dani closed the folder but kept her hand on it, as though if she let it go it might make its own way to the Deadlands and transform everything she'd ever known. She'd asked for Meg's help, and she knew she wanted a change. As she watched Meg move around the kitchen, talking about something Dani couldn't hear through the roaring of uncertainty in her head, she began to calm down. Meg's passion and spontaneity were so far from Dani's own personality it would be easy to dismiss her work. But she wouldn't. There might be aspects she'd decide against, but the truth was, Dani trusted Meg, and her sisters, more than any other beings in existence.

Meg flashed her a smile, and Dani's breath caught. *It would mean her spending more time in my territory. With me.* That thought alone made her open the folder once more.

Chapter Twelve

I love it. I think it's exactly what I wanted." Azrael turned in a slow circle, looking at the first level of hell. Formerly Limbo, it was now so much more. Overwhelmed by work, he'd asked Meg for more input and for some of her time to tell the designers what to do.

"I've suggested a few more dance clubs, all themed. There are some straightforward ones, with your basic alcohol- and drug-soaked interiors, and then there are a couple of sex clubs, catering to the more exotic and ambitious tastes." Meg motioned to the east side. "But over here, I've recommended something more sedate. I mean, you're bound to get some of the boring smarty-pants types, right? Now there's a library and some nice Zen gardens."

"That will make the old philosophers happy. They've been after me for years to provide better digs."

Meg nodded, enjoying the transformation. Limbo had been a drab, empty space, full of broken furniture and gray food. Now those who hadn't been saintly but who also didn't have any big sins on their records would have a place to go. It would be fun, and because Limbo wasn't necessarily meant as punishment, there was no reason they couldn't enjoy themselves here. It made her think of Dani's issue with the non-religious believers, and she wondered if she'd be able to do something similar with the Deadlands. "Several of the other floors have been divided into halves or quarters as well. One side for the less severe, one side for your bog standard version of Hell."

"I've already had a quick look. I love what you've done. Especially with level six. I mean, heresy is old school, you know? But I never thought of doing away with it completely, and when I mentioned it to the big guy, he agreed and has taken it off his books. The staff loves having their own level to hang out on." Az led the way to the elevator, and Meg followed. They went to level six and stepped out of the elevator to hear soft jazz.

"The best employees are the ones who are happy. Kera taught me that. If your staff has a place to relax after a punishment shift, they'll be more likely to be able to balance the new differences between the really bad folks and the ones who are in the less painful areas."

They stopped at a bar, and Az ordered them both a red cocktail of some sort. Meg didn't care what was in it, as long as it was alcoholic. The past several weeks had taken a toll, and she was ready for a break. They went to a large open area that had lots of thick, comfortable armchairs and loungers. A couple of demons were having energetic sex on one of the loungers, and Az and Meg chose seats far enough away not to get hit with bodily fluids.

They sipped their drinks, and Az said, "Any ideas on the next steps?"

Meg nodded and handed him a binder. "That's going to be harder. Convincing people to come here will be tough. I mean, you're supposed to be the world's best liar, right? Humans aren't going to flock to you because you promise things aren't so bad."

He sighed but continued to look through Meg's book. "I really wish J-ho hadn't come up with that bit of marketing right from the start. Imagine, trying to combat thousands of years of people thinking you've got hooves and horns and lie all the time."

Meg sipped her drink and tried not to stare at the demon couple, who had moved into a fascinatingly contorted position. Az's shortening of Jehovah to J-ho had made most everyone laugh, but the guy himself wasn't a big fan. Still, Meg liked it. "Hey, I worked for you, remember? I've been tarred with that rather smelly brush, thanks. We have to handle the marketing carefully. Personally, I think you start with page seven."

He flipped to that page and studied it for a moment. "Flyers?"

"Real estate information. You start with your own followers, who are already happy to tell other people about how great you are. You give them these, have them share them, hand them out, and so on. It's old school, but it's good for the kind of underground groups you're trying to reach. Maybe even make the rounds and tell them about the upgrades here. Then instruct them to tell other people."

"And then?"

"And then you hit the billboards. And maybe the talk show circuit. I'm sure Selene would be happy to have you on her show. We'll blow up social media too. We'll post photos on sites like Instagram showing the renovations, we'll Tweet about cool new drinks you're serving in the Devil's Lounge. Maybe we'll even throw on some vlogs where you can talk about the changes directly to the viewers. You're gorgeous, and that will play well with the vain who only want to be associated with attractive gods." She stopped to think, tapping the pencil against the edge of the binder. "Maybe you could even have a debate with the big guy. That would do amazing things for Selene's ratings, and it would get people to know the hot guy with the amazing body, instead of the old myth of hooves and horns."

He straightened, puffing up his chest and smiling widely. "You have no idea how much I like the sound of that." He caressed Meg's hand. "How can I repay you?"

His expression told her exactly how he wanted to pay, and she laughed. "You and I haven't locked naughty parts in a very long time. How about you tell other people how good I am and make a generous entry into my bank account, and we'll call it even?"

He put his hands over his chest and winced. "Turned down flat. I must be losing my touch." He grinned. "Consider it done. And really, thank you."

Meg downed the rest of her drink. "You can buy me another one of these too. It's—"

A small demon woman with enormous bare breasts came running up. Meg tried to focus on her words instead of her bouncing bosom.

"Tis has called an emergency meeting, Meg. She's asked you to come right away."

Meg stood, and Az got up too. "That doesn't sound good."

They headed for the elevator, and Meg wondered what could be bad enough that Tis needed an emergency meeting. She'd just been about to relax and simply enjoy the little bit of success she'd found in her new venture, but as usual, work called. *But not even work, not really.* It wasn't the kind of work they should be doing. It was all this political upheaval. Meg found it unfair and destructive, and she detested both those things. *But then, it's change and drama, so that keeps things interesting, like Dani said.* As usual, she was at odds with what she felt and wanted. The only time lately she felt at all centered was when she was with Dani. *But that's because she's...Dani.* As much as Meg wanted to move forward with Dani to see where it might go, she couldn't quite convince herself to take the leap. What if it ruined everything? She'd never been a one-person kind of girl; what if she jumped in with Dani and then decided she wanted something, or someone, else?

The elevator doors opened, and Az and Meg headed to Zed's office. Almost everyone was gathered around the huge TV on the wall. They went in and heard the news announcer speaking solemnly.

"And so, it seems yet another somewhat bewildering aspect of our new era has come about. Ancient deity Horus has joined with the Egyptian government, and they've said it's the beginning of a new stage of rule. The new system is being called a democratic theocracy, which means the government and Horus will work together to serve the citizens of Egypt. While ancient Egypt was ruled solely by Pharaohs placed in their positions by the gods, this new system will include the government already present in Egypt taking advice and instruction from Horus, the god himself." The reporter pressed on her earpiece and appeared to be listening to someone speaking. "And I'm now being told the Hindu god Vishnu has also joined with the government in India under similar conditions." She returned her attention to the camera, looking slightly shaken. "There's no way to know how this will play out, or what other theocracies may pop up. As has been the case from the beginning, all we can do is wait and see."

A commercial for Edesia's Italian Goddess Diner came on and everyone turned away. Zed motioned for them to sit.

"We should have seen this coming, but we didn't." Tis looked tired, and her wings drooped. "I didn't. It never occurred to me gods would actively work with governments, and it should have. I'm sorry."

Kera put her arm around Tis's shoulders. "Babe, no one could see any of this coming. I mean, damn, they only just left here. Who knew they'd move so fast? We just have to figure out what to do and what it might mean, that's all." She looked around the table. "Thoughts?"

Azrael spoke up first. "I like it, but it's my kind of game. It's going to cause all kinds of problems. And there isn't a god in existence who'd be willing to defer to humans for any length of time. As soon as they're in, they'll start pulling the strings until they snap. Governments will fall, and you'll end up with gods running everything. Except this time, they'll do it out in the open instead of from behind the curtain."

"Which takes away free will, at some point." Selene leaned against Alec as though for support. "Gods running whole countries will revert to what they know. They'll expect the people in their regions to pray only to them. All we've been working toward, with people able to choose which belief system to follow, will be for nothing. They've stopped fading, but at what cost?"

The room was silent as everyone took that in. Finally, Meg said, "Okay, let's think back. When a single god ruled a territory, they had their own staff too. They took care of their own. Things were sometimes too rigid, and sometimes the gods got out of control. But sometimes, it meant years of peace." She shrugged. "Just playing devil's advocate."

Az bumped her with his shoulder. "Always appreciated."

Selene shook her head. "I understand what you're saying. And it might have worked to some degree centuries ago. But in today's world, it won't work. There are too many variables. We've been telling people to choose freely, to think critically about what they want. Believers are now mixed together in specific locations more than they've ever been. To bring in a single entity in league with a government will mean many of the believers of other religions being ousted from their homes and countries."

"We did tell them to go out among their believers, to help them and try to get them to settle down." Tis rubbed tiredly at her eyes.

"Yeah, but you didn't tell them to leave Afterlife and stay there. The idea was to be out among *all* their followers, not just the ones in a particular region." Meg stuck her tongue out at Alec, who was looking at her as though she'd grown another head. "I pay attention, you know. Even if I'm not all serious Joe like the rest of you."

Alec laughed. "I love the way you always surprise us."

"Meg's right. The hot crazy ones often are." Kera grinned. "Not only couldn't we have predicted this, but it's not on anyone's shoulders here. The question is what do we do about it?"

"You wait."

They all looked up when Clotho entered the room from the hidden door behind the bookcase.

"For what?" Selene's eyes narrowed.

Meg sat forward, the tension in the room making her nerves sing. Everyone knew how much Selene disliked the Fates, who never provided answers but seemed to be in charge of everyone's life from the moment they took their first breath until they died in some tragic or ignominious way.

"For the eruption after the collision." Clotho sat beside Zed, her hands clasped, her silver hair pulled back in a bun, the epitome of elegance and the harbinger of things out of control.

Kera sighed loudly. "Again with vague ominous collection of words that don't mean shit to the rest of us. Would you even know how to give a real answer to anything other than your lunch order?"

Clotho gave her a tight smile. "Perhaps you should figure it out rather than bemoaning your lack of understanding."

Kera started to stand, and Meg's pulse sped up. She'd protect the humans in the room with her own life if she had to, but she'd very much enjoy watching Kera take a piece out of Clotho first.

Tis pulled Kera back down into her seat. "You're always welcome, but is there a specific reason you've come down?"

Always political. Meg sat back in her chair, slightly disappointed in the lack of action.

Clotho turned to look at Meg. "Find your place. Find your way. When the collision comes, be right where you need to be, and don't fail her." She went from looking intently at Meg to looking at the others in the room. "Don't forget what you are." She stood but stopped and looked at Tis, Alec, and Meg in turn. She seemed to hesitate for a moment before she said, "There are some things we can't see. Our mirrors are clouded, and the outcomes are uncertain. Often, there's more than one possible outcome in a situation." She put her hand on Zed's shoulder, almost as though to anchor herself. "But there's something of great importance involving the three of you we can't see clearly, as though the outcome is so uncertain not even we are allowed to see it."

She walked away from the table and back to the bookcase. "If we learn anything more, we'll let you know."

Selene made a slight scoffing noise, and Kera outright laughed. "And I'm sure you'll let us know in clear, concise language. Thanks for dropping by with your usual cheer and joy."

Tis elbowed Kera to get her to be quiet, but it didn't matter. Clotho left without another word.

"What the hell does that mean? Find myself? Don't let her down? Be where I need to be?" Meg gestured to the door Clotho had left through. "Why can't she tell me where I need to be? Maybe then I'd know where the hell to find myself." She grew more agitated with every thought. "And don't let who down?"

"I say we drag her back down here, and you three do what you do with those reptiles you carry around until she just answers the fucking questions." Kera scraped her chair back and moved to her desk, where she started moving stacks of paper from one to the other, clearly just needing something to do.

"I wish it were that simple. But you don't mess with the Wyrd sisters. Believe me, I know." Zed opened another bag of chocolate and dug in. "I tried once and watched as they nearly cut my string. Aside from the furies, they're the only other beings capable of taking out a god." He made a scissor motion with his fingers. "They cut any one of our strings, and *poof*. We're dust."

"I can't tell you how immensely I dislike the way they can play with all our lives. But I suppose they've given us some kind of warning, however nebulous it may be." Selene yawned, looking terribly human and fragile. "She said we have to wait, so I think we give it a little time and see what comes next." She turned to Alec and held out her hand. "Let's go home and relax for a while."

Alec took her hand, and they moved toward the door. Alec stopped and put her hand on Tis's shoulder. "You should go home too. Both of you. You look like worn-out rubber."

"Nice. Thanks for that." Tis smiled at her sister. "You look like your snakes are shedding."

Kera wrapped her arm around Tis's shoulder. "I think you both look like you need the kind of sex that happens fast enough you don't fall asleep during it, and then a hot bath. I'm only offering it to one of you, though."

"Damn right you are." Tis kissed her cheek, and the two couples left the room.

Meg, Az, and Zed sat there, apparently forgotten. Meg turned to Az. "I can't think of anything to compare you to in some kind of lovingly insulting way, sorry."

Zed waved them off. "You should get out too. It's not like either of you are hurting for bed partners. Ama and I have dinner plans, then I'm going to follow up on Kera's advice." He looked at Meg seriously. "We both know Clotho is never wrong. If something big is coming, you'd better be in the right state of mind for it."

Meg didn't know what state of mind that might need to be, but she wasn't going to find it in Zed's office, that was true.

Az turned to her. "Want to come back to my place? I've got some new staff who would turn you inside out and upside down. And it's always fun to watch a fury fuck."

She grinned, but that felt like the last thing she wanted to do. "Strangely, I think I'd rather be somewhere quiet for a while. Can I take a rain check?"

He kissed her cheek, and they both waved to Zed as they made their way back to the elevator. "You know you're welcome any time. I'm going to drum up some kind of crazy orgy to take my mind off politics for a while."

The elevator stopped at the foyer, and Meg started to get out, but stopped when something occurred to her. "I'm all for crazy orgies. But do you think you could check on something? It seems to me we haven't given the underworld gods much thought in this. But if they start joining governments too…"

He nodded. "Yeah. Worldwide shit storm. I'll hit some of them up, invite them over tonight, and see where they're at. I'll let you all know when I've got something."

She gave him a fierce hug. He felt more like a friend than he had in ages, and it was nice to have one. It made her think of Fin, and she decided she needed to go see him again soon. "Thanks. Have some fun for me tonight."

"Drop by if you change your mind." He waved as the doors closed.

Meg headed back to her place, her thoughts racing. *What the hell did Clotho mean?* It was true, she'd been feeling a little lost lately, but she certainly didn't feel the need to trade in her heels for flip-flops and go hang out at an ashram or anything, even though Jesus would welcome her. Clotho's words were ominous, and anything that unsettled a Fate had to be particularly bad. Still, none of them knew what to do.

She went inside and wandered aimlessly from room to room, flopping onto the couch only to jump back up and fling herself onto her bed. Restless, she decided only nature would calm her, the way it always had. But the idea of being alone was like sucking an old lemon. She grabbed her phone and dialed.

"Hey. I don't suppose you feel like going out? Anywhere."

"Sure. Things are a little crazy, and I might get called away, but I could use a break. Why don't I come get you in twenty?" Dani sounded happy to hear from her.

Meg tried to ignore the slightly giddy feeling that swept over her at Dani's immediate willingness to spend time with her. "Perfect." She hung up and grabbed a black pencil skirt and sheer red blouse from the closet. She paired it with a lacy black bra that showed perfectly beneath the blouse and knee-high leather boots. She liked the way Dani looked at her, and right now, she really wanted to feel that rush of adrenaline she got from being desired. *And cared for.*

CHAPTER THIRTEEN

Dis yawned and shook her head. *So predictable. So clichéd.* There were positivity posters on every wall bearing quotes about reason and logic and how religion was control, and on and on. Given the fire of their leader, she'd hoped she'd find something a bit more inspiring at the Humanity First offices. *But no. It's just like the Confucian section at Afterlife. Lots of meaningless phrases on pretty pictures.* She turned when Angie came into the room with a huge mug of coffee.

"Sure you don't want any? Or don't you creatures drink anything but flower water or whatever?"

Angie's ire was clear, and Dis liked it immensely. "I drink despair and feed on the fear of the weak."

"So, no, then. But at least you admit to being an asshole." She shrugged, looking distinctly unimpressed. "What do you want?"

Dis tapped a glass on Angie's desk, and it disintegrated into a pile of dust. She slowly stirred the pile with her finger. "I want to help your cause."

Angie didn't look away from Dis's finger moving in circles. "How? By destroying our drinking glasses?"

Dis pressed harder and the glass dust shifted, darkened. It turned to sand as pure as the kind found on pristine beaches. "Hardly, though destruction is fun. No. Like your silly glass, which I've returned to its natural state, I want to help humans return to their natural state as well. One that doesn't include the gods. Just humans being humans."

Angie finally looked up. She sat back in her chair and studied Dis. She glanced at the open door, but the rest of the office was empty. "You know as well as I do the gods aren't going anywhere."

Dis finally sat in the chair opposite the heavy wood desk. "But that's what you're preaching to your followers as the answer, isn't it?" "I don't have followers, and I don't preach." Angie sipped her coffee, looking exhausted. "Yeah, I tell people that. I think the world would be better if the gods were gone. If religion was no longer something people leaned on, they could learn to lean on each other and to depend on themselves." She pointed at Dis. "But you and I both know they're here to stay. We'll never get rid of all the believers. Some of the gods will stick around to get their narcissistic asses licked. But the more people we can turn to reason and philosophy, the more it takes away from the gods. One day, this world may be a better place."

Dis picked up a handful of sand and let it fall slowly back onto Angie's desk. "What if I told you I have a plan? A way to decrease followers exponentially."

"I'd say you're as crazy as, if not crazier than, the rest of them. But I wouldn't want to insult you and end up reverting to primordial goo."

Dis laughed. She hadn't truly enjoyed a human in a long time. "Star dust, actually, but point taken." She stood and moved to the window. "Do you know what I see when I look at humans? I see an extraordinary species that evolved from a combination of star dust and primordial goo, as you say. Animals who went from being water-breathing invertebrates to primates to humans. Humans who lived in caves and now communicate via satellites orbiting the planet. Truly, an exceptional species." Dis turned around to see if Angie was listening.

"I feel like there's a punch line coming." Angie opened a drawer and pulled out a bottle of pills. She popped two and leaned back in her chair again.

"Well. I also see a species almost completely taken over by a desire for more. More of everything. That's fine for those who hardly have anything, totally understandable. But even those with more than they could ever consume always want more. Your species is never satisfied with anything. In a way, it's helped you evolve incredibly fast. But it's also destroying you faster than you realize. You're heading for extinction, and you don't even know it yet."

Angie was silent as she stared at Dis contemplatively. Finally, she said, "And? What about it?"

Dis shrugged. "Just philosophizing. Not many people want to be around me. It's nice to simply chat."

Angie rolled her eyes. "Great. Glad to be of service. If you don't mind, I've got shit to do."

Dis came over and touched the sand once more, and this time it swirled, turned flame orange, and began to shift. It tumbled and spun until it was glass shaped, and with a final flick of her fingertip, it was a regular drinking glass again. "When you kill someone, what two places are sure to kill them the quickest?"

Angie sighed. "Weird question, but okay. Head and heart."

"And where would you say the head and heart are of one of the major religions?" Dis waited, knowing Angie would catch on quickly.

"There are a few. I suppose the most iconic would be Vatican City, in Rome. If, of course, you discount the Afterlife office itself. You know, where *all* the gods are."

Dis nearly clapped like a child at how easy this was going to be. "Exactly. Take out the heart and head, show how easily it falls apart, that the god who rules it is weak, and you'll have even some of the serious believers flocking to you." She could see Angie considering, could feel the part of her that wanted to see that flock come her way.

"I'm not going inside a building full of gods, so Afterlife is out. And the Vatican is protected, especially these days. There are a zillion tourists there all the time now. And you think God is going to just let us waltz in and take his place?"

Dis leaned forward over the desk and got close to Angie. She loved the disturbed feeling she got from her when she strayed into her personal space. "No. We're going to take it. I'm going to help. You see, humans believe what they see. They're already confused and frightened by having the gods walk among them. If we show how easily they can be brought down, that one of the most powerful gods in the world can have his largest temple destroyed, people will turn to non-belief. They'll think the gods are weak, that they don't deserve the loyalty they're asking for. And when that happens, when believers stop believing in their God… Well, the rest of the religions will fall like dominoes too. Mass hysteria that the gods can be defeated will mean humans turning their backs on their lackluster, disappointing deities. And then those deities will simply fade away, back into the realms of myth and imagination."

Dis could feel the plan coming together, could almost hear the screams and panic, could sense the beautiful fear and disintegration of faith. It fueled her and made her feel like she could ride a comet. "But I want you to act as the voice of the movement. Waving cute little signs outside Afterlife is adorable, but it won't get you anywhere. But if you make a big move, a serious statement, you'll be the savior of the human race."

"You're a nut case." Angie stood and pointed at a picture of two men on the wall behind Dis. "Both of those guys thought they could save us from the gods. Do you know what happened to Frey? A demon stabbed him through the neck. After some big underworld god used him, that is. If you think I'm going to work with you so I can end up like Frey or the other guy, who just up and disappeared one day, you can dance your crazy ass right back out the door."

Dis sighed, surprised that Angie hadn't jumped at the invitation for dominance. *Maybe not all humans are the same after all.* "Give me your hand."

Angie put both hands behind her back. "No."

"Don't make me ask again."

Angie held out her hand, and Dis was impressed at how well she hid her fear. Her hand hardly trembled at all. "Close your eyes."

Angie did as she was told, and Dis opened a little gateway into the future for her. It wasn't necessarily the real thing, but rather the way Dis thought it would come to be. It was enough.

Angie opened her eyes and looked searchingly at Dis for a long moment. "I'm in."

"Excellent." Dis dropped Angie's hand, glad to disconnect. Humans felt so…solid. Terribly dense and yet distressingly fragile. *Space dust indeed.* "I have some calls to make. I suggest you pack well and talk to a few of your most trusted followers. We'll leave as soon as everything is in place."

"I don't have followers. And I don't give commands. But I'll see if anyone wants to join me on your suicide mission." Angie brushed at her hand as though trying to wipe something from it.

Dis moved closer once again. She liked how something as simple as someone being too close physically made humans distinctly uncomfortable. "Oh, but you are, Angie. I saw how those people reacted to you. The crowd was responding to *you*. To your words. To your courage. To your desire for change." She lightly stroked Angie's cheek, and the answering flare of irritated emotion made Dis want to do it more. "You need to accept your place on top of this food chain, because when it breaks, there needs to be someone to step into the void left by the gods' absence. Someone to lead, to guide, to free." She stopped touching Angie's face, again impressed by her determination not to show her fear. Dis stretched, disliking the feeling of gravity more and more all the time. *Soon, I can go home.* She turned at the door and smiled at Angie. "Best get ready for some fun."

CHAPTER FOURTEEN

The ocean crashed below them, and the smell of ancient pines surrounded them. The wooden deck was strewn with oversized pillows and low deck chairs, and the view of the Pacific was unimpeded by anything at all. A few backpackers set their packs down on the far side of the deck and went in to order.

"Does this work? I love how quiet it is this time of year." Dani sipped her iced tea and watched as Meg took in Nepenthe, one of Dani's favorite restaurants in Northern California. The name meant *isle of no care* in Greek, something she knew wouldn't be lost on Meg.

"It's gorgeous. I think I came here once, years ago, but I'm not sure." Meg drew little shapes in the condensation on her glass. "I didn't know you surfed."

Dani smiled. "Since the first time I saw them doing it in Polynesia in the 1700s. A tribal chief there taught me, and I've been doing it ever since." She thought back to their recent conversations and didn't remember mentioning it. "How did you know?"

"I ran into Idona at a work scene, and she mentioned you had plans to go out."

"I'll have to talk to her about spilling things about my personal life." Dani laughed, but sobered when Meg didn't even smile. "Hey. What's up?"

"I hate that there's so much I don't know about you. I mean, you know everything about me and probably both my sisters. I don't know your favorite food, or the sexual position that gets you hottest, or what kind of women you like." She looked like she was almost going to cry.

"And now there's all this weird woo-woo shit with the Fates saying I need to find myself, and everything feels stupid and...and..."

"Out of control?" Dani took Meg's hand in her own and held it, slowly caressing her knuckles with her thumb. She tried to concentrate on speaking rather than how soft and hot Meg's skin was. "First of all, it's not your fault you don't know some stuff about me. I'm not the most forthcoming person, okay? Second, we all feel out of control right now. Imagine how Selene feels. She convinced the gods to come into the open, and it turns out most humans weren't equipped to deal with that after all. People are dying because of their inability to adapt. I can't imagine how terrible she feels."

Meg looked up, wide-eyed. "Oh shit daggers. I hadn't even thought about that. I knew Tis felt responsible, but I hadn't thought about how Selene was handling things. Damn, she even kind of said something in that meeting, but I wasn't really paying attention..." She pulled out her phone. "I need to call her—"

Dani gently put her hand over Meg's phone. "Aren't your sisters having some quiet time? You can have some too."

Meg lowered her phone and closed her eyes. "Why do I feel calmer around you?"

Dani hoped Meg didn't see how much the words meant to her. "I'm Death. You don't get a lot calmer than dead. Natural effect of hanging out with me, I think." She winked and was gratified when Meg laughed.

"That's totally not it." She held Dani's hand and studied it like she was doing a palm reading. "Everything is so crazy lately. But when I'm around you, I feel centered. Like things aren't frigging upside down."

Dani squeezed her hand and then gently pulled away. She needed to break the physical contact before she said or did something she shouldn't. *Be sensible.* "Things are upside down. And to be honest, they may get worse."

Meg threw her hands up. "Gee, thanks for that, Santa Darkness."

Dani grinned. "*But.* Listen. It's not like you're alone. We're in this together. All of us. Every god at Afterlife, your sisters and their partners. Me. We're taking this road together, and if it gets messy, so what?" She shrugged. "Yeah, we'll have to deal with it. Humans are messy. Life is messy, even for those of us who don't die. Upside down can suck, but it can also be interesting, right?"

Meg stared at her for a moment before laughing her trademark belly laugh. "I thought that same thing just a few hours ago. You know me so well. So, tell me more about yourself."

"I don't have a favorite food, but I could eat French fries for breakfast, lunch, and dinner. Dipped in mustard."

"Gross. What else?"

"My favorite color is the blue of the ocean in the Maldives. The way it goes from pale turquoise to darker turquoise to cadet blue. It's similar in Hawaii and Polynesia. And in Aruba, where the sand feels like grainy silk." She kept herself from saying her favorite colors were actually the shades of sunset trapped in Meg's wings and hair. The deep reds shot through with faint oranges and bruised purples were sensual and exotic. But as usual, the ocean was her safe place.

"And your favorite sexual position?" Meg bit her lip and leaned forward with her eyebrows raised.

"Nope. Sorry. Only people I have sex with get to know that one." Meg pouted for a second. "Does Idona know?"

Is that jealousy in her eyes? She shook off the feeling. *Of course not.* "Yes. She did, anyway, a century or two ago."

"So you're not together now?"

This time Dani was sure she saw relief in Meg's expression. *Interesting.* "She's my best friend, and I'm insanely lucky to have her in my life. But no, nothing romantic. I haven't been with anyone in a while. Too busy." It was a cop-out, and Dani hoped Meg wouldn't pursue it.

"Yeah, well, that's too bad and all, but I'm kind of glad. If you were with someone you wouldn't have time for me, and you know how much I hate not being the center of attention." She leaned across the table and took Dani's face in her hands. "And I really love spending time with you. Maybe we can help one another answer the questions of life and death." She kissed her softly before letting go and settling back in her seat.

Dani simply looked at her, at a loss for words. Her lips tingled like electricity was running through them, and her cheeks felt branded by Meg's hands. Before she could respond, though, Meg continued.

"You're super self-aware, right?"

"If by super self-aware you mean in a regular state of confusion and befuddlement, sure." She sipped her beer, wondering where Meg was headed, and if she'd be able to follow.

"I wanted to say something, but my sisters told me to leave it alone until you were ready to tell us…" Meg waited expectantly.

Dani stared at her blankly. "Yes? Tell you what?"

Meg sighed theatrically and blew a stray strand of hair out of her face. "Fine. I won't ask."

"Meg, I don't know what you're talking about. You know I'm pretty much an open book. Ask." She couldn't fathom what all three sisters wanted to know but wouldn't talk about. It was unnerving.

"Excellent. Why are you all glowy? What's going on? Are you having such amazing sex you're literally lighting up from the inside? I heard people who had sex with one of the Eastern goddesses could do that. I mean, they exploded shortly after, but it was a great effect for a minute or two."

Dani thought she saw a seriousness beneath the lighthearted question but wasn't sure. Apparently, she couldn't hide it anymore, and it wasn't like plenty of other people hadn't noticed. *Not that they're going to be upset. Why am I nervous? Because if I talk about it, it becomes real.* "Are you familiar with Santa Muerte?"

Meg frowned, clearly thinking. "That's the death cult in Mexico, right?"

Dani tilted her head, feeling foolish now that she was actually saying it out loud. "Yeah. Except it's not a cult anymore. There are nearly twenty million followers, and more coming through every day. Apparently—"

Meg leaned forward to grasp Dani's arms, her eyes wide. "Shit bricks and call me Susan. Seriously. You're becoming a goddess?"

"I have no idea why Susan and shitting bricks are associated." Dani was so embarrassed. It seemed preposterous, but it was true. "You know how it works. Enough people believe and a god come into existence. The thing is, I already exist, and the concept of death personified has been around for a hell of a long time."

Meg sat back down, looking fascinated. "So what does it mean? Can you do cool new stuff? Can you fly or kill stuff just by thinking about it?"

Dani flinched. "As if I'd do something like that even if I could."

"I'm sorry. Totally kidding, I know you wouldn't. But what does it mean?"

Dani sighed. "The truth is, I don't know. I feel different inside. Like you said, it's like something has been lit inside me. Maybe it's the effect of all those candles burning for me. I don't know. But my death-sight has become intense. I can feel the people praying to me like never before. Their voices are around all the time." She felt the tears well in her eyes and blinked them back. When Meg took her hand, she nearly let them fall. "There's so much desperation, Meg. The people praying to me seem to be the ones stuck in the middle. The ones who desperately want to believe and have religious leanings, but who don't feel like the gods of life are listening."

Meg stared down at their hands, suddenly serious. "That's incredibly sad. No offense, but if all they're looking forward to is death, that's a pretty difficult existence."

Dani nodded. "But now they're seeing me as not just death, but as some kind of protector. I don't get the correlation, but it's mostly the poor and the outsiders who seem to be praying to me. The thing is, I'm not a goddess. I take people from one world to another. I don't grant prayers, and to be honest, I wouldn't have the faintest idea how to if I could."

Meg let go of her hand and took a long drink of beer, finishing it off. "I'm going to get another. Want one?"

Dani nodded and watched as Meg walked inside to order. She was painfully beautiful. Her curves, her wings, her adorable short hair. She was full of passion and energy, and Dani was glad she'd been the one to ask. Meg's exuberance and way of seeing life made it easier to talk to her about it.

She came back and put the beer down in front of Dani. "Puberty."

"Sorry?"

"You're going through puberty. Without the zits and voice change, thank the gods. But that's totally it." She nodded sagely and grinned.

Dani's body responded the way it always did when Meg gave her that wicked grin, and she tried to ignore it. *Puberty for sure.* "Explain, please?"

"You've been around. You've seen things, done stuff. But now things are changing. Your body is even changing. So you have to grow up, change into something new. The problem, though, is that puberty takes time, right? I mean, it's not just a twenty-four-hour thing. You have to learn and figure things out." She smiled and fluffed her wings slightly. "Fortunately, you've got the most amazing friends ever to help you through it."

Dani laughed, feeling a million times lighter than she had been lately. "Seen things and done stuff, huh? That's probably the most delicate description of what I do that I've ever heard. And I'm not sure that Death goes through puberty, but I get what you're saying."

Meg laughed and flicked condensation at her. "No need to get all deep. You'll figure out the prayer thing. But you can't do it alone. You're going to have to talk to other gods and see how they do it."

The light feeling disappeared. "It just feels so presumptuous, you know? I didn't ask for this."

Meg rolled her eyes. "Please. Who the hell is asking for anything these days? I say ride the wave and see where it takes you."

Dani grinned. "Nice analogy."

"See what I did there? Totally paying attention." Meg stretched. "In fact, I have an idea. I'm craving poi. Know where I can get any?"

Dani laughed and followed Meg to the car. "Sure. Which island? And what kind of poi?"

"Hawaiian poi. And the island with no name."

Dani hesitated and looked at Meg over the top of the Mustang. "No one has been there in a long time. I'm not even sure I can properly open a road to it. Can I ask why we're headed there?"

Meg pointed at her. "Because you need to learn how to be a goddess, and I had some crazy fun times there when I was young." She got in the car, clearly marking the conversation as over.

Learn how to be a goddess. That's not something I ever thought I'd do. She concentrated on the ancient island, on the beautiful thick canopies and the calls of birds found nowhere else on earth. It was only when she focused on the warm, crystal clear waters around it that she felt the road open to it. She'd thought the gods there had faded long ago, but maybe Meg knew something she didn't. Even if it didn't work, it meant time with Meg.

Chapter Fifteen

The sunrise was surprisingly lovely. Granted, it was only because of the sunlight bouncing off the smog Rome was known for, but still, Dis enjoyed the strong reds and oranges puncturing the pale blue sky like blood from a wound. Ancient writers had said it was "rosy fingered dawn," but to Dis it was always a violent time, when the dark was forced to give over to the light as the planet spun on a needle tip in the vastness of space. It reminded her, to a small degree, of her home in the cosmos, and she was looking forward to getting back soon. She sat on the dome of St. Peter's Basilica and looked out over the packed city. She couldn't for a moment imagine living the way these humans did. Surrounded by noise, by crowds, by cars, by fumes…it was no wonder they turned on each other so easily.

Do they truly not see how they're hardly more than a beehive? The government is their queen bee, and all they do is for her. They even live in buildings that look like tall hives. It was truly baffling how they'd managed to pack themselves into massive centers this way. When she'd gone to visit Horus to see how he was moving forward in Cairo, it had been the same. Right in front of the ancient pyramids spread a massive city with more than six million people crammed into under two hundred square miles. Horus was happy with the crowding, as it made it easier for him and his siblings to slowly retake the city from the predominant Sunni Muslims. Those who didn't want to convert were being encouraged to leave. Horus would return Egypt to the ancient ways and make it beautiful once more. Dis had been happy to sow the seeds of confusion among the people while she was there, which would serve to drive people back to the old ways.

Just as she would rip Rome from the Catholics and bring back the old ways to Italy. Dis laughed softly. In truth, she didn't care who took over once she was done having her fun. Humanity First, the old Roman gods, or even no one at all. She just wanted to be the one to make it happen. A rumble of thunder announced her visitor before he appeared beside her, but she didn't bother to move. She was comfortable, and he was intruding on her quiet.

"May I join you?"

She looked up at Zeus and shrugged. "If you must."

He lowered himself onto the dome beside her. "No one else knows I'm here."

"What an odd thing to say." She watched with interest as a group of children threw rocks at a cat until it found refuge in an old building. "Why should I care about that?"

His voice rumbled when he spoke, and he was glowing like the god he was. "Because I wanted to have a private conversation with you, and I didn't want the others to hear it."

She slid her hand up his leg. "Oh, a clandestine meeting with an all-powerful god. I do like the sound of that."

He stopped her hand and moved away from her. "I've come to ask you what you want. What do we need to do to send you back where you belong?"

Dis thought about his words. "What do I want…" She closed her eyes and felt him beside her. *Godly fear. How lovely.* "What is the first thing you remember, Zeus? Or should I call you Jupiter?"

"Rome is Catholic. It belongs to the Christian god. We lost it a long, long time ago. A few still worship the old ways, but it's not ours. I won't go by Jupiter ever again, and I'm okay with that." He stared out at the city much like Dis had been doing. "My first memory is of my mother hiding me so my father wouldn't eat me."

She laughed, delighted at the morbidity of such a first memory. "Do you know what I remember?"

He shook his head.

"I remember the birth of this planet. I remember the rocks crashing together in space and the way this big chunk fell away on its own. I remember the asteroids hitting it, making craters and mountains. I remember watching it calm and grow. Volcanoes and earthquakes, storms that blocked its new sun for years. I remember when the first animal crawled from the water." She turned to him. "I remember the day the furies were born. Do you?"

He nodded, his brow furrowed as he clearly tried to figure out where she was going with her story. "I wasn't born yet. But I know their mother raised them to be as free as the wind and as fierce as fire."

"She did. What I couldn't have foreseen was that the day the furies were born, my existence changed. I lived among the stars, riding comets and exploring infant planets. But I'd come to Earth sometimes, just to see how the planet was evolving. It called to me constantly as it shifted and groaned under the weight of the evolution. It was doing so faster than any other planet I'd visited, and a particular type of ape began to walk on two legs. And then those less primitive apes eventually needed more than the chaotic, entropic world around them. More than me. They had questions, and they wanted answers. They developed societies. And then defined morals. Right and wrong, good and bad."

She drifted off, thinking of the changes she'd seen since the little planet had been born.

"And?"

She glanced at him and then back at the people of Rome, making their way like ants through an ancient anthill. "And so, the furies came to be. Born of the human need to package the vast beauty of their world into bite-sized morsels of action and consequence. When the furies began delivering justice, when humans saw bad things happen to bad people who had hurt them…the maelstrom of their lives calmed. Chaos became order, and I was no longer a regular part of this world. It's their fault I was cast off this planet. Sure, the universe is vast and I get to play in all of it. But this planet is special, and they took it away from me as surely as though I'd been banished."

She thought about the dark beauty of the world she'd lived in and what that meant. "I was alone. There are no other gods beyond this planet. They either haven't developed them yet or have never had the need. I've been alone, and that's all because the damned furies took control."

"So, what? You're lonely and you want to be part of the world again? You've certainly succeeded."

She restrained the desire to turn him to smoke. This wasn't the right time. "Thanks to you and the other godlings of this superstitious planet I was called back, and yes, I've enjoyed being here. But no,

I have no intention of overstaying my welcome. I'll come back in a hundred years, or three hundred, to bathe in the ruins of humanity and to see what comes after. Something will certainly come after. It's a tenacious planet, after all."

He was quiet, and she waited for his next question.

"You're leaving?"

He sounded hopeful, and she enjoyed being able to crush that. "Not yet. Not until I've done what I need to do here. After the eclipse, certainly." She motioned at the population below them. "They called me, yes. But your own kind has called me too. Did you know that? Many of your gods are scared because they no longer know how to be gods, and that's what you've asked them to be. But they're like declawed house cats. Fat and content to lie in the sun and be worshipped, but you've thrown them into the savannah. Now you have to deal with the consequence of that." She smiled at him. "Me? I'm going to help them see how to behave as gods again, but no planet can be reborn without an element of annihilation."

"Can you have an *element* of annihilation? That seems like an oxymoron." Zeus sighed. "I know you have very little respect for this world and its creatures—"

She held up her hand to stop him. "On the contrary. They're a fascinating species. They've only been walking upright for the blink of an eye, and yet, they've managed to almost entirely eradicate several other species and to do irreparable damage to the planet itself. I think they're extraordinary. Fortunately, it also means they're particularly open to my charms."

"And you'd watch them all die for your amusement?"

Thunder rumbled in the darkening sky above them and lightning cracked in web-like streaks around them. "Yes. I would. And because if they're let off this planet to live on others, they'll simply do the same elsewhere. They'll become a universal virus, and that can't be allowed to happen." She placed her hand on his shoulder. He looked deeply sad, as though already seeing the death of his precious humans. She'd forgotten what it meant to be among other immortals, and she almost felt bad for him. "I come when called, and I'm here to do what I do. When it's done, I'll leave. There's nothing I want that you can give."

He stood and stared down at her. "We'll try to stop you. Or at least, stop people from needing to call you. And I believe in my staff. They'll learn and grow the way they need to in order to be what the humans need them to be. We'll fight."

"As you should. You're their pet gods, their hope in an empty sky, and their love in an uncaring universe. Good luck. In fact, let's make it official, shall we? We'll meet back here in two days, on the morning of the eclipse. Just to add a bit of the dramatic. Who knows, maybe there will even be room to negotiate." She smiled sweetly and shaded her eyes as he disappeared into a bolt of lightning.

How absurdly benevolent of him to come to me to defend his little planet. He embodied the good side of humans these days, the part that sacrificed for others, though once he'd exemplified far more of the vices than the virtues. If he knew she'd be taking one of the furies with her when she left, he probably wouldn't have been quite so docile. He had a special affinity for the sisters. She wanted them to taste a morsel of the loss and loneliness she'd felt when she'd been cast away, and taking one of their sisters away from them would start that process. Taking the gods they worked with away from them, leaving them alone among the humans, would finish the job.

A group of people emerged from the underground station below, and she saw the iconic Humanity First T-shirts even from her perch on high. *We'll see just how misplaced his belief in the beings around him really is.*

She transported herself to the group on the ground, laughing out loud as they scattered like cockroaches when she appeared among them.

"I really wish you'd knock that shit off," Angie said, wiping her palms on her jeans. "It's really irritating."

Dis smiled at her favorite human. "That's why I do it." She studied the group Angie had brought with her. "Is this all?"

Angie crossed her arms. "No. More are coming tomorrow and the next day. We can't just pop up places, scaring the hell out of people. We have to make plans, travel. But yeah, more are coming. They know this is something big, and something that will probably get us killed. It wasn't exactly a reward-heavy offer, you know?"

"If you want rewards, go to the gods." Dis moved among them and felt their wariness, as well as their simmering rage. She stopped in front of one and listened to his deeply hidden emotions. "This one needs to go away."

He glared at her. "I don't have to do anything you say. You're no better than the others, ordering people around and waiting for them to do what you tell them to. You're probably just as weak too—"

His voice was high-pitched and irritating, much like that of the Christian god. Dis touched his forehead and turned away.

"Fuck. Fuck, fuck, fuck. Why did you do that?" Angie stood her ground but looked distinctly freaked out as she stared at the pile of speckled dust that used to be one of her team.

"I dislike being insulted, and his voice was nauseating. He wasn't one of you, either."

"What does that mean? One of us? And what gives you the right to take someone's life like that?"

Dis made eye contact with the followers directly behind Angie and smiled when they didn't back down. *Better.* "He was a believer. He didn't want to admit that deep down, he desperately wanted to believe in a god, any god. And he feared death. When the crucial moment came, he would have let you down. I simply returned him to his natural state." She was bored with the conversation now. *Humans and their petty concern for life.* "Go to your hotel. I've got some work to do here, and I'll meet you there later."

Angie motioned her group to head out and everyone steered clear of the mound of glittering ash that had once been a person. No one said a word as they headed to the Hotel Metropolis. Dis had suggested it would be large enough for a group but not far from where they needed to be once everything kicked off. She turned away from them and concentrated on the emotions throughout the Borgo area. The Vatican's shadow fell heavily over the surrounding cobbled streets and multi-floor housing. Graffiti ran the length of garden walls and broken bottles littered the curbs across from the Vatican's entrance. She felt the depth of belief surrounding her, but she also felt the seething turmoil of buried resentment. The people who lived here accepted the Pope as God's messenger, and many made a living off the tourists who flocked to the grand building to see the opulence of God's most devout. That didn't mean they weren't frustrated with having to live hand to mouth. It didn't mean the young people weren't bored and disillusioned.

Dis opened her hands and called the chaos of the universe to her. She fed on the energy created by the eclipse, felt her powers grow as she drank the cold moon getting ready to push itself between the little blue planet and the sun. She concentrated on the jaded feelings around her, the resentments, and the confusion, and she sent her special brand of being into the air, toward all those who were calling to her, even if they didn't know it. The cosmic dust would settle like the white plumed seeds of a dandelion, spreading like a weed until it brought forth every latent worry the believers had. The ecstasy of it was like a fire blooming in her soul, and she wanted to share it.

That meant her next stop would serve a dual purpose. She thought of Horus and was transported to Egypt, which was even hotter than Rome, though the cool tile under her bare feet was delicious. He was sitting on a throne beside Isis, but he rose when she appeared.

"Welcome, ancient one." He embraced her and bowed his head respectfully.

"Hello, love." She looked over his shoulder and nodded at Isis, who inclined her head but looked less than welcoming. *Jealousy in gods is far less interesting than it is in humans.* "Isis."

"I wasn't expecting you." Horus tucked Dis's hand into the crook of his arm and led her onto the balcony.

"I've come with an idea, and I'd like your assistance." Dis had known from the moment she'd reconnected with Horus he'd be part of the change to come but hadn't been certain how. Now she knew exactly what she wanted from him. "But first, take me to bed. I'm in need of release."

He looked over his shoulder at Isis.

"Bring her too. We'll enjoy her together." Sex was the only thing this planet really had going for it. She'd enjoy it while she could and then bring the world to its knees.

CHAPTER SIXTEEN

The road to the lost islands wasn't like Dani's other roads. It was like driving in a glass tunnel, and sea life moved all around them. Meg buzzed with anticipation as she watched Dani concentrate. She had no idea *why* she knew this was where Dani would find answers, but just the same, she knew the old island gods could help. Dani braked, and the road ahead of the Mustang simply stopped.

"Problem?" Meg tried to see what was beyond the car, but it was just...wasn't. There was nothing; no drop-off, no cliff or wall. It was almost like a still, grayish-blue fog. "What's out there?"

Dani looked to where Meg was pointing. "It's the area between. It only takes shape when it's created to do so. I haven't needed this area, so I've never bothered. I can't get a proper read on the island. I think they may have faded." She closed her eyes again, and her brow furrowed. "Got it." She waved and a road appeared to the left.

"What's above us right now? If we just popped to the surface?"

"About a mile of Pacific Ocean. Probably wouldn't be a good idea to check it out."

Dani smiled at her, and Meg's heart raced in response. "Would you take me surfing one day?"

Dani glanced at her, clearly surprised. "Sure, if you wanted to. But I didn't think it was really your thing."

Meg thought about it. "I don't know if it's my thing or not. I admit, even though I've watched other people do it, I never wanted to try. Too much salt makes my feathers itch and my snakes shed. But I really like the thought of being out on the water with you." Dani looked so serious Meg wondered if she'd overstepped somehow.

"Yeah. I'd like that. And if you don't like it, we'll put you on a boat instead."

Meg laughed. "I love boats. There's nothing like sunbathing out on the open ocean. There was this goddess, once, who owned a yacht she berthed in Morocco. Massive thing. The boat, not the goddess, obviously. We spent three months just cruising around the Med. I mean, I had to come and go because of work, but it was amazing downtime. She had a forked tongue, and oh my god, the things she could do with it."

Dani laughed. "And how did that end?"

"You know, I'm not sure. I think she might have met someone in one of the countries we stopped in." Meg thought back, trying to remember. "There weren't any emotional ties or anything, you know, I just made my way home. I was living in France back then, and there were plenty of people willing to lower their knickers." When Dani didn't say anything, Meg realized she might have stepped in it. "I'm sorry. Does it make you uncomfortable when I talk about sex?"

Dani shook her head. "Definitely not. I like hearing about your life when I wasn't around. You're so passionate. So…everything." The road began to ascend. "Did you ever have someone really special? Someone who stayed around for a while?"

The question had never bothered her before, but now it felt like a sewing needle pushed into her heart. "Not really. When I lived in Greece there was the occasional hero or queen, and with the world being small, it was easy to stay with one person for longer. But when we moved outside Greece and took on bigger roles, there was vast variety. Humans and gods both. There never seemed to be a need to cut myself off from that. And I can't imagine loving a human the way my sisters do."

"Why's that?" Dani asked softly.

"Mortality. I mean, Selene and Kera are going to die, and my sisters have given everything they are to them. At least when you're with the immortal set, you know there's a chance they'll stick around for a while." Meg had never expressed that particular sentiment to anyone, and she felt guilty about it now. Her sisters would experience the kind of love she never would, and for them, it was worth it. But Meg knew she wouldn't be able to handle that kind of attachment and loss. *Change the subject. Move on.* "Wow, you're really glowing. You

look like a firefly, except it's your head all lit up instead of your butt."
Meg took in the beautiful sight. Dani was effervescent. Her pale skin
looked like crystal in sunlight, and her eyes were… "I think you might
be turning into a raccoon."

Dani felt her face. "What does that mean? Am I getting a snout?"
Meg laughed. "That would be awesome, but no. Your eyes.
Instead of their usual ghosty color you've gone all beat-up boxer. Or
black holes."

Dani closed her eyes and smiled. "There's a festival going on in
Mexico. Lots of skulls and such. They're seeing me as a being dressed
in all white with huge black eyes to represent the vacancy of death."

She looked over, and Meg shivered. Dani's power pulsed off her
in sensual waves, and she had no idea how insanely hot she looked.
She was struggling to find something to say when they suddenly moved
into the sunlight and onto a road surrounded by an enormous rainforest.
Ahead, a long waterfall fell from a gorgeous rugged mountaintop. From
jades to emeralds to sages, the greens were offset by flowers that looked
like the sun in physical form. Birds in every shape and size called from
the trees, like something out of a child's painting. Meg lifted up from
her seat and breathed it all in, letting the warm sultry air flow through
her wings. "I'm hungry. I hope we find them soon."

"You're always hungry. And I wonder why we haven't seen them
in so long?" Dani slowed to let an enormous multihued parrot languidly
fly past.

Meg thought about it. "You know, it's weird. We live forever,
and you'd think we'd have the time to catch up with each other. But
then five centuries go by, and you realize you haven't gotten together.
Imagine being human and how hard they must have to try to keep up
with other humans?"

Dani flicked one of Meg's loose feathers away from her face. "It
means they have to decide who deserves their time. Though I can't help
but think many of them waste time on people and issues not worthy of
it."

They came to a fork in the road, and Dani turned left, heading
higher into the mountains. "Just a guess, but I know they used to like
looking out over the water."

Meg stood on the seat and spread her wings, loving the feel of the
tropical air on her feathers. She used to love it in her hair too, and now

it felt just as good on her naked neck. She flapped her wings and rose into the air over the Mustang. She held on to the edge of the windshield and drifted in the wind like a kite flown by a kid on a bike. Dani looked up and laughed, and Meg started to laugh too. Acacia leaves brushed against her wings and flooded them with a salty sweet scent.

Meg stopped laughing and listened as she perched on the doorframe. "Hey, hear that?"

"Ukulele music." Dani nodded and turned left at the next road. Within a mile, she stopped the car, and they stared.

"Well. That's unexpected." Meg settled back into the car but stayed standing on the seat as she looked down into a lush valley.

The hotel was varying shades of reds and oranges with what looked like a central hub in a long yellow column. A number of other buildings surrounded it, all shaped like gently curved flower petals. Long decks hugged each building, and a lazy river pool surrounded the yellow tower. In large, flowery script, a sign just ahead of them read *Akua Paradaiso*.

"God's paradise?" Dani started driving again, heading for the resort. "Have you heard about this place?"

Meg craned to look around, feeling like she couldn't possibly see everything she wanted to. "A resort for gods in a gorgeous Hawaiian island? Don't you think I'd be just about living here if I had?"

Dani parked the car next to lots of other convertibles and motorcycles, and she gave Meg a puzzled look when she spotted a golf cart. "Really?"

Meg shrugged. "It's a small island. Maybe it's easier. Though it's definitely not sexy."

They walked toward the main building and several people waved and smiled. Meg could feel Dani's discomfort and slid her hand into Dani's. "What's eating you, hottie?"

Dani smiled and shrugged slightly. "People aren't usually friendly when I show up somewhere."

Meg looked around. It was true. No one was flinching or turning away. "Hey, isn't that Lakshmi?"

The goddess in question was lounging by the pool, a book in one hand, a drink in another, a fan in a third, and an ice cream cone in the fourth. On hearing Meg say her name, she looked up and waved her fan at them before going back to her book and ice cream.

"I wonder if the other Tridevi are here." Dani looked as baffled as Meg felt. "I've heard rumors Kali is spending a lot of time with Hades these days."

Meg made a sound of approval. "That would be explosive sex. They both have a liking for the whips and chains stuff. In fact, I heard—"

"Dani! And Megara. Aloha! Welcome to *Akua Paradaiso.* We haven't had *haole* here in ages." Lono, the Hawaiian god of peace and rain, raised his arms and motioned them forward.

He was muscular and short, his grin was wide and his eyes kind. His skin was the color of golden pecans and his eyes were jade green. He reminded Meg of the old earth gods of the Druids, looking as he did like a living piece of the forest around them. She returned his tight hug. "Lono, you look amazing. What is this place? And do you have anything to eat?"

He laughed and linked arms with her before turning to Dani and linking her as well. "We always have food for you, Justice. Let's begin there." He led them to a table beneath a beautiful awning covered in flowering ivy.

Meg nearly moaned at the sight of the spread before her. She grabbed a plate and piled it high, noticing that Dani, as usual, took a modest amount. "I don't know how you can survive on so little food."

"You do know we don't actually *need* to eat, right? We're just in the habit as much as the humans?"

Lono laughed and shook his head. "Pleasure is a necessary part of existence, and food brings much pleasure, beautiful chaperone."

"Well said. See?" Meg took a huge bite of poi and pointed at Dani with a celery stick.

Dani took a bite of pineapple and laughed as the juice ran down her hand. "Chaperone? That's a new one."

"You lead the dead to their rightful places, do you not?"

Meg desperately wanted to lick the juice from Dani's hand but refrained in light of their company. *Focus.* "I like it, and it goes with your new marketing plan." She motioned around them with a carrot stick. "Tell us about this place."

Lono sighed, and some of the joy left his smile. "As you know, we were worshipped until the eighteen hundreds. When the country turned to Christianity, we began to fade. In fact, we were some of the first modern gods to do so. We still had followers but not enough to sustain us. The Afterlife company hadn't been started yet, so we had to figure it out ourselves. The old ways were dying, and we had a choice to make. Kane, Kanaloa, and I decided we wanted to give gods like us a place to go. Somewhere they could relax if they were still active, and a place to retire if they were pre-faders. It felt like *pono*: total balance. Once Afterlife got started, we were already settled here, and there was no reason to leave."

Meg peered closely at Lono. "But you've still got your god glow."

Lono sipped a glass of awa and offered some to Meg, who nodded. "More so lately, thanks to those of you at Afterlife who decided to walk among the humans again." He relaxed back onto the lounger and motioned at the resort. "Even if we're answering prayers again, we won't give this up. Too many gods have come to depend on it, and in truth, we enjoy running it."

Dani set aside her plate. "Why haven't we heard about it? I mean, I couldn't even find the road here at first. We thought you might have faded."

Lono took Dani's hand. "Darkness, those in the West forget about those of us who live between. Our islands are far from any mainland, and the old ways long forgotten. You go on with your lives as we go on with ours. You focus on what's happening in front of you, understandably."

"Why only the West?" Meg asked around a mouthful of salmon.

"Because the old Eastern religions have continued through the centuries, and their gods aren't so different from us. We've asked that the gods who visit us here keep it to themselves so we can keep the resort a place to really chill out." Lono handed Meg another coconut shell full of awa. "But you didn't come for a lesson on ideologies." He stood and stretched. "I'll let Kanaloa know you're here. But I hope you'll still join us tonight as guests of honor. We'll have a luau and sing some of the old songs. And you can tell us about life on the mainland."

Dani nodded, and Meg jumped to her feet and gave him a tight hug. "I'm sorry we've been away so long. We'd love to come for dinner."

He left, and Meg continued to eat, moving so she could see the different guests.

"How did he know?" Dani said softly.

"Know what?"

"Why we're here. He's sending Kanaloa, and I'm guessing that's who you wanted me to talk to. But how did he know that?"

Meg shrugged and popped a strawberry in her mouth. The sweet juices coated her tongue and made her want to have sex. "Who knows? The Hawaiian gods aren't as old as some, but they're old enough. Maybe they've got extra-special powers because they live by volcanoes, like some kind of superhero kryptonite or something. Or maybe they just know stuff, like I do."

Dani laughed and reached out to wipe a bit of food from Meg's lip, making her shiver. "Yeah, maybe."

Suddenly, someone leapt over the food table and picked Dani up in a bear hug, swinging her in a circle. "Dani! *Make*, it's good to see you again."

Kanaloa finally set Dani down, his beautiful cherry wood skin offsetting her pale skin like sun against snow. He turned to Meg and opened his arms. "Beautiful terror. It's been far too long."

She hugged him, and as she had long ago, liked the secure peace she found in his embrace. "It really has. I'm so sorry."

He held her at arm's length and studied her briefly before turning to Dani. "I think we've got a ton of things to talk about, old friends. Let's go down to my place and catch up."

They followed him to an area just beyond the tree line around the resort, where he stopped at a hole in the ground. "Jump in, and when you come up, we'll be at my place." He jumped in and disappeared. Dani followed, and Meg went in after, hoping her wings wouldn't get stuck.

She seemed to fall for a short time, and when she emerged, the ocean lapped lazily before her, diamond studded by the sun. A simple beach house was nestled in a cove nearby, with a canoe bobbing at the edge of the jade water.

The easy beauty of it took Meg's breath away and made her long for her childhood home in ancient Greece. She forced herself to pay attention, but when she did, she wondered if her heart could actually stop. Dani stood at the edge of the water, looking out at it as though she were pondering all of life's mysteries. She looked so beautiful, so peaceful, it was painful in the way poets wrote about. Surreal and divine. It was a lot like the photo of Dani she'd put on the project file, but this moment she knew she'd never forget.

Kanaloa put a hand on her shoulder, but his focus was on Dani. "I'm glad you came to me. She needs this."

Meg was about to ask what he meant and how he knew, but he shook his head.

"Later. For now, just enjoy." He left her and headed toward the beach cottage.

Meg sat down in the fine, warm sand and closed her eyes. Still, she could see Dani looking contemplative. Her obsession with Dani was a first, and she wasn't sure what to do about it. All she knew was that she was glad she had this time with her, whatever came of it. Her cell phone buzzed in her pocket, the "Hotel California" ringtone on silent.

"Hey, Sis. What's shakin' in the world of politics and weirdness?"

Tis sounded tired. "Weird is right. A group of underworld gods have created a coalition of sorts. They're using the chaos caused by Dis to bring followers to them. It's not a bad marketing ploy, frankly, and it is getting some of the more disturbed people settled down. But laws about religion and who people can pray to are already coming into effect in some of the countries where the gods have joined with governments. We're expecting to see migrations on a massive scale soon."

"Are people fighting back yet?" Meg had seen enough of history to know there were always people who stood their ground and refused to leave what they considered their homelands, even in the face of persecution.

"Not yet. I'm actually calling on Kera's behalf. She was wondering if Dani has had any news on more group death scenes or more people without souls?"

Meg stood and fluffed her wings to get the sand out. She hated to disturb Dani, who looked more serene as she stared out at the ocean than Meg could ever remember seeing her. "Hey. Sorry to bug you. Since you don't send out a newsletter, Kera wanted a dead and lost report."

"Sure. Hold on a second." Dani dug her toes into the sand and closed her eyes.

Meg could all but feel the energy pulsing off her and wondered for the zillionth time why she'd never noticed it before. *Is it the goddess thing, or am I just finally paying attention?* She put the cell on speaker so Tis could hear Dani's response.

"Less. The bodies entirely without souls have slowed down quite a lot, but the deaths caused by general confusion are about the same. My department has had an influx of the in-between souls. But there don't appear to be any unusual upheavals anywhere at the moment. Some of my staff are even taking vacations." She reopened her eyes. "That's good, right?"

There was a moment of silence on Tis's side. "It feels like the edge of the storm. Like we can see it coming, but we just have to wait and see how big it is. We know she isn't gone, and if she's grown tired of messing with the smaller groups of believers and the war zones, she could be up to something bigger and worse." She sighed. "We're still trying to figure out our next move, but without knowing what her game plan is, we're in the dark. Like you said, Meg, there's nothing to really fight against yet."

"You know how much I hate to say I told you so…" Meg grinned at Dani and wiggled her eyebrows.

"I'm pretty sure those were your first words." They heard Zed's rumbling in the background. "By the way, where are you guys? Meg, you feel strangely far away."

"Hawaii. Did you know there's a hotel just for gods to get away and relax? Can you imagine how much fun I'd have had here if I'd known?"

"Why do you think no one told you about it?" Tis laughed, sounding less stressed. "That island is deep in the in-between, no wonder I can't really feel you. Say hey to Kane and Kanaloa for me. And try the Tropical Itch. It's amazing. Love you, feather butt."

"Love you too, chipped fang." Meg hung up, trying not to show that Tis's comment had hurt her feelings.

"You okay?" Dani asked, putting an arm around her.

"Totally. Of course." She shrugged and swallowed back tears. "No."

Dani took her hand and tugged so they were sitting on the sand together. She put her arm around Meg's shoulders again. "Tell me."

"Am I so terrible that people don't want me around?" Meg hated the pitiful tone in her voice but couldn't help it. Tis's offhand comment had hurt.

"Terrible isn't the word. Passionate. Wild. Energetic. Curious. Those are the words I'd use."

She stroked the top of Meg's wing, sending electric shivers through her feathers. "Then why didn't she tell me about this place? What did she mean?"

Dani was quiet while she thought, something Meg was used to when it came to Dani, though it drove her crazy when it came to other people.

"Let me ask you something. When you're in a great mood, would you rather have a quiet dinner and read a good book, or would you rather hang out with friends, listen to music, and eat and drink the night way?"

"You know the answer to that." Meg liked the feeling of Dani's arm around her. The warm strength that emanated from her made her want to immerse herself in everything she had been and was in the moment and would be in the future.

"This place is dinner and a book. It's a place of quiet and reflection and time to get away from everything." She hugged Meg to her. "Your passion for life is exceptional, like everything about you. I know you like occasional time by yourself, but I also know how fast you'd get bored with no drama and no one to have sex with."

Meg sniffled against the tears she couldn't quite keep at bay. "I've never felt unwanted before. I don't like it."

Dani laughed softly. "Believe me, you're far from unwanted. And if you felt like staying here, I'm sure they'd welcome you. But I think any place where you'd have to blunt your beautiful energy isn't the right place for you, let alone them."

They continued to sit there watching the waves slowly lap at the shore, and Meg curled into Dani's strength. She thought about what Tis had said, as well as Dani's take on it. Always one to take things at face value, she rarely stopped and really thought about the deeper sense of things. Now, though, she wanted to understand. Dani was right. She did get bored quickly, and although she was happy to lie in the sun for a few hours doing nothing, it was usually with a thousand things she wanted to do later going through her mind. And, yeah, sex was often in the mix, if she wasn't already having it on the beach. Lately, however, the parties had started to pall, the sex had become rote, and the alcohol was more sour than sweet. *Who the hell am I?*

The sun hovered at the edge of the horizon, slowly sinking beneath the waves and casting sherbet splatters across the duck egg sky. They both looked over when they heard Kanaloa call to them.

"Hey! How about a little wave play with my old friend Death?" He held two surfboards under his arms.

Dani looked down at Meg, still tucked under her arm. "Want to have a go?"

"Now? Isn't it about to get dark?"

Dani stood and pulled Meg to her feet. "It is, but there's a full moon tonight. And surfing under a full moon is something else."

"Sharks? Other bitey things? I know we can't die, but I don't want to see how hard it is to grow back a limb. And I'm not getting my feathers wet just to have something sting or chomp me." Dani's laugh made Meg's stomach flip, and she started to smile. She could think deep thoughts later. It was time to play again.

"Bitey things tend to say away from me. I can't speak for the other gods, but every living thing avoids death. It's a beautiful aspect of evolution, the intrinsic desire for self-preservation. The smaller fish don't mind me as much because their brains aren't as evolved. But the big things tend to steer clear."

There was no sadness in Dani's voice the way there used to be when she talked about the loneliness that came as part of her job. *I wonder if that's because of the believer thing.* "In that case, I'm in. Let's do it."

She held Dani's hand as they made their way to Kanaloa, who was kneeling in the sand to wax his board. The idea of doing something important to Dani was exciting, and she couldn't wait to try something new. The fact that she'd be wet and pressed against Dani out on the water didn't hurt either.

Chapter Seventeen

A ngie eyed the newcomers with distaste, and yet Dis could also feel her deeply hidden fear. Though Angie knew exactly what she wanted and why, it didn't make her immune to the knowledge that the gods were powerful, regardless of why or what they did with that power. Dis liked that she functioned within her own tightly controlled chaos.

"Seriously? I thought you said you were going to help us. Not make us the chess pieces in a game of power." She motioned at Osiris and Horus. "He's green, and he's a bird. That guy keeps looking at me like he's going to feed me to some weird pet he probably has." She pointed at Iblis. "And you...I still haven't figured out what the hell you are." She glared at Dis, her arms crossed over her chest.

Iblis leaned forward to say something, but Dis held up her hand to stop him. "Did you think we could vacate the Vatican with a few meat-bag humans? Don't you think God will show up to defend his house and followers?"

Angie slumped into a chair. "I'd hoped for something like that, yeah. That's how you made it sound when you convinced me to follow you into this black hole of a plan."

Horus moved to her side and placed his huge hand on her shoulder, almost gently. "The world is a confusing place, small woman. Your desire to rid the world of the gods might happen one day. Today is not that day. But we will rid the world of the gods who have failed their followers for centuries, who have demanded war but not cared about the aftermath."

Angie looked at his hand on her shoulder and then up at him

before she slid from beneath his touch. She looked shaken, but her true mettle continued to shine through.

"I'm not convinced. In fact, if you're going to war with other gods, why do you need humans? Can't you just snap your fingers and bring the Vatican to the ground? Then you can fling lightning bolts and tridents and owls and whatever the fuck else at one another all you want. Why should I put my people in the middle of this?"

Osiris opened a cooler and handed Angie a beer with the Eye of Horus symbol on the label. Dis thought it was both disturbing and hilarious that he and his son Horus had decided to take Tisera's suggestion about rebranding to heart. As gods of creation and harvest, they'd established a brewery that developed beer laced with a mild aphrodisiac. Not only did people get addicted to it, they also began to flock to the gods as followers, just as the fury had predicted would happen with good rebranding.

"There are two rules when it comes to another god's temple. First, we can enter if they specifically invite us in. That's the way it's most commonly done, and a tenet we've lived by for millennia. But the sanctity of the structure is also protected by the faith of those within, the ones who have created their gods in the first place. That's what really makes the structure strong. If you shatter the faith of those within, if you can make them think that their gods have truly deserted them in their time of need, then the invitation becomes unnecessary. Take down the followers, and the god will fall with them. As gods, we forget that there are few rules without loopholes of some kind. Even for us."

He handed bottles of beer to the other gods. "Paradoxically, faith has been weakened by the gods coming into the physical world. They've always been told theirs is the only one, and now they know they've been lied to. It serves our purposes, because the believers inside those walls are already in a state of confusion, which weakens the structure. We simply need humans to get into the building and remove the faithful. Once the believers are dead or their faith broken, you can open the doors and invite us in. You believe in us, you see, which allows us passage within. Just as the Christians took over Pagan sites and claimed them for their own use, so too will you then claim this site for yours."

Angie sipped her beer and looked at them contemplatively. "People were burning temples all over the place not so long ago, but it didn't do any good. The gods just rebuilt them. I guess their followers were still strong, huh? None of this shit makes any sense to me. I hope you've got a better plan than that for this particular building. And then after? What about us?"

Iblis scoffed and was about to answer, but Dis cut him off once again. "You leave. Or stay. Whichever you want. Stay and watch the fun or run away like those grotesque poultry things you eat on this planet."

Angie frowned, clearly thinking. "Chickens? You'd call us chicken for not getting in the middle of a war between gods? You've got some nerve, lady." She set down her beer and stood unsteadily. "I'm going to let my people know we're on a suicide mission. They can decide whether or not to get on this ride to nowhere. All we can hope is you all cancel each other out." She stumbled from the room, holding on to the wall as she went.

"I forget how quickly humans are affected by the drink," Horus said, sipping his beer through a straw, since they hadn't yet created bottles made for beaks.

Iblis glared at Dis. "I dislike being silenced. I don't suggest you do it again."

Dis stepped into his personal space, her eyes open wide so he could see her world and her power. "I silenced you because you would have said something to tip the human off and send her scuttling away."

"There are more humans. We don't need that one." He was clearly trying hard not to step back and averted his eyes, though his jaw worked angrily.

"As narrow-minded as the humans, you are. Think." She poked his forehead. "Humanity First is a major player in the world. They defy the gods on every continent. They are a mass of faithless who could get us into places of worship all over the world. She's the voice and face of their movement, and she's got power of her own." She stepped back, bored with his fear. "And when humans die in huge groups, people won't know what to do or to believe. Humanity First will be working with gods, dying for gods, all while extolling their belief the gods shouldn't exist. The confusion and chaos it will cause will be magnificent. Non-believers will turn on each other. Believers will kill believers thanks to the development of theocracies. Most importantly, true belief, the kind that created the gods in the first place, will belong to those who have proven their strength and validity."

She turned to Horus and caressed his beak. "I'll draw in the power from the solar eclipse and use it to slow time. Not for long, but long enough for us to attack in darkness, to shroud the world in fear. And to give you and the others who follow me time to drink that power from me. When the eclipse is over, when the sun shines once again, you'll not only have the power of your believers, you'll have the power of the universe. The gods still standing will step in and take true control of the humans left."

Osiris opened another beer and relaxed in a chair. "We'll rebuild. The world will be as it once was...with better plumbing and electronics."

Dis looked at the few underworld gods beside her. They were a small group but powerful nonetheless. She'd hoped for Hades and Freya, but both had been able to dismiss the seeds of doubt she'd planted among the gods. Azrael had as well, but she'd figured he would. He had been an angel, not born to rule the underworld and the dead as the other gods were. Surprisingly, Yama had yet to answer her call. The blue-skinned Hindu god of death had seemed a sure bet, but apparently he was less power-hungry than his contemporaries. He remained in India, actually talking to the followers about what they wanted in an afterlife. It was baffling that he appeared to truly care for the believers of his religion. *Silly god. If he gets in our way, another underworld god will simply have to take over his territory.* She liked that notion, full of complexity and strangeness as it was. Maybe she'd suggest it, just to get the ball rolling. There were other gods, smaller ones relegated to bit roles among outlying religions who might come along for the ride. She decided to visit some the next day, since they had to wait for the rest of the Humanity First group to arrive.

Iblis stared out the window at the tall walls of the Vatican in the distance. "What's the plan?"

She definitely hadn't been surprised when Iblis had shown up. He'd always been a narcissistic goat, and the jinn were known mischief-makers. He'd refused to bow down before man and been cast out by his cloud god, and he'd been pissed off about it ever since. She wasn't sure what he wanted more: power or simply revenge against the humans he felt had wronged him.

From her position in the stars, she knew he was simply playing out a story that had been created when humans could imagine something bigger than themselves but had to relate it to their own small lives in order to fill in the incomprehensible gaps. A wayward son disobeying and being forced into an unkind world wasn't anything new, and every religion had a version of it. Still, he was unlikely to see past his own vitriolic nature or the fact that his story was one created by the humans who had thought up the gods in the first place.

"We're going to bring the cloud gods to us. We'll show them what power looks like, and when humans begin dying in the process, they'll have no choice but to back down." She smiled at Horus and Osiris. "They'll have to be dealt with, of course, in order to keep them from taking power back at the first opportunity. I recommend releasing them into my domain."

Stunned silence greeted her statement, as she knew it would. She gave them time to digest it.

"Yes. I suppose it makes sense. I hadn't truly considered the death of another god at my own hand, but there's no other option." Osiris picked at the label on his beer bottle. "What's to keep the believers of those gods left here on earth from creating a new version of that god?"

Dis finished her beer, glad he saw it her way. The other two were younger and would be easy to manipulate. "We'll make it a spectacle. The white fury wanted them to be visible, and we'll make their exile visible as well. We'll play it on every screen on the planet. Humans believe what they see, especially on that mind control machine they keep in their homes. When they see their gods gone, when they see one of the most iconic religious buildings reduced to dust, they'll turn to the gods left. Even if a few still have hope, the numbers won't be there to help re-create the gods. At least, not for a very long time." She held her hand out to Horus. "The drink is singing in my blood. Take me to bed." She led him from the room, anticipation and excitement an unlimited aphrodisiac. She could almost taste the despair and devastation to come. *Come, uppity godlings. Fall at my feet and weep.*

CHAPTER EIGHTEEN

Warm water lapped at her legs and moonlight stroked the ocean like a lover. But Dani hardly noticed, thanks to the beautiful woman straddling the board in front of her. Kanaloa had just taken a wave to shore and was paddling back, leaving Dani and Meg to float gently by themselves. Meg leaned back against Dani, and her energy was quieter than Dani could ever remember it being.

"This is amazing. I don't know why I've never done it." Meg scooped some water into her palm and let it fall over Dani's leg. "Sometimes I get so caught up in the day-to-day stuff, I forget how much I need nature. It makes everything quiet but brings it all into focus at the same time."

Dani shivered and tried to concentrate. "Wait until we catch a wave. That's really something."

"So how do I do it?"

Dani hadn't ever tried tandem surfing, though she'd watched plenty of other riders do so. Surfing was mostly a solitary sport, just a rider and her board in the vastness of the ocean, but sometimes people found it fun to experience it together. Dani had never thought she'd have the chance, and now that it was here, she could barely breathe. "When we're ready, we'll position the board in front of a wave. You'll scoot forward and kneel toward the front. Once I've popped up, you can carefully stand up. Your right foot will be at the front, pointed forward. Your back foot will be turned sideways, toward the side of the board. Make sense?"

Meg's brow was furrowed in the way that always said she was

really absorbed in something. "I'm with you. Like the warrior's pose in yoga?"

"Yeah, pretty much exactly like that. Soft knees, relaxed body. Because I've done this before and I'm in the back, I'll do most of the steering. Once we've done it a few times we can try turning, and you'll use your balance to lean into the wave slightly."

Kanaloa waved at them to take the next wave, and Dani felt her kinship with the former god of the underworld, in the loose way the Hawaiians had thought of the afterlife. He was also an ocean god, and Dani had always felt an affinity for the ocean deities. Poseidon rarely came by Afterlife, preferring the ocean's depths to walls and concrete, and he tended to keep to himself. He employed a huge number of nymphs and mer-people to carry messages all over the world, and he was fully aware of how necessary he was, though he didn't have the number of followers many of the cloud gods did. Unlike Poseidon, Kanaloa had a chilled-out, serene energy that called to Dani's desire for peace.

"Okay, ready? Knee onto the board and put your weight forward." Dani leaned down and started paddling. When she caught the crest, she popped up, but without her usual space to get into stance she was off balance, and when she went to correct it, she caught Meg's wing. The board flipped and sent them both into the water.

The wave passed, and Dani could hear Kanaloa's bellowing laughter across the water. Meg spluttered to the surface, wiping water from her eyes.

"I don't think that's how you do it." She grinned and began to laugh.

Her laughter was infectious, and Dani joined in. They rose and fell with the swells, hanging onto the board, until they eventually calmed. "Okay. Let's try it again. Sorry, I've never done it before."

Meg looked surprised. "Really?" She splashed some water at Dani. "I like being your first. It's not often that gets to happen when you live forever."

Dani was glad it was dark and Meg couldn't see how the words affected her. "True." She climbed onto her board and then helped Meg on. "Scoot forward a little more." Meg did as she was told, and Dani tried not to stare at the perfect swell of her perfect butt, which had no business looking so damn good in the wetsuit Kanaloa had loaned her. "There. Okay, let's go."

Dani paddled again, and this time kept her balance as she popped up. Meg got up carefully and stood exactly as Dani had told her to. Gently, Dani pulled her back so Meg's back foot was slightly behind Dani's and her back was pressed to Dani's front. She inhaled the spicy scent she'd always associate only with Meg, and when Meg wrapped her front arm over Dani's, it became the most exotic, most sensual dance Dani had ever moved to. Every miniscule move Dani made, Meg followed. They glided along the wave in an effortless duet of motion, and when the wave ended, Dani loathed that the moment was over. The board lost momentum and they fell to the side of it. When they surfaced, they stood with the board bobbing between them, the ocean lapping at their thighs. Neither of them spoke, and the moment felt weighted with a thousand questions that could only be asked and answered by their bodies. Caution and hesitation no longer felt like an option, and Dani cupped Meg's face in her hands and leaned forward. Their lips met, and Dani's place in the world suddenly made sense. There in the moonlight, standing in the warm tropical waters by an island that didn't really exist, she knew she wasn't alone anymore. Death had found life, and the universe belonged to her.

Meg pulled back, and her eyes were wide and full of tears. She touched her fingertips to her lips and seemed like she was about to say something, but then stopped.

Kanaloa paddled up beside them and dropped into the water. He nodded, and his smile was understanding. "We can talk more tomorrow. For tonight, let go." He pointed down the beach. "Just around that rock is another cabin like mine. It's yours for as long as you're here." He picked up his board and splashed toward shore, leaving them to answer the night's questions.

Dani knew what she was feeling, but Meg had yet to speak, and she felt a sudden pang of insecurity. "Meg, if—"

Meg shook her head vehemently. "Don't." She took Dani's hand and started to splash toward shore.

Dani picked up her board and followed. Meg's sunrise red wings caught the moonlight and turned it into a crimson promise. They walked along the beach together in silence, and when they spotted the beachside bungalow, Meg made a small noise of appreciation. Dani left the board beside the steps and continued to follow Meg into the house. She'd always thought she'd be nervous to the point of incapacity if anything ever happened between them, but all she felt in the moment was deep, ardent desire.

Meg went straight to the bedroom and turned to Dani when she was beside the bed. Their kiss was desperate, devouring, and full of need. Meg's mouth was hot and her hands were all over Dani's body. She pulled away and almost roughly turned Meg around so she could get to the zipper on her wetsuit. Once it was down, she tugged the material off Meg's shoulders, then slowed her movements. She'd seen Meg naked before; Meg wasn't shy about her body and showed it off whenever the moment was right. But this was different; this was for her, for them. Dani slid her hands over Meg's shoulders, paying attention to every inch of her silky porcelain skin. She pushed the wetsuit down slowly to bare Meg's breasts, and when her palms brushed against Meg's nipples, she moaned and pushed into Dani's hands. But Dani skimmed over them and slid the wetsuit lower, letting her palms stroke Meg's soft stomach until she reached her hips. Impatient, Dani turned her around and pushed her gently onto the bed. She tugged the wetsuit the rest of the way off and flung it to the side.

White sheets glowed beneath Meg's spread wings, her curves perfect and begging to be touched. Dani's breath hitched as she stared at the woman she'd desired for so long, though never to this degree of painful aching. Her own clit throbbed, and she needed her skin against Meg's. She shrugged out of her wetsuit and dropped it on the floor. The look of hunger and appreciation in Meg's eyes told her everything she needed to know. She'd never felt sexier, more desired, than she did because of that look. They danced with flames, and she looked the stunning, magical creature she was. Terrifying, magnificent, passionate Meg reached for her, and Dani stopped thinking. She climbed onto the bed and lowered herself onto Meg, kissing her way over Meg's chest, along her collarbone, over her neck, and finally to her mouth. She tasted of the sea, salty and real, and she tasted of excess and sex in its most primal form.

She moaned as Meg's wings encircled her, the feathers like silk over her raw nerves. She shuddered and pressed her leg against Meg's hot wetness, and felt Meg's answer in the way she pressed herself to Dani's leg.

"Fuck me. Gods, Dani, fuck me." Meg's voice was breathless, her eyes half-lidded.

Dani didn't need her to ask again. She slid her hand between Meg's legs, entered her with two fingers, and took her quickly, pumping hard and fast. She'd heard Meg talk about her escapades often enough to know how she liked it, and she was damn glad she'd paid attention. Meg rode her fingers with abandon, writhing and moaning. She came but kept moving, and Dani gladly kept going. Being immortal was a blessing when it came to stamina. It took a lot to tire a god.

Dani pulled out and moved to turn Meg over. She pulled her onto her knees and then entered her from behind. Meg's scream of pleasure nearly made Dani come right then. She'd dreamed of taking Meg in this position, and a zillion others, for centuries. Now that it was happening, she wasn't going to miss a moment. If it never happened again, she'd always have tonight.

By Meg's fifth orgasm and as many new positions, she finally began to grow quiet, and Dani pulled out. She pulled Meg back onto the bed and into her arms. Meg wrapped a wing around Dani, and she smiled at the feel of the feathers. She knew Meg's snakes were in there somewhere too, but she couldn't feel them. She liked the way Meg's red feathers looked against her own bone-white skin. *Death and passion.* She closed her eyes and enjoyed the simplicity of the moment, trying to ignore the distant warning bell caused by the words.

"Can I taste you?" Meg asked quietly.

Dani grinned at her. "Have you ever had to ask before?"

Meg shook her head, looking shy. "Weird. No, I haven't. But I feel like I should."

"By all means, beautiful. I'd love to have your mouth on me."

Without another word, Meg made her way slowly down Dani's body, kissing and nibbling her way to Dani's clit, which was throbbing almost painfully. The moment Meg's tongue lightly touched it, Dani nearly shot off the bed from the intensity. Instead, she grabbed fistfuls of the sheet and closed her eyes. She wanted to feel—every caress, every move, every breath. Meg stroked in soft, swirling circles, and Dani knew she wouldn't hold out very long. Sure enough, within minutes, she crested the wave and came with a hoarse cry, one hand buried in Meg's hair, the other knotted in the sheets. When Meg went to continue, Dani tugged on her hair. "I'm not quite as quick to recover as you, beautiful. Give me a minute."

Meg pouted but crawled back into her place at Dani's side, her wing once again draped over Dani's body.

Dani kissed the top of her head and held her until she felt Meg drift to sleep. Her heart felt like it could burst from the knowledge that Meg was really in her arms. It wasn't a hot dream or a vivid fantasy. Not this time. No matter what the next day brought with it, no matter what the future held, this night would be the most precious of her life. Did she dare hope they could fashion some kind of future together? The world beyond their little island bungalow was full of chaos and an encroaching darkness. But the Fates had told Meg to find herself; could she do that with Dani at her side rather than behind her? Dani wanted to believe that it was possible.

She breathed in Meg's scent and pulled her as close as she could. Dani had her own stuff to do, but somehow, she knew Meg would be there to help her through it. It was Meg, after all, who had thought to bring her to Kanaloa. Was this part of the Fates' plan? Did they foresee this? Or was this part of their cloudy vision? The thought of a blinded Fate was truly disturbing, and though Dani's job would continue as long as there were humans, for the humans' sake she hoped it wasn't going to be as bad as the Fates seemed to think it could be.

Meg stirred and groped for Dani's hand. "More." She put Dani's hand right where she wanted it and ground against it.

Dani was happy to oblige. The world and its future could wait. Tonight, Meg was hers and the world was magical. Tomorrow, she could learn how to be a god. Tonight, she felt like one.

Dani woke with the sunrise. Meg lay curled on her side, looking beautifully serene, even with her fangs poking out slightly. They'd made love throughout the night, stopping to doze, only to meld into each other again later. Dani closed her eyes and focused on her realm. She felt her crew everywhere, doing their jobs, bringing souls back and delivering them to the right afterlives. Those without a place were in her own realm, where she'd set up a small receiving room not unlike the ones the other gods had. Her phone buzzed, and she grabbed it.

She slowly moved out of the bed so she didn't disturb Meg and took the phone outside. The cool tropical air felt amazing on her naked body, and she flopped into the hammock beside the porch. She saw the text message from Idona and called her back.

"Hey, boss. All good?"

Idona sounded concerned, and Dani knew she'd never ask directly where Dani was, as she'd consider it rude. *Even after all these years.*

"I'm good. Really good. Best I've ever been, in fact." She smiled widely and was glad Idona couldn't see it.

"That sounds promising. You coming back soon? I've got something I'd like to run by you."

Dani looked out at the waves. She couldn't leave her realm for much longer, and she knew Meg would need to get back to work too. "I'll be back by tonight. But what's up?"

"You know that idea you had about rebranding? I want to take the first step."

"Yeah? How so?" Dani left the hammock and wandered down to the sand, watching the sun's rays light paths along the oceans crests.

"These souls in receiving. Can we allow them to take form again and open a space in the Nexus sector for them? I'm thinking we can let them start figuring out if they want to stay with us or if they want to check out other sectors or whatever."

Dani laughed. "Why do I get the feeling you've been talking to Meg behind my back?"

"Not behind your back, exactly, because you weren't around. Just…talking. And I think she's got some stellar ideas. She explained them way better than you did."

"Yeah, okay. I get it." She thought about the ramifications and knew it could work. "Let's do it. But I want you to have some of the more experienced Sundo on hand to greet the souls. Do it a few souls at a time, to make certain they get personal attention. They'll need help adjusting." She pictured the other things in Meg's rebranding folder. "Get the library set up as quickly as you can, and if you liked some of the other places in Meg's plan, run with it. I trust you."

"I won't let you down. Thanks for giving me some say."

Idona sounded as excited as a kid with a new trampoline.

"Yeah, well, remember you have to take my place at some point in the very, *very* distant future. Make sure you're happy with it. But don't stress, either. I imagine we'll hit some bumps along the way and have to do some learning. We can talk tomorrow morning, and you can tell me what you've got going, okay?" Dani had made Idona wait longer than any other deputy Death in history to take over. The least she could do was give her some autonomy in the rebrand. Not to mention it took some of the pressure off if someone else was helping make it happen.

"So frigging awesome. See you tomorrow. Tell Meg I said hey."

She hung up before Dani could ask how she knew she was with Meg. It didn't matter, but she wasn't sure how she felt about Meg talking to Idona about the rebranding plans. A flare of jealousy hit her when she remembered Idona's comments on Meg's sexiness, but she quickly quashed it. Idona wouldn't go there, and she felt certain Meg would've mentioned it had anything happened between them.

She heard a whistle and looked up. Kanaloa had his board under his arm, and he pointed to the water. She waved before heading inside. Meg was still sound asleep, and though the desire to crawl back in beside her was strong, she knew she needed to talk to Kanaloa about the god thing before they left. Plus, Meg really hated mornings, and a grumpy fury wasn't a fun fury. She grabbed her wetsuit from the floor and took it outside so she wouldn't make any noise. She picked up her board, jogged out to the water, and paddled to where Kanaloa sat on his board, waiting for her.

"Dolphins. And a few orcas to the north of us."

She watched as the dolphins dove and played all around them, the clarity of the water allowing her to see them passing under her feet. "Weird. They usually stay away from me. I don't think I've ever been this close to them."

He nodded and patted the nose of a dolphin that popped up next to him. "Things are changing all over, aren't they?" He turned to look at her. "Even Death is transforming."

She nodded and spoke past the lump in her throat. "I'm not sure how to handle it. The persona of death has always had a small following in various places in the world. But never enough to give me deity status. Lately that's changed. I've got millions of followers, and if I go through with the kind of rebranding Meg is talking about, it could be a lot more."

"Rebranding of the gods. A sign of the times for sure. Tell me something, Dani. Why do you want to rebrand? Personally."

She'd given it a lot of thought, and the answer came easily. "Human lives are fragile and short. They're here for an instant, and some of them manage to leave some kind of legacy for other generations to follow, while others simply live out their given time without really noticing the gift they've been given." She smiled as a dolphin nosed at her leg and clicked at her before dropping back into the water. *Not alone anymore.* "But pretty much all of them are afraid of leaving their existence because they don't know what comes after. That fear has lessened a little bit, thanks to the gods walking among them, but now that they have a choice of where to go when they die, they're confused. That confusion has called Dis back to the world—"

He hissed slightly. "She's hit our islands as well."

Dani nodded. "But the fact is, they *did* call her. And now they're afraid of dying because not only do they not want to leave this life, but they don't know *where* they want to go. Death isn't just scary anymore. It's terrifying." She looked out at the vast ocean and imagined the human population. "Human life is difficult enough. They face obstacles every day, some worse than others. I want to help ease their way into the afterlife. Maybe that way they can stop worrying about what's to come and just enjoy where they are."

Kanaloa was silent for a while as he clearly considered her words. "I've always liked you, Dani. I think you're one of the kindest, most ethical Deaths there has ever been. And I like your logic. Once the humans have settled down, your hypothesis will be put to the test. Don't you think fear of death gives them a reason to fight to stay alive?"

It was a question Dani had turned every which way and still didn't have an answer to. "Maybe. I think that's evolutionary. But maybe they can evolve to live in the moment if they don't fear death to the exclusion of living life as best they can." She shrugged. "I think some of them fear leaving life behind more than they fear actual death. If they can set aside a fear of the afterlife, maybe they can really pay attention to life in the moment. I think making their world an easier place to live would help give my own job more meaning too."

He squeezed her shoulder. "And that's what's going to make you a god worth praying to. I hope you're right, and I'll be behind you all the way if you need anything. Let's talk about the other stuff. What do you want to know?"

"Honestly, I'm not entirely sure why Meg brought me to you, out of all the gods. But basically, I don't know how to deal with becoming a god. I don't know what I'm doing, and I don't want to let down people who believe in me."

Two orcas surfaced in the distance, blowing water high into the air before they submerged again. Their size and beauty took Dani's breath away, and she wondered if she could actually swim near them now.

As though reading her mind, Kanaloa said, "Those aren't the vegetarian type. They might mistake you for a snack." He motioned behind them. "Let's catch a few waves before we get stiff."

He moved away to catch the next wave, and Dani admired his grace and form as he rode the small tunnel to the end. She started paddling and popped up on the next crest. The water flowed past her, over her, under her, and she felt like part of the planet. She laughed out loud when the dolphins joined her, riding the wave beside and in front of her. When she fell into the water at the end, she got nose and fin bumps before they darted back into the ocean.

"That was awesome in the truest sense of the word." She felt tears of appreciation and serenity fill her eyes. It was like her body was too small to contain the wonder of her world now.

"Come on."

She followed Kanaloa back out to beyond the point break, where they just floated on the light swells.

"You've had people praying to death for a long time. Have you never answered them?"

She shook her head. "I don't think so. I mean, many prayed their loved ones would be delivered to the afterlife they wanted, and I deliver the soul no matter what, although I never helped dictate if they went to the cloud gods or the underworld. Some prayed for the health of their loved ones, and like any god, there's nothing I can do about illness."

"And now?"

She sighed. "Now they want protection, health, for my scythe to sweep away every obstacle from their lives, to stop their enemies. They pray for money and success. Some are even praying to me about lost love."

He nodded knowingly. "Generalities. Those aren't too bad. Like any god, you can't answer the ones about enemies because there's a conflict when it comes to the fact that enemies might be praying about each other. You could answer the first one to come in, like some gods do, or you can forgo answering the general prayers. That's what we do here. If someone asks for something really specific, we look into it. If it's something we can help with, like making sure someone comes to someone else's notice, or that a building stays upright for just one more year, then we do it."

"Do you personally do it? How do you have the time?"

"Gods, no!" He laughed, a great big belly laugh. "Like any god, you'll have to develop a section of staff that help solely with prayer. They'll come to you with the prayers, and you can sift through them and figure out which to grant and which not to."

He paddled to catch another wave, and Dani waited for him, thinking. Developing the staff to take on that section of her new role was something she hadn't considered, but it made the job seem far less daunting. She liked the distinction about generalities too. It might be a little sideways as far as answering prayers went, but with millions of people invoking nearly the exact same prayer or ritual, it made it impossible to answer them all. Kanaloa paddled back to her.

"Hey, this could work with your rebranding, you know?"

"How so?" Dani wasn't that far ahead yet.

"Just like the other gods, go be with them. Let them know your face, and tell them what kinds of prayers you grant. Like being able to help with specific stuff and not being there to kill enemies. Set parameters, just like the other gods are doing. Heck, maybe even come up with your own guidebook."

She thought about it. "That would make my job clearer, if not easier. People asking for something specific would mean no wasted prayer. I like it." The thought of being among the humans praying to her, visible for all to see, made her tremble slightly. Death only showed herself to people who were about to go with her. *Until now.* "If I wanted to answer a prayer directly, how do I do it?"

Kanaloa put his hand on top of the water between them. "And now we come to why Megara brought you to me." He tapped the water, and they watched the ripples it created. "She knows you well, I think. You may not be a water god, but you love the ocean like one. Water is part of you, so she brought you to a water god who surfs." He smiled at her. "When you want to grant a prayer, you figure out what needs to happen to make that work. For instance, if someone wants their business to get more clients, you use your magic to make sure a certain number of people see the advertisement in a particular place. And you plant the idea that they want to check it out, and then maybe tell a friend or two." He splashed water in the air. "And just like that, prayer answered."

"But how will I know who the right people are to tap into?" As logical as it sounded, it also sounded completely bizarre.

"Use the water. Humans are made of it; the planet breathes it. Use your love of the water to feel it flowing everywhere. Not just the ocean, but rivers and streams and fountains. Connect with it and then direct your connection outward to the people. Let the energy of your intentions flow from the water."

"That sounds impossible, unlikely, and somewhat outrageous."

"You're Death, sitting on a surfboard, in front of an island that doesn't exist, with an ancient god of water. Implausible is the name of the game, gorgeous. You have to just take the leap."

They spent the next three hours practicing what he'd told her. They'd catch a few waves and give Dani time to think, then practice some more. Instead of focusing on water specifically, she concentrated on the flow, like the drawing of water into a wave and then the way it folded over and rejoined itself. Like that flow, she listened to prayers and created a kind of ripple and flow beyond the person, affecting the areas that needed affecting. At first, it took a lot of energy, and it was hard to focus on a single voice, but he taught her how to concentrate on a single point of the ripple rather than on the whole thing, and she got the hang of it quickly. Kanaloa was incredibly patient, and being able to be on the ocean while she learned made it seem far less worrying than it had when they'd arrived the day before. Just when she felt like she had a reasonable handle on it, they heard a shout from shore.

"I'm going to eat my own wings if you don't feed me soon!" Meg shouted and fell back onto the sand dramatically, her wings spread beneath her.

The sight made Dani's pulse race, and her heart almost hurt from the beauty and memory of their night together.

Kanaloa nudged her. "There's more to her than she shows people. She brought you here because she understands you. I bet she understands a lot of people, and they have no idea. This thing between you? Be patient. Learning to tame the waves takes time."

Dani shook her head. "I'd never want to tame her. She's perfect wild."

He laughed. "And you never really tame the waves, do you? But you come to an understanding, a mutual admiration." He shoved her and she fell off her board. "And remember to get some sleep occasionally too."

She sputtered water, laughing, as he caught the wave to shore. She followed him and was never as gratified, or grateful, as she was when Meg bounded back to her feet and threw herself into Dani's arms.

"By all that lives and breathes, please feed me," she mumbled against Dani's chest.

Kanaloa laughed. "No matter what else happens, some things never change. Let's walk up to the hotel. I'll tell you about some of the animals we've got here."

They followed him up a long, winding trail toward the hotel, and true to his word, he told them about the various species around them. Some of them, he and his brother had saved from extinction by bringing them from the other islands. Now some of the plants and animals couldn't be found anywhere else on the planet.

"It really is a special place." Meg reached out, and an American Lady butterfly landed on her wrist. "Stunning. She looks like something out of a steampunk novel."

Her black and white wings looked like the insides of a clock, and her beautiful pink stripe at the top made her wings look like modern paintings. "She's like you."

Meg looked at her curiously.

"Strong, delicate, unusual. Complex and colorful."

Meg hooked her arm through Dani's. "I like that you see me that way."

They arrived at the hotel, and Meg shot off toward the food table. Dani and Kanaloa followed at a slower pace, both smiling as Meg filled her plate and talked to everyone around her.

"Did being here help?" Kanaloa asked as he picked up a piece of pineapple.

"I can't thank you enough, Kan. It really did."

They sat next to Meg at a table, and Dani laughed at the expression of ravenous delight on her face. When she took a moment to breathe, she sat back and looked around.

"I wanted to ask you. How did you know we were coming?" Meg asked.

"The volcano told us."

"Sure. Makes total sense." Meg rolled her eyes and held out her hands as though requiring more information.

"Hawaiian gods are tied to the land and the sea, especially to the volcanoes. Those same volcanoes run deep into the earth and are surrounded by water, and they're part of our spirit world as well." He tossed a blueberry at Dani. "Like our Death, here, who is both part of the world because of her work with humans and part of the spiritual world because of her work with soul delivery and prayer. The volcanoes began to whisper that death was coming."

Dani raised an eyebrow. "That can't have been very reassuring."

He laughed. "Nah. We know their language, and we knew they meant it literally. Or metaphorically. Whichever it is." He finished his breakfast and stood. "Stay as long as you like, although I know you've both got jobs to get back to. If I don't see you before you go, come back soon, okay?" He gave them both a massive, tight hug. "Don't forget about us again."

Dani held him tightly, unable to voice how much she owed him. "Never."

He left, and they sat back down. Meg sipped her coffee and slipped her hand over Dani's. "I say we go see how hard it is to have sex on a hammock."

Dani jumped up from the table, grabbed Meg's hand, and they ran down the road back to the shore like wild teenagers. Once they left here there was no telling what would happen; this little bit of haven from their daily world felt like a gift, and it wasn't one she'd take for granted.

In this moment, I can have it all.

CHAPTER NINETEEN

"Make it stop." Meg pulled the pillow over her head, but the ringing just kept on. She threw off the pillow and sat up. She stretched to pick up her phone off the floor and fell off the bed. With her cheek pressed to the floor and her legs still on the bed, she answered it. "What could possibly be this important?"

"We've been trying to reach you mentally, but you're too far between. We need you to come back to the office."

Tis sounded even more stressed than usual, and that was saying something. "What's up?" She slid the rest of the way off the bed and wondered where Dani was as she tried to untangle herself from the sheets.

"Dis, mostly. But we've been doing a lot of talking, and we need your input. And Dani's too."

She finally disengaged herself from the sheets and jumped to her feet. "Sure, Sis. We'll get there as soon as we can." She hung up and walked down to the sand. Dani was riding a wave, looking relaxed and confident in a way she never really did on land. The mellow sunset made her dark silhouette stark against the wave, and she looked both powerful and mysterious. Meg didn't know why she'd thought of the Hawaiian gods when Dani had told her about the whole goddess problem. She'd just known it was the right thing to do. And although it turned out sex in a hammock was even harder than she thought it would be, sex on the beach, on the porch, in the bed, and finally, on the roof under the moonlight, had been perfect.

Dani rode the wave to shore and tucked her board under her arm as she ran back toward Meg. When she was close enough, she dropped the board and wrapped Meg in a wet hug.

"Much as I love being wet, hot stuff, this isn't exactly what I had in mind." She grinned and pulled away. "And Tis just called. We're needed back home, pronto."

Dani sighed and looked disappointed. "I knew we'd have to go back today. And now I fully understand why gods come here to really get away from it all." She took Meg's hand in her own and kissed the top of it. "It's been more than I could have imagined."

Meg shivered at the intensity of Dani's gaze. The sex had been magnificent, electric, passionate. Their connection was what she'd hoped it would be. But now, faced with returning to real life, would it hold up? Or would they go back to being friends? Dani would go back to running the world of the dead, and Meg...Meg would go back to having few friends and lots of sex with random people. The thought was deflating. *I can't imagine my bed without her now. Or my life.*

Dani kissed her forehead softly. "Hey. Deep thoughts can wait. Let me take a quick shower, and then we'll head out, okay?" She started pulling her wetsuit off as she headed to the bathroom. "Kanaloa left a tray of food on the porch for us. I put it in the kitchen."

Meg wasn't sure what she wanted more—to join Dani in the shower or food. Given the time constraint, she decided food was a more responsible option, and she dug into the plate of fruit and pastries. When Dani came out from her shower, Meg swallowed hard.

"You're glowing even more than when we came." She wasn't just glowing. She looked effervescent. Her pale eyes shone brightly but seemed in constant motion, and Meg realized she was seeing souls in the whites of Dani's eyes. She exuded power and strength, and beyond that, she looked at peace.

"I feel amazing. I've been practicing what Kanaloa taught me yesterday, and the feeling I get when I answer a prayer..." She shook her head, smiling. "I can't even explain what it feels like. I've always taken life away, and now I'm making life itself better before I have to take it. If this is what being a god feels like, I understand why they fight to stick around."

Trust Dani to be humbled by granting prayers. The beautiful simplicity of it brought tears to her eyes. "We'd better get on the road."

Dani nodded, and they dropped into the hole that took them the quick way back to the hotel, where they headed straight to the Mustang. As they drove back to the shore where they'd come in, Meg longed to stay right where they were. Dani opened a tunnel ahead of them, and Meg turned in her seat to watch the island fade away. She waved back at Lono and Kanaloa, who stood on the rocky outcrop, watching them leave.

With a sigh, she turned back into her seat. "I wonder when we'll see them again."

Dani took her hand. "It sounds like we're going to be busy for a while, but I know I can't wait to come back. Maybe when everything has calmed down we can take some time for ourselves."

Meg loved the way Dani's strong, slim hand felt over her own. "Think they'll let me come back?" The idea of not being wanted in such a beautiful place still stung.

"I'll keep you so busy they won't even know you're there." Dani gave her a wicked grin and licked her lips.

Meg laughed, feeling better. They drove in silence for a while, and Meg murmured in awe when the silhouettes of a pod of whales surrounded the road they were on.

"Beautiful, aren't they? A pod swam close this morning. First time ever the mammals haven't been afraid of me. What a feeling."

Her smile was genuine and open, making Meg's stomach flip. She couldn't remember feeling this way about anyone, ever, the morning after. Not even after a really, *really*, good night. "I can imagine."

Dani looked over at her, her expression serious. "How did you know to take me there?"

Meg shrugged. "I just knew."

"Can I ask you a favor?" Dani frowned as she watched the road.

"After that thing you did with your tongue last night? You can ask about fifty." Meg didn't want to seem flippant, but Dani's seriousness made her uncomfortable.

Dani laughed. "Glad you liked it. Really, though. I'd like you to think about why you took me there. I know you said you just knew, but...well, will you try to explain?"

Meg shook off the feeling that there was a question beneath the question. "Okay..." *I can talk to her. She doesn't judge. Let go.* "My sisters are the serious ones, right? Alec is all hot and broody, Tis is the smart, sensitive one. And I'm the fun goofball. That's what we were as kids, and that's what we've always been."

"But?"

Meg sighed. "But that doesn't mean I don't think. I may not bury myself in books or be a hero, but sometimes, I *really* know things. I don't think about them, but I know the answers if I just kind of zone out and let it come to me. If I get all thinky the way my sisters do, it shuts down." The blue-black ocean hue around the road ended, and they were once again back on land with the houses and trees of Dani's realm around them. There wasn't much more time to talk. "Like when you said you were having a problem, I just relaxed into it, and I knew where you needed to go. It didn't matter that I didn't know exactly who we were going to see, or exactly where. I just knew the general place, and that it would be okay when we got there."

Dani nodded, apparently thinking about the answer. They pulled onto the road that led to the Afterlife gate. "I feel like you've given me a whole new life."

"I'm glad to hear it." Meg had helped people before but never someone whose happiness mattered quite so much. It left a residual feeling inside she wasn't used to, like a warm stream flowing through her veins.

Dani parked and turned to Meg. "Thank you for our time together too. I can't tell you what it means…" She took a deep breath and smiled. "I'd like to keep doing it, if you'd be interested?"

Meg flung herself into Dani's arms, relief swamping her. "Yes! Now. Later. Tomorrow."

Dani kissed her gently. "Probably not now, since there are people waiting on us. But later I'll take you up on that."

They got out and headed inside, hand in hand. Meg had never been much for genuine displays of affection. Public sex was fantastic, but real emotion always seemed too intimate, too private. Now, though, holding Dani's hand made her feel grounded, and she hoped everyone on every floor saw it. When they walked into the conference room, she saw pretty much everyone notice, but no one said anything.

Kera shoved a box of donuts toward them. "Thanks for coming."

Meg grabbed a jam-filled donut and slid into a seat next to Tis. "Always. What's going on?"

Instead of taking a seat, Dani stood in front of the giant wall map, her head tilted as she studied it. Meg liked watching her think.

"We've had a report that Dis is in Rome with a few of the Egyptian gods, as well as Iblis. We also know there's been a sudden cessation in deaths attributed to her influence. Less of that weird spaghetti black stuff in people's souls." Tis had files open in front of her and tapped on them constantly with a pencil.

"Less death and muck is good, isn't it?" Meg asked around a mouthful of donut.

"When cosmic-crazy-fuck goes quiet, you have to wonder what's about to explode." Kera motioned at the map Dani was studying. "And when she's hanging out with Beakface and Mr. Grumpy Butt, seems like there's other stuff at play."

Selene leaned forward. "Is it okay to finally ask what's going on with you, Dani? Forgive me, but you're radiating light like a full moon."

Dani laughed and turned away from the map, though her eyes were still serious. "Sorry, everyone. I wasn't ready to talk about it before, but thanks to Meg, I've worked some things out." She shrugged almost apologetically. "Because of the amount of people who believe but who don't have a god they feel represents them, many have started praying to Death. My followers have quadrupled—"

"And you've become a god." Zed stood and clapped her on the back. "Well done, and welcome to the club!"

She nodded slightly. "Thanks. It probably won't last once the humans calm down, but it's a nice feeling in the meantime."

"So, what? You were in Hawaii celebrating?" Kera asked, her tone a little sharp.

"No, not at all." Dani looked around, seeming less certain of herself now. "I didn't really know how to deal with it or what to do. Meg took me to see Kanaloa, so he could teach me."

"I would have taught you." Zed looked put out and grabbed another donut from the box.

"I needed a water god, one who gets me." She smiled at Meg, and this one reached her eyes. "Meg knew that."

Zed snorted and waved his hand. "Okay, yeah. Let's get on with it."

Meg knew he'd have forgotten his pique by tomorrow and ignored it. "So why did you need us to get back here?"

Tis and Selene looked at one another, and Selene spoke first. "We wanted to talk to you about the rebranding you've been doing. Especially with Dani's department."

Dani moved around the table and sat beside Meg. "What about it?"

"We're wondering if the humans can handle it. We're trying to understand the ramifications of this kind of massive change."

Meg frowned. "You were the ones who suggested it in the first place."

Tis nodded and closed her eyes. "I know. And part of me still thinks it was the right thing to do. But the other part of me is wondering if we haven't taken into account just how fragile the human balance between life and death really is."

Selene nodded. "Faith is mutable. While humans might be having trouble with the gods walking among them, they're capable of handling a choice of who to worship. But the human fear of death is what keeps us from doing dangerous things. It's what keeps us moving forward. If we no longer fear death, if it's a destination of its own, then what makes humans strive for more?"

"That's stupid, and it's not giving humans enough credit." Meg leaned forward, aggravated and having one of those moments where she simply knew what she was saying was true. "A whole heap of them really, *really* believe in an afterlife of some sort. But just because they knew there was a reward at the end, they didn't stop doing stuff and trying to be better in some way. It's not like death comes as a surprise. That's the one thing all humans seem to accept, that death will come for all of them at some point."

"Cheery." Kera flung a rubber band across the room.

"True. I mean, you didn't have any faith in the gods at all. But it didn't mean you stopped being a good human because of it. In fact, you tried even harder because you didn't think the gods were doing enough."

"I like this line of thinking. Do go on." Kera leaned back and propped her feet on the desk.

"If you knew you could spend your afterlife in Dani's realm, where you don't have to believe in any god at all, but you also don't have to turn to atheist dust, how would that stop you from being the good person you are now? What if, instead of seeing the afterlife as a reward or punishment, but simply as another step, people could focus on making the world better because they want to and not because of the consequences after death? And would it make a difference to you wanting to live in Dani's sector after you died?" Meg had no idea why she felt passionately about it, but she had to make them understand. They were on the right path with the redesigns.

Kera stared at her thoughtfully. "Hell, I like the idea right now, frankly. I hadn't thought about it."

Tis shook her head. "I agree, there are people like Kera and Selene who don't need fear to inspire them to do and be better in this life. But they're extraordinary, and I think knowing life is finite makes it precious to humans overall, whether they know it or not."

"What are you saying, Tis?" Dani asked softly.

"I don't know." She shrugged. "All I know is that by giving humans a vast array of choice among gods and by taking away their fear of death, we may have taken them to a place they can't function. And by doing so, we've played into Dis's hands."

They all sat silently, but Meg wasn't buying it. "I don't think we could have averted this." She looked at Selene and Alec. "From the moment the Fates put the two of you in an oracle together to save us all, I think this moment has been coming. We all know how seriously messed up the Fates and their oracles are. This time they can't see beyond it, but that doesn't mean we aren't still doing exactly what we're supposed to be doing. I mean, that's the whole fucked up thing with oracles, isn't it? No matter what you do, you're going to do what you're supposed to do. We just have to ride the wave as best we can."

Dani smiled slightly at Meg's use of surfing jargon. "I agree. The Fates have set us on this path. Second-guessing ourselves isn't going to do any good." She took Meg's hand in her own. "I like Meg's plans, and now that I've got my own followers, I think there's no way to go but forward."

Zed nodded. "Agreed. What are we going to do about the problem in Rome?" He stared out the window while munching a huge bar of chocolate.

Kera still looked at Dani thoughtfully but turned her attention to Zed. "I think we can assume she's going to do something stupid with the Vatican. The question is, will more gods join her?"

He sighed and turned around. "I hate that I feel guilty. It's one quality no god should ever have. But I feel the need to tell you something."

"What have you done, big guy?" Alec asked.

"Nothing, really. Clotho told me Dis was in Rome. I went to see her, to see if she'd open up to me, without any audience."

"And did she?" Selene leaned back into Alec's arm draped around her shoulder.

"Kind of." He slumped into a chair at the conference table. "I asked her what she wants. I thought if we could find a way to give it to her, she would go away. But the truth is, there's nothing we can give her. She wants to do what she does and see it done to an extreme. She thinks the humans are a virus that needs to be dealt with, and her way of doing it is the only way."

"And did she say why she was in Rome?" Dani said.

He winced. "She said she'd meet us there in two days, at the start of the eclipse. I didn't bring it up right away because I wasn't sure I wanted to play into whatever trick she has up her sleeve. But I don't think we have a choice. And now that we know there are underworld gods with her, we can assume it isn't something that goes with the Afterlife constitution." Zed motioned at Meg and Dani. "That's also why we called you back. If we need to move quickly, we want to do it as a group."

"You kept the fact that we've been invited to a rumble to yourself?" Kera looked like she was going to burst.

"Hey, I'm still in charge, and the lives of the gods are in my hands." He glared back her, his eyes sparking. "And I'm telling you now. I only saw her this morning."

Kera rubbed at her head but didn't say anything else, and Zed grumpily shoved more chocolate into his mouth.

"None of this is news, is it?" Meg said, looking around the table and focusing on the big picture. "We pretty much knew this was a shit show with her around, and yeah, it sucks that gods are becoming her merry little band of psychos. But all we have to do is figure out how to get the humans to be less confused, which is exactly what we're doing, and what we'll keep doing. Why do we keep going around and around this?"

"I suppose because we don't know what to do next, and we're just trying to find the answers. *How* do we get the humans to be less confused? How do we keep them from feeling so lost and overwhelmed that they call to Chaos? Do we go to Rome and meet her on her terms? Why the eclipse?" Tis closed her eyes, looking terribly tired. "What's the right move?"

"I want to move forward with the rebranding. I'll get other departments going. Not only that, but I'll talk to the heads of those departments and really get them to lay out what they're offering in simple terms." Meg nodded slowly, that feeling of rightness building inside her. "That's it. Simplicity. Not overwhelming them with sparks and circuses but giving them the absolute basics. It will help with the confusion and relegate some of the other stuff into white noise."

Dani squeezed Meg's hand. "Death is a big question. I think Meg's right. Simplifying what I do will make it less scary, but it's not going to make life any less precious. I think the desire to live is built into their genetic codes."

"Okay. Our plan includes…" Kera stood and started writing on the white board. "Dani is rebranding to explain death and make it a journey instead of a penalty, probably by using posters with motivational sayings on them. Meg is going to help the gods simplify their offers to help abate confusion, essentially editing every religious text in existence. I'm going to stand here writing things, and Zed is going to eat so much chocolate he'll turn brown and lumpy and look even more full of—"

The door opened and Petra, pre-fader Nabatean goddess and Kera's new right hand at GRADE, came in. Close behind her was Fin, who winked at Meg. They both sat down, and Petra smiled at Tis. "I hardly hear from my boss anymore. I can't tell you how grateful I am."

Tis grinned and leaned over to kiss Petra's cheek. "Glad to be of service. What brings you to our constantly stressed conference room?"

"Information. I was listening to prayers at temple yesterday, and a young man was praying for guidance. It seems several of his brothers have joined a religious movement that involves removing certain deities from certain places. He wanted a sign whether or not he should join them."

Fin held up his hand to keep them from asking questions. "Wait. Let me go first. Once you all start babbling, there won't be any room for a ginger Irish ex-god. Freya and I had a visit from Dis, the scary old bitch herself. She wanted to know if we were interested in joining her expedition to Rome. Seems they're interested in removing the powers that be."

"And replacing those powers with what?"

He shrugged. "Sheep fucks if I know, lassie. But I can tell you I wasn't about to jump on her crazy train. She was talking about changes of power and needing to save the planet. Proper megalomaniac stuff."

Meg leaned across the table to get near him. "What were you and Freya doing in the same place? Did the old biddy upstairs not do it for you anymore?" She propped her chin on her fists and wiggled her eyebrows at him.

He laughed and turned pink. "Apparently, Freya likes a taste of Irish almost as much as she likes a taste of fury. And as for our resident Fate…well, lovey, she's got more important things on her mind right now than sex. Even I couldn't distract her."

"I think you're way better off with a Viking goddess than a woman who speaks in riddles and controls the whole of destiny. And Freya's insanely strong, isn't she? Did she do that thing with her pinkie—"

"Um, Meg? I think we might need to talk about something else at the moment." Dani tugged on Meg's ankle to pull her back to her seat. Strangely, them discussing Meg's other sexual exploits didn't bother her. In fact, she could easily picture Meg astride the Viking goddess…

"I want to know about the pinkie thing when this is over." Kera turned to Zed. "Does the Catholic god know his golden throne is about to be overthrown?"

"I can't believe she'd go this far." Zed looked stunned. "I doubt he knows, or he'd be in here. Or already there."

"We've got to stop her. And the gods who have joined her. Which means we meet her just like she knew we would." 'Tis stood and began to pace. "If she's recruiting humans to fight, she's going against everything Afterlife has worked for. We can't let humans die fighting some kind of weird power grab between gods."

"It's not just a power grab, love." Fin stretched, but the casual move didn't disguise his worry. "She offered me my powers back. Said if I fought for their side she'd make sure I was a full-blown god again."

"She must be desperate." Kera tilted her head apologetically. "No offense. But if she's even asking the pre-fader gods to join up, she must not have much of an advantage."

"We need to go to Rome." Selene said it so quietly everyone stopped to listen. "In force. Every god willing to stand for Afterlife needs to be there to say 'no more.' Every god willing to give humans freedom of choice and movement needs to stand up and say so."

Alec frowned and shook her head. "If they fight back…"

"Then the gods go to war. It's exactly what she wants." Dani felt the tension in every person in the room and hated being helpless to fix things.

Silence filled the room as they all took in the implications.

"Has it ever happened?" Kera asked.

"No. Not on this scale, certainly. Gods within their own departments have always squabbled. Sisters baiting brothers, aunts drowning nephews, that kind of thing. And before we came out and modernized, we told our followers we were the only ones and to disregard the others. But we've never openly warred against one another. I mean, our followers have often misinterpreted our texts and killed each other in our names, but that wasn't us telling them to. And that's exactly what we've been trying to fix since we've been among them. But it's a long process. Most of us are still writing fourth and fifth drafts of our department rules." Zed, the oldest god in the room, knew his world history, and no one doubted him.

"Dani, what happens at the death of a god?" Fin asked.

"It's hardly ever happened. But they basically return to a molecular state. Humans create gods in their image, manifesting them through thought, creating them out of consciousness combined with atoms. When the god dies, they return to that atomic beginning. But it usually means their followers have been decimated in some way as well, so they can't be re-created."

Selene looked around the room. "If she can turn followers against their gods on a massive scale, she can kill off humans and the gods they believe in." Once again, the implications were monumental. "But there's a small difference now. Thanks to people believing more strongly in their gods now that they're among them, the gods have also developed a certain level of autonomy. People expect their gods to protect them, and now is the time to show them that belief is founded in truth. If the gods have to sacrifice themselves to keep the humans safe, then that's how it has to be. If believers see their gods die, it will wipe out their belief instantly, and that god won't be reborn. Not for a long time, anyway. But that's a chance we're going to have to take. We can't allow chaos and gods of destruction to rule the world if we have a chance to keep it from happening."

Zed stood slowly, looking as though the weight of the world rested on his shoulders. In a way, it did.

"We'll call an emergency meeting for the whole building. Gather everyone in the main hall tomorrow morning and tell them what's going on and what needs to be done. Megara, you should be there to talk to them as a whole about the simplicity idea. You can talk to them individually later to help them spell things out, but start the process tomorrow. No more lingering over drafts and word choice. There's no more time."

"In the meantime, everyone else get some rest. Get whatever things you need to bring with you and be ready to fly by tomorrow night." Kera started stuffing things in her briefcase but looked up when Tis sighed.

"You can't come with us." She looked at Kera and then at Selene. "You're driving forces behind this place, and you're the ones who know every aspect of what's going on. The gods trust you. If everything goes to cosmic hell in Rome, we need to know you're both safe here."

Kera looked at Tis disbelievingly and then at Selene, who began to laugh. Kera smiled and began to laugh too, and Dani was left wondering what she missed.

"As if." Selene gathered the files on the table and pushed them into Alec's chest. "You're right, you do need us. But if things go to hell in Rome, our last concern will be running Afterlife. You think they'd let us live? You think we'd be able to hide anywhere she couldn't find us?" She poked Alec in the chest. "You think we'd live without you? No chance, buddy. You go, we go."

Alec wrapped her big black wings around Selene and closed her eyes. "I'm fully aware I can't stop you. Promise me you'll stay behind us, though?"

Kera snorted. "We're in love, we're not stupid. I'll hide behind your feathers any fucking day."

The tension lifted slightly, and everyone began to file out. Meg took Dani's hand. "My place?"

"Anywhere you want to go, beautiful." Dani meant it. She'd follow Meg wherever she wanted to lead. She was also aware that Meg had said very little about the plans and wondered if Meg was doing the Zen thing she did, knowing things deep down but not sharing them.

They walked to Meg's hand in hand, and when they got inside, Meg went straight to the fridge and opened them a couple of beers.

"Want to talk about it?" Dani asked. She sat on the sofa, and Meg sat at the other end with her feet in Dani's lap. Dani began to massage them, and Meg moaned.

With her eyes closed, she said, "Selene and Kera shouldn't come with us. Tis is right."

"Is that one of your gut feelings?" Dani hated the thought of the humans in her chosen family being in danger.

"Yeah. I just know. But there's no way in hell they'll stay behind. Maybe it's all part of the big stupid plan, right?"

Dani continued to massage Meg's feet, knowing there was no real answer. Tomorrow would be a frightening step toward a possibly more frightening future. "You and your sisters can kill gods. The three of you, together." She hated bringing it up, but it needed to be said.

"We can. We will, if humans are being used as shields or pawns." She shrugged and took another sip of her beer, still with her eyes closed. "But it takes a lot of energy. It's not easy to kill one, and there might be a lot more than that up against us. Gods fighting gods can damage one another, though. Enough to make them slink away to heal. But given that we're the only ones who can kill a god, it makes a lot of sense for those same gods to make sure we can't do what we do." Tears started slow trails down Meg's cheeks. "I'm scared. Not for me, necessarily, but for my sisters. For the gods I love."

The thought of the serious harm that could come to her colleagues hadn't occurred to Dani, and now that it was spoken, it was real. And terrifying. "I'll be right beside you, okay?"

Meg pulled her feet from Dani's lap and crawled into her lap. "And I'll be right beside you. But right now, I'd rather be under you."

She leaned in for a kiss, and as the passion ignited between them again, Dani stood and carried Meg to the bedroom. If tonight could be their last night together, she wanted it to be full of the years they'd lost.

CHAPTER TWENTY

The cacophony of noise made Meg's feathers tingle and her snakes restless. She looked out over the panorama of gods in the meeting hall, and it reminded her of old times, when they all worked out of the same building and had plenty of time for sex and lounging around. Today, even those who had been among their followers had been called back to the office. Normally, it was Tis or Alec on this stage, but it was Meg's turn, and as much as she loved being the center of attention, the importance of what she was doing made her chest ache a little. She smiled when Selene walked onto the stage, and the room began to quiet.

Selene pushed her glasses up on her nose and gave Meg a quick hug. "I'm not entirely sure what we're doing, but I'll follow your lead."

"Thanks for trusting me." Meg turned to the group of gods assembled in front of her, their skins such an array of color they looked like a huge box of multishaped crayons. "Hey, everyone. Thanks for coming. We know how busy you are, but we've got some really important information we needed to get to everyone at once. We won't keep you here long."

"Take as long as you want, red wings. I could use the rest!" shouted a god whose black skin was laced with red cracks.

"Who's that?" Selene whispered.

"Kagu. He's the old Shinto god of volcanoes, and he's coming back into existence thanks to the rumbling volcanoes in Japan," Meg whispered back as the other gods laughed along with Kagu. "In a way, that's kind of why we're here, magma breath." Meg winked at him and steam rose from his skin as he grinned back at her. "We know you guys are out there working hard. We know you're helping your followers, and you've been thinking of new ways to write your sacred laws and texts. Thanks to you, wars and murders are way down. Humans are behaving better than they have any time in history. You should totally pat yourselves on the backs, if you have one."

The group broke into applause and shouts of agreement. Meg knew full well gods loved having their egos stroked. She waited until they quieted again.

"That said, there's always more work to do. As you know, there's been a problem with Dis, or Chaos, as some of you know her—" She nodded and held up her hands to acknowledge the hiss of dissension that filled the room. "I know. She's messing with both humans and gods, and we have to find a way to fight back. We don't have the luxury of waiting to see what happens, because humans don't have the kind of time we do." She was glad to see they were paying attention. She focused on that feeling she got when she knew she was on the right track and let it flow through her like cool water.

"We've got two things to talk about. One is your rebranding, and the other is your focus." She turned to Selene. "Would you mind saying a little something about the importance of people understanding the rules of their religions?"

Selene looked surprised, and she bit her lip, a sign she was concentrating. "Sure." She stepped forward and addressed the group. "As many of you who've been on my weekly show know, I'm interested in the philosophy of religion. That is to say, the examination of the need for humans to believe and the ways in which they connect on both a sociological and personal level with their spiritual belief systems. Religion is a set of defined parameters which a believer chooses to follow based on their own ideological and often geographical circumstances…"

Meg let Selene continue and watched as the gods began to shuffle and yawn. She even saw a few take out their phones and start tapping away. She gently tapped Selene on the shoulder. "Thank you, babe. I think you've made my point."

Selene shrugged and stepped back, looking curious.

"Hey! Put your phone away and pay attention, trunk face." She pointed at Ganesh, who had the sense to look as abashed as an elephant could as he slipped his phone back in his shirt pocket. "You know those hefty books you wrote a long time ago, full of stories about things happening to people who didn't do what they were supposed to? Full of rules that contradicted themselves because the humans who wrote them down were coming at it from different angles?" She made sure to make eye contact as she looked around the room. "That's kind of what Selene does. She uses big long words, and although she's always totally, completely, right, you start to zone out because she's not talking like the rest of us plebes."

Laughter greeted her statement, and she gave Selene an apologetic smile. "Sorry, beautiful."

Selene shook her head and smiled. "Not a problem. Nice way to illustrate."

"Thanks. I'm good like that." She turned back to her audience. "It's time to get shit done, folks. You need to write your new rules and regs in plain language. Today's language. Write it down exactly the way you'd tell me or your coworker what you're up to. And seriously, tell them why. No one likes to be told to do things just because Mom said so."

She uncovered a large white board on the corner of the stage that listed three bullet points. "Rebranding means simplifying. No more vague, ominous stories. Sure, keep your origin stories. Everyone likes a good origin story. But when it comes to today, keep it simple. Let them know all the fabulous things that come with following you, and let them know the less-than fabulous stuff too. You want them to follow you, you want them to believe in you. That means you lay it out in ways they can understand every word. And don't hire a batch of humans to do your work for you. That's how things get messy, and we're trying to keep messy at bay. Sit down with someone you trust from your department, and get these things written down. Spell out what folks should and shouldn't do, what you want from them in the way of prayer, and what they can expect in the afterlife."

Selene looked contemplative next to her, and Meg could tell she wanted to say something. She raised her eyebrows to see if she wanted to say it now or later, and Selene shook her head slightly. *Later, then.* Selene was one of the smartest people she knew, and as a demigod and the bridge between the humans and the gods, she had an understanding of the way humans ticked that Meg never fully grasped. *I hope she doesn't think I've put my foot in it.*

"That's the first thing. Your rebranding needs to be simple and direct, and your new texts need to be drafted *this* week. Seriously, there's no give on this. Sit your gorgeous godly asses down and get this done before Dis can make things a heap of shit worse."

She could see that although some of the gods looked stressed or disturbed, most seemed to accept her proposal as doable. "The next thing is something I'd like you to think about but not something that's required." She concentrated on the intuitive flow and took strength in its sureness. "There are two major things humans are facing on this planet. One of them is war. They've been doing that since they started walking upright, and it probably won't change. But the thing is, since you've been at their sides, they've actually fought a lot less. One suggestion is to make a part of your new texts an initiative on peace. Put in a few simple, clear rules about not making war on other people or places, for any reason. I think we've got a real opportunity to give humans a chance at living peacefully for a while."

Kali's necklace of human heads shook as she yelled from the back of the room. "And what does that mean for the war gods, fury? Would you have us fade into the void or go work as accountants?" Her red eyes flashed with fury.

Meg felt her snakes bristle, but she kept them down. "Of course not. But how many of the war gods are solely gods of war? I mean, you're also a mother of creation and time, right? Play on those instead. If people want war, they're going to go to war. And you'll still be there to deal with them. But don't instigate it and do what you can to prevent it." She waited for more comments, but none came, so she moved on, feeling a little less certain and not liking the feeling at all. "The second issue is the environment. As you know, humans eradicate between two thousand and ten thousand species per year. They've begun drilling into the earth's core in order to provide the shit they use to run machinery." She motioned at Kagu, who watched her intently. "They're destabilizing the earth to a degree they're even waking the volcanoes." Kagu nodded, and she could see him sigh. "They're headed toward a path of extinction themselves. And if they die off, where do you think we'll be?"

Total silence met her statement. Every god knew that a mass die-off of followers meant fading. But the concept of humans dying off altogether was a different matter.

"So my second suggestion is that you put something about behaving responsibly toward the earth into your new texts, in order to get the humans on a path that doesn't lead to their extinction. And those followers who choose greed and destruction over the planet they live on can be guaranteed a place in the afterlife they don't want."

The flow she tapped into started to wane, and Meg wanted nothing more than to sink into a hot bath with a glass of wine and Dani on top of her.

"To sum up. Get your asses writing, and make things super simple. If you can, add in something about the need for peace and something about the necessity of walking gently on this big blue ball in the sky. You've got until the end of the week to have your first drafts on Zed's or Kera's desks. Once those are done, I'll come in and help you with your new brochures and marketing plans. Oh, and one more thing. We need to talk to the heads of the departments about the situation with Dis. Please head to Zed's office after this for an update." She made a shooing motion with her hands. "Off you go, you lovely creatures great and small. Have fun."

The gods began to file out, and the mood in the room was somber, but not angry as she'd feared it might be. She turned to Selene and was gratified when she gave her a big hug.

"You did great. I think that's exactly what they needed to hear." Selene pulled back and studied Meg's face. "Are you okay?"

Meg nodded and fluffed the stiffness out of her wings. "I'm glad it's over. I've never been the one telling people what to do before. It's exhausting. I don't know how you do it all the time."

Selene raised an eyebrow.

"Shit. Sorry. I don't mean you're bossy or anything. I just know you have to tell gods what to do and how to do it when they come on your show, and I know you help Tis with the legal stuff—"

Selene laughed and put her finger over Meg's mouth. "I know what you meant. Don't worry about it." She hooked her arm through Meg's and led her from the stage and out the side door. "I think it's time for a drink. Tis and Zed can handle the meeting with the department heads to tell them they'll be needed in Rome."

Meg relaxed as they headed across campus to her place. Selene was clearly lost in thought, and Meg was glad to let her stay there. She was done talking. Sex, alcohol, and food were necessary, and not in that particular order. She thought of the numerous of religious departments sitting down to write out their new texts, and how she'd be the one to help them get those new texts to their followers. It was daunting to think they'd be depending on her, but when she thought of Dis and the dark dread she felt at the thought of going to Rome, she knew she would do whatever it took to keep the humans safe. *Who knew I had such a soft spot for them?*

CHAPTER TWENTY-ONE

S o we're going to do it?"
Dani could feel Idona humming with excitement, a feeling she was beginning to share. "Yeah. Let's start putting things in place. How's Nexus going?"

Idona stretched and put her feet on the coffee table. "Good. The library is up, we've put in a coffeehouse, and the open-air theater will be ready by next week."

Dani tossed her a beer. "I've hardly been away. How'd you get all that done?"

"I brought in some builders from Azrael's remodel. They're really enjoying the extra work, and not a lot of folks get to see the Deadlands, so it was an opportunity to check us out." She shrugged and took a long drink of her beer.

"I get the library and coffee shop. What's with the cinema?"

Idona grinned. "Informational viewing. Folks who learn better visually than by reading will be able to see the marketing videos produced by the other religions. It could help them make an informed decision."

Dani laughed and stretched out next to Idona on the couch. "When did you get a teaching degree?"

"Hey, I have hobbies too, you know." Idona laughed and nudged her with her shoulder. "Want to see?"

"Your hobbies? I've known you long enough to know your hobbies often include strap-ons and no clothes. I'll pass for today, thanks." The thought of sex made her think of Meg, and thinking of Meg made her wish she was with her.

"Idiot. Not my hobbies, although you're missing out when it comes to the twins. I meant the changes at Nexus."

"Sure. Let's go."

Dani led the way outside and opened the road into the new sector. They strolled along, drinking their beer, and Dani took in the changes. Houses were going up in orderly rows, and when she saw the name of the café she laughed. "Wake the Dead?"

"I thought it was catchy. But we can change it if you don't like it."

Dani didn't miss the hint of vulnerability in Idona's voice, even though she tried to look like she wasn't bothered. "It's great."

They went past the library to the amphitheater and sat on one of the high stone rows.

"Onyx?" Dani loved the way the long black rows looked as they climbed above the staging area below.

"Obsidian. Easier to get in sheets."

They sat silently drinking their beer before Dani said, "Are we doing the right thing?"

Idona nodded without hesitation. "We are. The world is different now that the gods are out there. People know their afterlives exist, and it makes death a different journey. Now we can have a say in how people view that journey." She tapped her bottle to Dani's. "I think it's fucking awesome."

Dani smiled but kept pondering out loud. "I can't get rid of the idea that death makes humans more aware of how precious life is. General bad behavior resulting in deaths has reduced massively, which is great. But there are still bad people out there. Human behavior isn't always regulated by religious belief. Does that mean we'll be overwhelmed with people who don't believe but don't belong anywhere? Should we allow the bad people to mix with the good people?"

They drank while Dani waited for Idona to answer.

"No. We have a separate place for the bad eggs, one where various gods will have to take some responsibility. Make it a cooperative of Limbo, where the bad ones don't get the cinema or amazing coffee. Just books and books, so all they can do is read about what shitheads they are."

"I'll have to see if the other gods will go for it, but I like it." Dani thought about what she'd learned in Hawaii. "Idona, I need to talk to you about this new stuff going on with me."

"Finally. I was worried you'd wait another eon."

Dani sighed. "I might have, if it weren't for Meg. But she's helped me figure some things out." She spread a drop of moisture from her bottle on the shiny obsidian step. "I'm going to be spread a little thin for a while. My new position as goddess means I've got to pay more attention to the folks praying to me. I think we need to change your position."

Idona looked up from her beer, her expression guarded. "Are you retiring?"

Dani took a deep breath and dipped her head slightly. "Kind of. I don't know. I think I'm asking if you'll co-run the Deadlands with me. I'll still be Death, technically, but you'll begin running the day-to-day stuff. I'll dedicate time to my believers and to the marketing thing, and you can handle scheduling and the reports from the Sundo." She stared at the amphitheater, feeling the weight of the coming changes in her old soul. "I don't know how long the goddess thing will last. But if it dwindles, I'll step down and finally retire. In fact, I take it back. We'll get through the rebranding together, and then the Deadlands will be yours. I'll continue on as a goddess for as long as that lasts, but you'll officially be Death."

Dani had expected Idona to be her usual exuberant self at the news, but instead, she looked almost in shock.

"Well, damn." Idona picked at the label on her bottle. "I thought I couldn't wait for the day you finally went to play golf in the old fogies home, but now that it's here…" She swallowed hard. "Fuck."

"Hey." Dani bumped her shoulder. "I'm not leaving yet. The rebranding thing will take time, and I don't think my followers are going to just disappear, especially once the real marketing campaign starts. I'm going to be around for a while yet. But I'd like you to start taking lead on stuff. I'll be here to bug the crap out of you, I promise."

Idona began to smile, and soon she was laughing. She jumped up and did a weird little jig. "Now I'm excited. You go have sex with your excessively hot and terrifying girlfriend and grant prayers to people who see you as a better option than gods they've worshipped for centuries. I'll keep things running down here."

Dani laughed. "I like that idea more than I can say, although this goddess gig is a bit overwhelming. I need to go see Poseidon to see if he's willing to work with me."

Idona frowned. "Better you than me. He's always given me the creeps."

"I know. Which is why I'm not asking you to come with me. I think you give him the creeps too."

Idona puffed out her chest. "No way. Everyone wants a bit of this." She grinned and flexed her biceps.

"Whatever. Go celebrate with your twins. I'll see you later."

Idona ran down the amphitheater seats and called back up from the stage. "Good luck. I won't be thinking of you for the next several hours."

She waved and disappeared down the road she opened. Dani made her way down to the stage and looked around her. She thought of the ancient Greek plays, the Roman comedies, and Shakespeare's tragedies, all done in places a lot like this one. *All the world's a stage.* She'd always been a shadow player, the one quietly chasing humans down the time tunnels of their mortality. *Now I'm on stage. I hope I don't screw this up.* She opened a road and headed to Poseidon's home in Atlantis.

Muted blues and greens ebbed and flowed over and around the tunnel, the shadows of sharks and millions of fish sliding ghost-like past her. She loved that the tunnels through the ocean were more like clouded glass than the earth-based ones she used. Occasionally, she wanted to let the tunnel open and let herself get swept into the current, to be part of the ocean. Today, though, she concentrated on the walk to Poseidon's place.

When she got to the city gate, she nodded at the guards. She'd always found their silver armor over-the-top and even a little crass, but the god of the ocean liked his bling. They nodded back at her and let her pass without question. Few denied Death entry, and those who tried were usually the ones she'd come for. She went straight to the enormous white palace and appreciated the smell of honeysuckle and jasmine, though she wondered when he'd started cultivating land flowers instead of the beautiful flora of the sea. The rainbow coral exhibit he'd done last century had been stunning.

She loped up the steps and into the hall, a tiny bit of anxiety kicking in. Poseidon kept apart from the other gods. He'd always been a little put out that although most of the planet was covered in water, humans gravitated to the sky gods rather than the ocean gods. When he was in a particularly bad mood, he messed with the currents and sent sharks into populated areas just to mess with the humans. He didn't seem to get that creating fear of the ocean didn't mean he'd get more followers. But then, he was one of the oldest gods, Zeus and Hades's brother, and logic didn't always matter as much as ego.

"Dani! What a lovely surprise."

Dani turned and smiled. "Hey, Reef. How are you?"

He enveloped her in a huge embrace, his opalescent scales catching on Dani's T-shirt. He held her at arm's length, his yellow eyes narrowed slightly and the tips of his razor-sharp teeth showing. "I think it's literally been an age since you were last here. Should I be worried?"

She shook her head and hooked her arm through his as they made their way toward the office. Reef had been Poseidon's lover and confidant since Dani had taken office, and few beings knew the kind of love and devotion they shared. She'd envied it herself. *Until Meg.* The thought made her tingle, and she forced herself to focus. "Far from it. In fact, I'm here to ask for a favor."

He looked surprised and slowed his pace. "Your timing might be a little off, Soul Collector. He hasn't been in a great mood since the gods started walking among humans again. You know how he feels about sky gods." He ducked his head slightly and whispered, "In fact, he was even considering Dis's invitation to join her little party in Rome."

Dani stopped and stared at him. "But he didn't?"

Reef shrugged. "In the end, he decided to let the sky gods kill each other off, and then he'll be there to say I told you so. You know how he gets."

The information was disturbing. They'd simply assumed Poseidon wouldn't want to be a part of the new course Afterlife was taking. But no one had thought to ask him, and it could have been disastrous to have a god with his kind of power and resources on the other side of the Vatican issue. She wondered if there were other gods they'd overlooked who might feel similarly slighted. She thought quickly and hoped she wasn't making a bad decision.

"That's part of why I'm here, actually. Although I've got a favor to ask, I also wanted to talk to him about where he stands with all the changes going on."

Reef smiled. "I can't tell you how glad I am to hear that. We used to go on land occasionally, hang out in the thermal hot springs in Iceland, or at the ones in Lesbos or Cyprus when we wanted to spend time with Athena. We used to swim to the Caribbean and watch the turtles. But lately, he just sits in his office and stews like a musty mussel. Maybe you can help."

They walked the rest of the way to the office in silence, and Dani's thoughts were a hurricane of options and possible outcomes. Reef opened the door to the office and ushered her inside, before giving her an encouraging smile and closing the door behind her. She turned to Poseidon, who looked up from the massive charts on his desk.

"Soul Collector. It's been a long time. Sit."

He got up from his desk and went to pour them drinks. The ocean god preferred a unique brand of salted whisky Dani had learned to tolerate, and she wouldn't say no now. He handed her a glass of the pinkish concoction, and she took a sip, trying not to wince at the sharp flavor. He poured himself a larger glass, and she realized she'd forgotten how much he looked like Zed, except for the crown with a triple trident on his head. His white beard, unlike Zed's, also looked slightly more like coral than hair. She wondered if it was scratchy when he kissed Reef.

He sat and tilted his glass at her before taking a sip. "To what do I owe a visit from Death herself?"

"There are a few things I wanted to chat about. But first things first, how are you, Salty?"

He grinned at the nickname she'd been using for him for years, then his expression turned somber. "Worried. Frustrated. Occasionally as pissed off as a seahorse trapped in an octopus tentacle. I know it was my choice not to work at that ridiculous building in California, but you can't imagine what it feels like to not be consulted on a matter as important as gods walking among humans." He stood and began to pace. "And then, to be ignored when things get out of hand, as though I'm not a viable ally." He pointed at Dani. "Dis thought I'd be a good ally, and she's eel-shit insane. But my own brother didn't have the decency to call."

Dani relaxed slightly. If he considered Dis nuts, it was a step in the right direction. "An inexcusable oversight. But also, part of the reason I'm here today."

He looked at her suspiciously. "He sent you to talk to me?"

"Not specifically, no." She held up her hand to stop him when he started in on a tirade again. "Hear me out, Salty."

He frowned but sat down, his arms crossed and his expression petulant. "Fine."

"You've heard about the rebranding most of the departments are doing?"

He leaned forward, and Dani could swear she heard the ocean rumble around them.

"That's another thing! No one consulted me on that—"

"I know. And I'm here to see if you'd be interested in working with my department on a kind of co-rebranding." She hadn't known she was going to say it until it came out, but she knew she'd hit the right key.

He looked surprised. "With the Deadlands?"

"I've developed goddess status, and I'm rebranding the Deadlands at the same time. Idona will be taking over the day-to-day running while I concentrate on the god stuff. But I think we could make an amazing team. By combining my Sundo with your mer-people and messengers, we could develop a unique new system where the journey to and from the Deadlands would be via the oceans and waterways. The most powerful, most complete presence on earth." Dani wasn't above pandering to his ego a little.

He sat back and studied her for a long moment, and she let him take his time. Rushing a disgruntled god wasn't the way to get what she wanted.

"Water and Death. Giving and taking life. Why haven't we considered it before?" He nodded slowly, clearly considering the concept in full. "What do you propose?"

She wasn't completely ready for the question, but she homed in on the feeling Kanaloa had taught her to focus on and jumped in. "Megara mentioned simplicity in a meeting the other day." He began to glower, and she rushed forward. "I think that together we combine the beauty and power of the oceans and waterways with the inevitability of death. I want humans to become less afraid, and therefore less focused, on death. By showing them how their souls move from their bodies to the Deadlands, we can take some of that fear away. At the same time, we can use that to rebrand your own realm a little and show them what a magnificent god you are."

He puffed up slightly, his chin lifted. "I only tend to get sailors or sea cultures in my afterlife areas. It's not a high-growth area for me."

"Do you want it to be?" In truth, Dani hadn't considered his afterlife sector at all, but she wasn't about to admit to it.

"I haven't thought about it. I don't think so...too much work and too many rules. But I like the idea of working with you on your portion of the afterlife journey, and I wouldn't say no to more appreciation. Humans are mostly water. They're like thinking cucumbers. They should appreciate that more. Not being cucumbers. Being water." He reached across to his desk and pushed a button on the phone. "Reef, come in here, would you?"

Within seconds, Reef entered the room, and Dani grinned at the idea he'd been hovering nearby, hoping to be invited in.

"Dani has an offer I'm entertaining. I'd like your thoughts on it." He motioned at Dani, who went on to repeat what she'd said to Poseidon.

"Wow. That's great news about your god status, Dani. Congrats." Reef kissed her cheek and then settled onto the arm of Poseidon's chair. "How are you going to approach marketing, and what do you need from us?"

"I'm still working out the details. But first, I want to know if you'd be willing to allow me, as part of a cooperative between our realms, to use water as my way to answer prayer." This was the part she was worried about, and when Poseidon frowned she knew she'd been right to be.

"Granting prayers through water has always been the specific domain of the water gods, Dani. I'm not sure how I feel about a non-water god using it for that reason."

She nodded. "I understand that. I really do. The thing is, I seem to be a bit of a hybrid. My natural connection to the planet is through the oceans. I learned that from Kanaloa recently, and it feels right. And if we create a partnership, people will see your messengers helping deliver prayers and possibly even assisting with soul collection with my Sundo. It would be good for both of us." She wasn't sure if it sounded as weak as it felt saying it, but she really couldn't come up with a better reason than it felt right.

Poseidon stared at the wall, seemingly far away. Reef studied Dani, but she got the feeling he was thinking more than actually looking at her.

"A lot of your followers are near large bodies of water. If not the ocean, they're near lakes and rivers." Poseidon's far-off gaze returned to her, and he nodded. "I can see them, and I see why you've gained god status." He looked at Reef. "What do you think?"

"I like it on pretty much every level. We need some fresh air down here." He touched Poseidon's arm when he began to protest. "You know we do. It's time for us to take our place at the table with the other gods, and I think Dani's plan means we don't have to do nearly as much rebranding as the other departments, because we don't want an influx of people. But it will get your face back in the minds of humans who aren't water-bound. It will also tie you to one of the most powerful concepts, and now deities, on earth. Maybe not everyone will pray to Death, but there isn't a person on the planet who doesn't respect her."

Dani had always thought of it as fear rather than respect, and the different wording made her a little heady. "Kanaloa taught me the basic elements of granting prayer, but I feel like I've still got a lot to learn. Would you be willing to teach me? I can't imagine a better mentor."

Once again, Poseidon looked like the god he was when he smiled. "I'd be happy to. And that way I can see the kinds of prayers you're granting and make sure you're using water the way you should be."

Reef rolled his eyes. "Of course we'll help. And you're welcome to begin using the waterways for soul retrieval too, if you want to. Our mer-people and naiads can help your Sundo use the water for travel. It's faster than your roads."

"I want my face on the marketing materials." Poseidon crossed his arms stubbornly, as though expecting resistance.

"Obviously. That's the best way to show us working together. If you don't mind, I'm going to leave some of the rebranding and marketing stuff to Idona and Meg. I think they're better at the conceptual stuff than I am."

"I haven't spent time with the fury sisters in centuries. Meg used to come to some of the parties we had here back when she was just a little fish, but once they got their official duties, she stopped coming around as much. I think she enjoyed the company of a certain mer-woman who I recall had a particularly versatile tail—"

Reef squeezed Poseidon's shoulder and said, "It would be great to see her again. Maybe she and Idona could spend some time with us one day soon to get started."

Dani wondered if her expression had given her away. It wasn't that she minded hearing about Meg's sexual exploits; rather, it was that she preferred to hear them from Meg, when she could picture all the sexual energy and play and put the imagery to good use.

"Thanks, guys. I'll let them know, and they'll get in touch to work things out. And if it's okay, I'll get in touch soon to talk through some training with you, Salty?"

He nodded and leaned forward. "Fine, good. Now, tell me what's going on with Dis? Does my hammer-headed brother need help, even though he'd never admit it?"

She thought about their imminent trip to Rome. "I think we could use every god possible on our side. We don't know what's waiting for us. It could come down to a simple discussion. Or…" Dani left it, not wanting to voice the possibility of something far more serious.

Poseidon stood. "That's what I thought." He turned to Reef. "Start making preparations. We'll leave tonight and meet everyone there."

Reef gave Dani a quick kiss on the cheek. "See you in Italy when the sun disappears, dark goddess."

The title made Dani laugh. "Thanks, Reef. See you there."

He left, and Poseidon turned to Dani. "Tell my brother and the fury sisters I'll be there." He put his massive hand on Dani's shoulder. "And thank you for coming to me, Soul Collector. Reef is right. We need fresh air. I think you and I will do good things together." He clapped his hands together, and the ocean rumbled around them. "Now. I'll see you to the gate, and then I've got to get things in order before I leave."

They walked to the gate, and Poseidon talked about possible tag lines for posters, along with musing about dying his beard to capture light better. Dani couldn't wait to get home to Meg and to fill in Idona on the plans she'd set in motion. *Meg would be proud of me for moving forward this way.* The thought made her skin tingle, and she jogged back along the ocean tunnel. Tomorrow was uncertain, and she wouldn't waste tonight.

CHAPTER TWENTY-TWO

Sunrise brought a finger painting of pinks and oranges bleeding into a clear blue sky. Dis stood on the highest remaining wall of the Coliseum and looked out over Rome. Time meant nothing to her, but yesterday she'd watched from the shadows as a human had looked out over this same view and been reduced to tears. The disheveled, fragile-looking human had explained to the guide how small she felt and how insignificant her life looked from this vantage point.

The human was right, of course. She, and all the lives lived alongside her, were little more than dust specks, brief flickers in an uncaring, cold space. Almost everything they did would be forgotten, unless they built something like the building Dis was standing on now. Even then, it too would be reduced to rubble one day, nothing more than the rock ripped from the earth to build it, returned to the soil from which it came. The tract of ruins below her were a perfect example of that. Though the shells of some buildings remained, the people who'd used them, who knelt and prayed and wept in them, had vanished into time, not even a memory or whisper of them remaining.

She'd seen civilizations these humans didn't even know existed rise and fall, to be buried beneath the seas and mountains that constantly shifted around them. Briefly, she wondered what this next stage would bring with it. Who would be remembered, and who would fade into nothingness? The coming conflict made her entire being hum with the energy of the universe, like a newborn star about to burst into the night sky with its blinding light. This feeling was what created her, what kept her alive and moving through the cosmos. Change on a massive scale demanded movement into the next stage of development. Or death. She didn't care which, as long as she got to experience it. And to be able to do so under the light of an eclipsed sun, with all that pent-up energy just waiting to crash back through the darkness, was even more thrilling. She did so love the drama of it all.

With a quick thought of the Vatican, she stood in the square before St. Peter's Basilica. Around the tops of the porticoes lining the square were various gods, standing like ominous shadows over the statues of saints. She'd been surprised when a large group of them had showed up the night before. Most were an amalgamation of good and bad rather than simply underworld guardians, secondary or tertiary gods in pantheons with cloud gods who treated them like upper-level humans rather than the gods they were. The main surprise had been Anubis, the jackal-headed god of the Egyptian underworld. Osiris had essentially usurped his position many centuries ago, but he was slowly regaining power, and the two would likely have to fight for the position once more. Others, like Apophis, with his snake tongue; Kuk, the personification of darkness; and several of the petra loa from the Haitian belief system were secondary gods with closets full of resentment. Their gods had mistaken their apparent subservience for acquiescence, and those smaller gods had decided to fight for a place at the big kids' table. They knew the stakes; if they won, their place among their people was assured. If they lost, there would likely be dire repercussions. Gods could severely maim one another, and the heads of religions could excommunicate their rebellious secondary gods in an instant. Dis knew only the fury sisters had the power to kill off gods, though, and she was determined to make that triad a duo, if not obliterate it altogether. They would feel her pain and know what loss truly was.

Whatever was to transpire, Dis was fine with the outcome. She wanted to bathe in the destruction and chaos, and then she'd leave them to do whatever it was they would do with the remaining humans. She'd likely be called back repeatedly, but that wasn't at all problematic. It would keep things interesting for a little while, anyway.

Angie strode up beside her, her coat pulled tight against the early morning chill. Though her expression was determined, Dis could sense her simmering fear and concern for those following her.

"There's been a development. Last night I got a call to meet a train. There were a hundred more people who wanted to join us. It's a weird mix of believers who are disgruntled and want to see the gods suffer, believers who think they're fighting for the gods they believe in, and a few more non-believers who are more in line with Humanity First's ethos and just want to see the gods gone."

Dis considered the information. "That means we have enough people to enter the Vatican today."

Angie squinted at the gods lining the porticoes. "Looks like you got a few more recruits too."

"Indeed. It seems we're ready to begin. We've dealt with the police force here as well as with the Swiss Guard. They're currently… immobilized by the power of the gods, and they won't be there to stop you. Our gods will break the doors so your people can enter. As I said before, we can't go straight in, but once our believers outnumber their believers, we have right of entry. Have your people remove any obstacles in their way until they reach the inner sanctum. Particularly with regard to the believers. Take the Pope hostage and bring him to the roof. When you've cleared the majority of the believers, open the doors and invite us in. From there, we'll see how things play out."

Angie looked at her incredulously. "That's a pretty shit plan. I was going to ask if your gods would protect my people when things go sideways, but I think I know the answer." She turned and walked away, her shoulders hunched.

Dis smiled when the sounds of destruction began a short time later. Angie's people, all armed, ran in and the shouts started seconds later. She closed her eyes and relaxed into the fear emanating from the building. *And it begins.*

She raised her arms and addressed the gods surrounding her, her voice echoing off the ostentatious marble all around them. "Today is the day you say *no more*. No more kowtowing to your sky gods. No more bowing and scraping, no more waiting for your place at the front. Today you fight back and take what is yours by right. When the others arrive, the world will change. When the sun shows its face once more, be sure *you* are the ones it shines on. Fight well, and show your worshippers you are the gods they need, the gods they'll follow into the fire. Make the world bow to *you*."

A roar of support greeted her words and various powers lit the sky. *Too easy. Made in the image of man, they share man's propensity for jealousy and destruction.* She shook her head and went to find a place where she could watch things unfold.

❖

"This has to be the weirdest shit ever." Kera sat beside Tis on the private plane and looked around.

Meg grinned, following her line of thought. Gods of every color and shape were arrayed throughout the cabin. Some with animal heads, some with several limbs, a few with tails that were occasionally in the aisle and getting stepped on. Confucius was busy writing his new texts, constantly crossing through things and struggling for simplicity. He'd come along to provide wisdom, should they need it, since he wasn't technically a god. Durga and her eight arms took up two seats, and Hades sat beside her talking about a new restaurant he'd set up in the underworld. Azrael and Jesus were involved in an intense game of chess. Yama and Buddha were discussing a new philosophy text, and Fin and Freya kept sneaking off to the bathroom together. Although she knew Kera was seeing it from the human point of view, she agreed it was weird to see so many religious leaders gathered together outside the office. Italy was nearing, and everyone was getting geared up for the coming confrontation, though no one was certain what it would entail. Some primary gods had chosen to stay with their followers, wanting to be in place to protect them should things go badly. Assistant gods, like Zeus's kids, had stayed behind for similar reasons. Though it was doubtful anything would happen to their dad, he wasn't taking chances on leaving the leadership empty. Ares had been particularly unhappy about it, and as the god of war, he would have been useful, but war was what they were trying to avoid, and he had a tendency to push things into explosive territory.

She and Dani had spent a glorious night together, fucking into the early hours of the morning and making use of several of the toys Meg had forgotten she owned. When Meg had left to catch her flight with the others, Dani had headed back to the Deadlands to talk to Idona about her conversation with Poseidon and to plan for potential casualties in Italy. Although Meg wished she was on the plane, she understood that Dani had responsibilities Meg could barely comprehend. Dani would meet them in Rome as soon as possible.

Selene looked tired and distracted as she leaned against Alec.

Once again, Meg's intuition told her that Kera and Selene shouldn't be there, but she couldn't voice why, and she knew neither of them would listen to her anyway, not with the stakes so high. Something about the solar eclipse made it feel extra important Selene should be home in bed, curled up with one of her wordy books. She looked at Alec when she nudged her with boot.

"You're awfully quiet, worm face," Alec said to Meg with a concerned smile. "Don't tell me Dani actually exhausted you into silence."

Meg threw a peanut at her. "Did you know Reef and Poseidon are still together? And is it possible for a fury to have an allergy to rubber? Because let me tell you, that new toy has made me itch—"

Tis stuck her fingers in her ears. "Way too early for that kind of information, Sis."

Kera leaned forward, her elbows on her knees and her hands under her chin. "I disagree completely. Do tell."

The ding of the seat belt sign coming on stopped the conversation, and Meg winked at Kera. "Remind me later."

Zed stood at the front of the plane and motioned for attention. "Listen up, everyone. We're not sure what we'll face when we get to the Vatican, but we know it won't be good. Be on your guard, and watch one another's backs. Any information you get, pass on." He looked at Meg and then at her sisters. "We all know what might need to happen, and if it comes to that, stay out of the way, and let them do what they need to."

Suddenly, God stood, hitting his head against the ceiling but not seeming to notice. "They're in the Vatican. They've already killed several Cardinals. I'm trying to tell the others to get out, but they can't hear me over their fear."

Meg could tell he was watching the action play out even though he was there with them, and he looked truly distraught. The plane bumped down on the runway, and as soon as it stopped, the gods leapt from both exits, not bothering with stairs. Meg was one of the first to get off, and her relief at seeing Dani waiting on the tarmac was instant.

Dani raised her hand and shouted loud enough for everyone to hear her. "I'm opening a road to just outside the Vatican. There are a large number of dead inside and more dying. I don't know where the gods on the other side are positioned, but I can tell you there are more than we expected. When you come off my road, be prepared for anything." She waved, the road opened, and the plethora of Pantone gods made their way toward the unknown.

"Go team!" Meg murmured and took Dani's hand as they walked behind the other gods. The road was short, and she could see the strangely dimmed light at the end of it already. The eclipse was in progress. She stopped and turned to Dani. "Whatever happens—"

Dani put her finger over Meg's lips. "Whatever happens, we'll be there together at the end."

Meg swallowed the confession. Emotional outpourings during climactic scenes were so clichéd. She'd save it for a less tense moment, like while eating a salad on a random Tuesday. "I was just going to say that no matter what happens, I still want to try having sex on a hammock again."

Dani's smile was gentle, and Meg didn't think she was fooled. "Perfect."

They turned at the same time when a thunderous crash sounded ahead of them as the first gods emerged from the road. Meg leapt into the air and flew over the gods still making their way to the opening. Below her, the gods had their weapons of choice ready, some glowing, some not, all looking deadly. At the entrance, she landed and spread her wings to block the others from coming out. A massive piece of the stone wall surrounding the Vatican lay in front of her, and all she could see sticking out from beneath it was a pair of hooves. She looked to her left and saw several gods using the entryway of an apartment building for cover from more debris hurtling through the air at them. Stone crashed against stone, and the screams from the humans around them permeated the air. She saw a herd of humans running down the side street, but some fell as yet more stone hurtled from the sky.

Zed pushed aside her wings and looked out. "Bastards. All of them. They deserve to stew in oil in every hell ever created."

Meg took a deep breath and felt her intuition rise. "We need to get to that building, over there." She pointed at a particularly tall apartment building facing the Basilica. "We'll empty it of humans and use it as a base. From the top, we should be able to see inside without trapping ourselves within the city itself."

Zed turned and told the rest what to do while Meg flew to the gods who'd taken shelter and told them where to go. She flew into the darkening sky and did her best to hide them from view as they ran down the street and into the building. She looked down at the road and saw Kera, Selene, Dani, Alec, and Tis waiting in the doorway. She landed in front of them.

"I don't know why, but I can't open another road into the building. It could be that one of the gods has managed to put up blocks of some kind." Dani shrugged, looking frustrated.

"Then we carry Kera and Selene and fly hell for leather to the building. I'll take you," Meg said.

Without any further discussion, Selene climbed onto Alec's back, Kera climbed onto Tis's, and Dani wrapped herself around Meg.

"Stay low and try to stay near the wall. Cross over at the last second." Meg pushed off the ground and heard her sisters do the same. They made it to the building just as a massive stone crashed into the pavement beside them. Two gods inside opened the doors to let them in and quickly shut them again behind them.

Kera brushed herself off. "No offense, babe, but the next time I ride your back like that, I hope it's under different circumstances."

Meg followed the rest of the group up the stairs to the rooftop, where the rest of the gods were waiting after having sent mental messages throughout the building to evacuate. Dani stood beside her but looked a million miles away.

Suddenly, God turned and sprinted back into the building without a word.

Dani said, "The Pope and a few Cardinals made it through some old underground escape tunnels to the back of the city. He's going to get them."

"Not alone." Ama turned and went after him, quickly followed by Mohammed.

Meg looked out over the Vatican wall. "Who are those gods? Why don't I recognize them? And why haven't they ever come to one of my parties?"

Selene stood on a chair to see what the non-humans saw. "They're almost all lesser gods belonging to the various pantheons. Although I see an angel or two in there as well, and I think a few of the Vodun variety are playing. Horus and Osiris are there, and Anubis is guarding the gate."

"And that explains why they don't go to your parties, and why we don't know them. Lesser gods are usually left behind to do the bulk of the work, but they never get credit. And the Egyptian gods have always kept mostly to themselves." Tis sheltered Kera with her wing when a blue bolt of energy sizzled a bit of the rooftop in front of them.

Zed's thunder shook the building, and his lightning bolt electrified the air. "I won't stand for it. The hierarchy is there for a reason. This happened before, when my own kids tried to tell me I was outdated. I showed them, and I'll show these bastards too."

"Look." Selene pointed at the ground far below, where several news vans had pulled up. Within moments, reporters were swarming the area, their cameras pointed at the rooftops. Police sirens wailed and military vehicles poured into the area. When the Vatican walls shattered in front of them, even the heavily armed guards took cover. Screams of pain and fear filled the air.

The God, Ama, Mohammed, and the Pope joined them on the rooftop. The Pope's white frock was covered in dirt, and a long cut on the side of his face dripped blood onto the front. Meg wondered how it felt to be rescued by the god you prayed to in such a literal fashion. That his mind hadn't melted into Dis's little black strings suggested his faith was absolute. Maybe he'd even expected it.

Tis turned to him, and Meg nearly laughed out loud when he took a step back. They were all in their natural forms, and although he'd just been saved by not one, but three different deities, the sight of a full-blown fury was obviously more terrifying. She didn't bother to analyze why she liked it.

"Have they taken control?" Tis asked him.

"I was in the last vault, leading to the tunnels, when I saw them come in. They weren't shooting at everyone, though. They seemed only to aim for religious leaders. Some lay people have been spared, though they remain trapped inside." He bowed his head. "Thanks to God."

God patted his shoulder in acknowledgment.

"We're out of time," Zed said.

They all turned toward the Vatican, where the tops of the walls had all been crushed or blown to bits, allowing them a direct view into the city. The moon covered the sun completely, and the gangrene sky looked like it was holding its breath.

Dis stood on the Dome, an array of multicolored gods around her. She waved like she was greeting someone at a picnic. "Nice of you to come!" Her voice carried across the distance easily, echoing against the stone and marble around her, reflecting the empty feeling of the blocked sun. "Feel free to join us!"

Thunder rumbled, and the sky darkened. Zed raised his thunderbolt. "We'll send you back to where you belong, and we'll deal with those who dared join you."

Dani touched his arm to stop him. "She'll be gone from that space before your bolt gets there, and you'll just end up destroying the building."

Her laughter reached across the space like an oil slick leading to an inferno. "I'll have to finish this conversation later. It seems I've been invited to lunch." She disappeared from the Dome, only to reappear at the huge gold doors of the Basilica, which were slowly being pushed open from the inside. Armed people stood aside as a woman strode out to meet Dis.

She appeared to say something. Dis turned to the gods following her. "Why yes, I believe we'd love to come in."

Rain fell from the sky in sheets and lightning cracked the black clouds above them as Meg and the others watched the gods below file into the venerated building.

"That's mine!" God grew and glowed, looking like the all-powerful being he was meant to be. He raised his hands as though to throw his power at the building.

Meg looked down and saw the multitude of cameras pointed their way. "Stop! Do anything that brings down the building and you'll kill the innocents they haven't. You'll play right into their hands."

"Not to mention kill your own believers, which won't do much for our cause. They want you to attack your own building and have the world see you as a monster." Dani was glowing, her eyes dark pools.

He shifted back into his normal godly size, his expression showing his rage. "Then what do we do?"

"Go get them." Confucius stood staring at the building. "Quickly and as quietly as you can. A few of us can go with you. We'll get the innocents out ourselves, right now."

Meg nodded, glad they'd brought him along for this quick thoughtfulness devoid of normal godly ego. "They're expecting a visible assault. But if you go in and get the ones you can, and leave them on the sidewalk with the media before you come back up here, it will serve two purposes."

God didn't need to be told twice. Ama, Jesus, Buddha, and Fin followed him down the stairs.

When Meg saw them on the sidewalk, she turned to Zed and Hades. "Let's provide a distraction."

Zed grinned and threw a bolt of lightning into the air that exploded like a firework, raining down smaller bolts on the Basilica. Durga raised her bow and let fly several arrows, while Azrael sent flames climbing over the porticoes. Hades raised his hands, and screaming shadows threw themselves against St. Peter's doors.

Meg's pulse raced and her heart beat so hard she thought it might pop out of her chest. Although she and her sisters could send their mists and snakes into the building, without being able to see, they couldn't be certain they'd avoid innocents.

The building they were standing on began to rock and tremble, and those who could took to the air, while the others braced themselves against the earthquake.

"Rūaumoko. It figures he'd find a way to join that group. He's been on the edge of fading from the Maori system for years." Zed's skin was crackling with electricity.

Meg looked around, energized by the drama unfolding around them and ready to jump in somehow. It felt like the eclipse was lasting forever, and she wondered if Dis could actually slow the movement of the cosmos, given that was where she'd spent most of her time. The building rumbled harder, and this time there were more screams and terror as the buildings beside and behind them began to crumble.

"Look!" Alec pointed at the street.

Humans were being ushered out a well-hidden door in the side of the wall, flanked by the gods who had gone to save them. The cameras were turned their way, and reporters began shouting questions as soon as everyone was within range.

The ground shook harder this time, and the gods on the street quickly rejoined the gods on the rooftop.

"There are many dead. I think we reached all those who aren't already on the road to the afterlife." God sounded deeply grieved, and Ama gently put her arm around his shoulders.

Dani turned to Meg. "We need to do something quickly. Humans are dying all around us."

"Maybe I can help?" Poseidon and Reef made their way onto the rooftop, looking utterly out of place with their shiny scales and gills.

"Do it," Zed said, clearly not bothered how his brother planned to do so.

"I'll burst all the pipes and cause the underground rivers and wells to surge into the building. No self-respecting cloud god, secondary or not, wants to rule from the water."

Meg heard the slight bitterness in his voice and hoped it wouldn't be a thing now. Later, she'd gladly sit back and watch that particular fight, but for now, they needed to work together. "I'm not sure that will work. Not while we have humans in there, even if they're the ones working for Dis. There are already plenty of dead in there, and more are going to die. We shouldn't go full force until we don't have a choice. We need to keep them safe, while disabling their gods. And we need to do it before the eclipse is over."

"Easy, right?" Selene rolled her eyes and pushed deeper against Alec's wing, wrapped around her to keep the rain off.

"In the old days, we wouldn't have cared about casualties. We'd have done what we needed to do and let the humans clean up the mess." Poseidon crossed his arms and looked out at the Vatican.

"I'm afraid it's no longer the old days, my friend," Dani said as she moved to stand beside him. "We're lucky Dis didn't think through the fact that most of the gods' weapons are handheld. Swords and hammers aren't going to do much good from a distance."

"No, but the spears and arrows can. We saw them in action when empires were busy rising and falling, and they're no joke." Meg stared down at the reporters below, an idea forming.

Dis appeared on the remains of the wall across from them. "You should simply step down, you know. Let us do what we want to do. Then pick up the pieces. That's what humans have come to expect from you anyway."

"What do you mean?" Selene asked in her usual calm, contemplative way.

Dis barely glanced at her. "Humans pray, and few get answered the way they're hoping to. Bad things happen, and there's usually a god to give some semblance of hope or consolation, though it's almost always after the fact." She looked pointedly at Jesus, who just glowered back at her. "And since you can't help them with the big stuff like disease, weather issues, or war, they've come to rely on you more out of habit than true belief."

"Your seeds of doubt won't work here, Chaos." Alec moved in front of Selene, and Tis and Meg moved up beside her. "You've started a war you can't finish."

Dis's laughter was harsh and loud. Meg wanted to punch her, hard. "You think I care who wins? Look around you. Gods are fighting gods, and it's being broadcast all over the world. Who will humans follow when this is over? When the eclipse is done, and the building is in ruins with new gods inside, all they'll see is how weak the old gods were, and they'll turn to the ones who have taken what they wanted. The sun will shine on the victors and highlight the weak. And the best part is that humans are going to die regardless. Fight, and they'll die. Don't fight, and they'll still die. I've rid the planet of some of the excess, and they'll turn on each other once they've watched their chosen gods perish or flee. You lose no matter which way you turn, and the planet gets to breathe a little easier. Isn't it delicious?"

Her laughter echoed in the darkness as she disappeared once again.

Dani felt the deaths of the humans around her. She felt their fear, their cries for help, and most of all, their desire for life. If more humans were going to die because they were standing on this rooftop, then they needed to move. But if they moved, and Dis's crew targeted this area anyway, they wouldn't be able to shield the humans at all. "What if we take the fight inside?"

"Go on?" Zed said.

"If we lessen the reach of the target, there will be fewer casualties around us. Make them focus on us right in front of them, and maybe they won't have a chance to get to the humans. The media will see us moving in, actively trying to help, instead of standing by and waiting."

"It's not a bad idea. And when the three of us get close enough, we can work to stop the gods who are misbehaving." Tis shook her wings free of water and gave Kera an apologetic look when she accidentally showered her.

"I want to try something before we do that." Meg took Dani's hand and looked at Poseidon. "Come with me?"

She led them down the stairs and out onto the street. She marched straight to a female reporter with long blond hair and intense blue eyes. She looked vaguely familiar, but Dani couldn't place her. When the three of them stopped in front of her, Dani was impressed she didn't step back, though no one would have blamed her if she had; it wasn't every day the god of the sea, the god of death, and a fury in full form came over to talk to you. Cameras kept rolling all around them, and the tension in the air was heavy.

"Madison Ford. It's nice to meet you." Meg stuck out her hand and Madison shook it, though now she did look slightly bemused. "How would you feel about exclusive access to this story? We'd like you to come to the rooftop with us."

There were some grumbles and protests from the other reporters around them, but no one dared step forward to voice them clearly. Now Dani recognized the reporter. She'd won major prizes for her work on human rights in other countries, and the fact that she was covering this story made Dani incredibly sad.

"Lead the way," she said and motioned for her cameraman to follow. He didn't look nearly as enthused as she did.

"Great. But first, I have something to say." Every camera focused on Meg as she turned to the bevy of reporters. "The gods who have taken over the Vatican do not represent you, nor are they representative of the rest of us. The Pope is alive and with God, and they're discussing a way forward. But know this…" She looked into each of the cameras individually. "We are not here to fight. We want peace, which is what we've always wanted, and what your gods have been talking to you about over the past year." She gave one of her sweetest smiles, one that hid her fangs. "Please don't come down here. I know it seems exciting, and there's something very Marvel versus DC about it all, but we're begging you to stay where you are until we announce that it's over."

She turned away and headed back into the building. Poseidon followed, then the reporter and cameraman, then Dani. She wondered why Meg had asked her and Poseidon to accompany her, rather than Zed or her sisters. Or even Kera, who, as a well-known human, might have carried some weight. But she trusted Meg's instincts, and she'd follow her right to the end of the line if need be. More distressing were the souls left waiting in the buildings around her. They were confused and frightened. But Dani didn't want her Sundo caught between gods lobbing their powers at one another like angry toddlers with grenades. Mentally, she contacted Idona and told her to help with evacuation the moment she and the others had entered the Vatican. Death didn't wait for anyone, but maybe this time it could be actively delayed by death's workers.

Meg led them all back to the roof, and Madison stumbled a bit when faced with the group of multi-limbed, colorful-skinned gods waiting in the heavy rain. Dani placed a gentle hand on her shoulder to steady her and was gratified when instead of pulling away in fear, Madison gave her a grateful smile. When she turned back to face the rest, Dani saw the expression of determination on her face and knew Meg had chosen well. *Big surprise there.*

"Everyone, Madison Ford, journalist extraordinaire. Madison, everyone not on the other team." Meg waved in both directions to indicate who she was talking about. "Madison is going to show people what we're doing up here, and why." She turned to Dani and smiled. "I can't think of a better god to start with than Death."

Dani winced inwardly. She'd have liked to watch the other gods talk first, but she wasn't going to balk at the first hurdle. She nodded and moved to Madison's side.

"What's going on here? What do I call you, first?"

Dani let the powers Kanaloa had helped her refine flow through her and felt the cool spread of them run through her. She lifted her chin and looked at Madison. "You can call me Dani, but officially I'm known as Death. I'm goddess to some, but I'm caretaker of everyone when their time comes."

Madison stared at her for a moment but cleared her throat and carried on. "Okay. Dani it is. What's going on? What's happened inside the Vatican?"

God rumbled, and Madison looked toward him. When she seemed to realize who he was she swallowed almost audibly, and Dani felt her fear rising. She touched her shoulder to get her to focus. "There's a being inside who has been making trouble for pretty much the entire world. Her ancient name is Dis, though most people would recognize her as Chaos. She's been the source of many people's angst and frustration about their belief systems, and today she's gathered several gods who feel underappreciated, or who want more power, to stand against the gods who are well known and beloved." It sounded strangely succinct and far too simple, but that really was the gist of it. Except for the bits about humans' brains turning to mush and doubts causing the gods to fade...

"Gods fighting gods. Does this mean some kind of deity-based civil war?"

As if in answer, a flash of silver flew through the sky, only to separate into individual arrows when they hit the building, causing yet more of it to disintegrate around them. The humans on the roof were thrown to their knees, though the gods kept their footing. Dani reached out to help Madison and her cameraman up, though she noticed him flinch away from her touch.

Meg moved to her side, as did Alec and Tis. Selene and Kera moved forward as well, while Zed, Poseidon, and Ama hovered behind them. The rest of the gods created an outward facing ring around them, watching for incoming attacks. Meg took over talking.

"Sadly, it appears that way. But here's the thing." She pointed over her shoulder at the gods behind her. "They're fighting for the humans. For their choice. For their lives. For their freedom to move freely through the world. The gods on this rooftop, as well as those who are out taking care of their communities right now, care about the humans who pray to them." She pointed dramatically at the Vatican, which was now partially illuminated by the returning sun. "Those gods care about being worshipped. They want you to fear them, they want to control where you go and who you pray to. They don't care about you as people. They want to go back to the old ways, where people in particular locations didn't have the right to choose who they wanted to pray to. They want your fear, not your respect."

Selene stepped forward. "The gods on this roof are fighting for *you*. All of you, whether you believe or not. Because for them, that's what belief and faith are about. Taking care of humans who pray is something they all have to do. The ones in the Vatican have gone against those sacred tenets, and the gods who care for you can't allow that to happen." She spoke clearly and firmly in front of the camera. She was a well-known face on TV, and her word on this would be invaluable.

This time the sky lit up, and as the ground shook beneath them, arrows and spears came flying through the air like deadly slivers of brutal rain. Rock and mortar flew to pieces, dust filled the air, and cries of pain and terror bounced off twisted metal and rock as massive chunks of the building exploded around them. The eclipse was nearing its end, and the gods were no nearer to stopping Dis and her desperate disciples. Dani knelt and stared at the returning sun, wondering how they were going to make it in time. Everything around her felt like it was in slow motion, the people she cared most about in the world lost in a haze of dust and smoke.

"Fight back!" Zed yelled.

The world turned right again, sound roaring back in, the shouts of those around her filling the air. The lights were too bright to look at as the fighting gods did exactly as Zed told them to. The pacifist gods, Jesus, Buddha, Confucius, and Fin, formed a protective barrier in front of the humans. There were going to be casualties inside the Vatican, and Dani could only hope those humans with Humanity First, as well as those who had joined them in a strange coalition, had gone in knowing they wouldn't come back out. Lightning bolts, waves of water, and their own sets of arrows and bolts of power were pounding against the Vatican. The Dome began to buckle, and with a last furious throw of lightning, Zed managed to collapse it. Vatican City fell to rubble and ruin, the limbs of marble statues sticking out grotesquely beside the bodies of those who'd chosen the wrong side. The gods who'd fought against their primaries had lost, and there was no trace of them through the clouds of dust.

Dani let the tears fall as she felt the death count rising. But when she heard Alec's scream, followed by Tis's howl, bile rose in her throat. She knew before she turned around what she would find.

Alec knelt in the dust and rubble, cradling Selene's limp, bloody body in her arms. She screamed her agony and fury, her pain radiating out from her in waves of anguish, her body heaving with sobs as her tears fell onto Selene's still chest.

Tis, too, knelt beside Kera, who had an ugly piece of metal sticking out of her leg, though she was still unmercifully conscious. The stream of inventive profanity coming from her would have been funny in a situation less life and death. Ama rushed over and placed her hand over Kera's eyes, putting her to sleep before she pulled the metal from Kera's leg and quickly placed her hands over the pumping wound. Within moments, the bleeding had stopped, and the wound had closed. Meg stood beside Dani, her shock evident. "I knew they shouldn't have come. I should've made them stay behind."

Dani wrapped her arm around Meg's shoulders and pulled her close. "You know as well as I do the Fates have a hand in every life, especially those involved with Afterlife. They came because they were meant to."

Meg turned to Dani with flames in her eyes, her snakes hissing in her feathers, and her fangs fully extended. "We need to end this. Now." She turned to the other gods on the roof. "Find any gods who might be in the rubble and see if there are any humans you can help. Call in your secondaries if you can. Send paramedics to the wounded." She turned to Dani. "Ready?"

Dani nodded, understanding. She let her full power flow through her, drawing it into her like a tsunami hitting shore. She wrapped her arms around Meg from behind and held on as Meg flew into the ruins of Vatican City.

CHAPTER TWENTY-THREE

Meg did her best to block off her sister's pain, though it pounded against her head and heart. Rage like she'd never experienced suffused every inch of her being, and she was going to put the bitch down any way she could.

They landed at the edge of the rubble, and Dani let go of her, only to take her hand once she was beside her. Her cool touch grounded her, at least a little bit, and she was grateful for it. When someone appeared at her shoulder, she started.

Tis looked as serious and grim as she felt. "Kera's with Ama. You two aren't doing this alone."

Alec landed beside Dani. Her eyes were pools of wet tar, and she was trembling. Her snakes were wrapped around her arms, awake and hissing, fangs bared. "And you're sure as fuck not doing it without me."

Meg's snakes hissed along with those of her sisters as they entered the building. Frescoes once stunning and colorful lay in muted shards. Religious relics lay in mangled pieces beside equally mangled bodies. They stepped over and around them, searching.

"Are we sure she's here?" Tis asked.

"I can feel her. She's here." Meg was certain, and she wasn't about to question where the knowledge came from. Not now, not ever again.

Everyone followed Meg down long, empty corridors that were usually filled to the brim with tourists. Now they echoed with the hissing of snakes and the sounds of rubble under their feet. It was a silence Meg knew she'd never forget.

Meg focused and knew exactly where to go. Down a set of stone stairs and yet another, they reached the entrance to the Sistine Chapel, which, probably thanks to its special place below the palace, was largely untouched. Meg had watched Michelangelo and Botticelli paint the Sistine Chapel, and to see it here, untouched among the ruins but housing the foulest creature in existence, made her skin crawl.

Dis sat alone on one of the far benches, staring up at the ceiling, looking calm and contemplative. Meg wanted to rip her throat out but stopped when Dani took her hand.

"Remember what the Fates said."

Meg thought back. It felt like a billion years ago they'd been spouting their usual ominous warnings. *Wait for the eruption after the collision. Don't let her down. Find yourself.* Well, hopefully, she'd managed at least two of those things. And it looked like the third was about to take place. She held Dani's hand tighter. Dani's power surged up her arm and merged with her own, making her wonder how her body could contain it. She liked it. She liked it a lot.

"You're done, you interfering asshat of a murderous monkey shit. We were told to let you do your thing, and we have. But you've gone too far. No one murders humans on this planet and skips off into the bloody sunset." Meg's voice bounced around the small rectangular room.

Dis sighed, sounding genuinely disappointed. "I thought we had a chance, you know. Obviously, I didn't care one way or another, really, but I thought it would be a far grander experience. Drawn out like the battles in the old days. But bring down one little building and the little gods scatter like roaches. It's no wonder they're lower on the deified food chain. Even my beautiful Horus flew away. The ancient gods fear losing more than they desire to be gods. Incredibly disappointing."

"You're a fucking monster," Alec roared. She moved forward, only to be stopped when Dani put a hand on her shoulder.

"Call me what you wish. I'm bored now. Your gods are as weak as your humans, and if even a big war isn't interesting, there's really no reason to stay." She raised her hands and dust rose from at her feet, coalescing into ribbons of reds, blues, and yellows filled with clusters of bright stars. As they grew and spread around her, Dis sighed and closed her eyes as though she was alone and at peace.

Meg raised the hand she'd entwined with Dani's and quickly grabbed Tis's as well. Alec slipped her hand into Dani's. "You can fuck right off if you think you're leaving this place."

Old power, the kind they hadn't used in centuries, rose. Meg let it spread through her body like a wildfire and felt Dani's power, the power of death, destruction, but also of healing and life, mingle with theirs. Nothing overpowered Death, and it was the first time Meg really understood that. "Focus on her, keep her in place."

They did, and Meg knew they could all feel Dis fighting it. She was the strongest entity in the universe, and they wouldn't be able to hold her for long. The cosmic energy flowing around her began to pop and sizzle under the pressure, and Dis screeched like an angry animal. Meg saw a heavy chain dangling from beyond the door and mentally pulled at it. Levitation had never been her strong suit, but she'd damn well figure it out now. She felt Dani's connection, and the chain moved swiftly into the room. They wrapped it around Dis, who struggled and screamed as it bound her from ankle to neck. The red and blue ribbons fell to gray ash around her, the sparkling stars blinking to nothingness.

When she fell to the ground, writhing and berating them, they were able to lower their power.

"Sanctified metal. How did you know?" Dani asked softly, never taking her eyes from Dis.

"The usual. I just did. Blessed as it was by someone with absolute faith, she won't be able to break out of it, though I don't want to depend on it for long." Meg's power hummed through her, the exhilarating mix of capture and defeat making her feel like a god. Then she looked at Dani, who was a god, and was brought back to earth. She looked far away and incredibly sad. The goddess of Death was taking the terrible amount of dead around them to heart. Meg knew there wasn't anything she could do to ease that particular burden except be at her side when Dani needed her.

Alec jerked forward, her eyes wild. "I say we make her into the star dust she reminds everyone else they are."

Tis shook her head and blocked Alec's path. "We can't kill Chaos, Alec. She'd simply be reborn at some point because of human nature. But we can damn sure send her back to where she came from. I don't care what the Fates say."

Dani left the room and came back quickly with a huge tapestry she'd clearly taken from a wall. "Let's wrap her in this, gangster style, and take her back to Afterlife."

Meg nearly clapped like a kid she loved the idea so much. "She'll hate it. Let's do it."

Carefully, they moved around Dis, who continued to threaten, plead, shout, and generally abuse them until she was muffled by the heavy ornate tapestry depicting the massacre of the innocents. Dani shrugged when Tis looked at her with a raised eyebrow.

"It seemed fitting."

Dani opened a road to Afterlife, and her Mustang was at the opening, waiting. They hefted the bundled Dis into the trunk, where she hit with a satisfying thump.

Dani looked thoughtful and turned to Tis. "My road is faster than a plane. Why don't you get Kera and Ama, and the three of you can drive back to Afterlife as fast as you can possibly go? I need to be here right now."

Tis nodded, looking exhausted. "Sure. Is there a faster way than the jet to get the rest home?"

Meg gave Dani a small smile. "How about the water?"

Dani closed her eyes, and when she reopened them, she turned to Tis. "Poseidon can get everyone home once they've finished searching the ruins. They should arrive shortly after you, with the bound gods in tow." Dani turned to Alec, who sat slumped against the wall, her wings closed around her, her shoulders shaking. "I need you to come with me, Alec."

Meg watched as Dani held out her hand, and Alec looked at it for a moment before taking it. They didn't know what would happen when Selene died, and they sure as hell hadn't intended to find out so soon. Based on the way she'd looked in Alec's arms, it wasn't promising.

They left the decimated Vatican City behind them and went back to the rooftop where the others waited. They'd found a few of the gods who'd fought against them buried in the rubble, and they were bound on the ground, kept there at the ends of the other gods' various weapons. Others had fled, though they'd soon be found as well. They were all strangely quiet, as though no one knew what to say in a situation like this one.

Now, though, there was another god among them. Selene's mom, Chandra, goddess of the moon, knelt beside her daughter's body. Meg had always found her remote and dull, but now she stared at Selene's body and tears like crystal fell onto Selene's chest. Alec knelt beside her and gently pulled Selene's body into her lap. Tears cascaded down her cheeks, mixing with Chandra's. Meg's heart broke for her sister, who had finally found the love of her existence, only to lose her.

Dani whispered in Meg's ear, "I need to do this. I might need you to hold Alec so I can do what I need to do, okay?"

Meg nodded, hating the idea and part of her wanting to stop Dani herself. Still, she moved behind Alec, ready to take her shoulders if necessary.

Dani knelt beside Selene, and her hands hovered over Selene's head. The last sliver of moon slid away from the sun and bathed the scene in surreal sunlight. Alec's sobs grew louder, her body jerking as she howled. Chandra watched silently, but her pain was clear in her pale eyes. And then Meg watched as Selene's soul slowly left her body. But instead of the usual electric blue, Selene's was the glowing silver of moonlight, and when Dani moved away with it cradled in her hands, she opened them as though to let it go.

Alec cried out, but Meg held her in place. She watched as Selene's silver soul cascaded from Dani's hands and slowly, increasingly, took shape.

Alec nearly collapsed under Meg's hands as Selene looked around, clearly puzzled. She'd been a beautiful human, but as a demigod, she was…exquisite.

"Alec? Baby, why are you crying—"

Meg flinched at the moment Selene saw her own limp body lying in the rubble. If Selene had been able to go pale, she probably would have. The drama of the moment was electrifying, and Meg watched with fascination. She let Alec go when she stopped straining and leaned against Meg.

"Oh." Selene stared down at her body, and then looked at Alec, who gently placed Selene's body on the ground before stepping over it and moving to stand in front of her glowing spirit. Chandra sighed softly and closed her eyes before moving away from Selene's body to stand beside Zed, who put his arm around her.

Alec looked at Dani. "Can I touch her?"

Dani smiled. "Why don't you try?"

Alec held out her arms and Selene moved into them. They

wrapped their arms around each other, and Selene certainly looked solid to Meg.

"Thank the gods," Alec said into Selene's hair. "I thought I'd lost you."

Selene pulled away slightly. "Do I feel any different?" She looked down at her body on the ground. "That's extremely disconcerting."

Meg moved to stand in front of Selene's body so she couldn't see it. "Does she feel different?" she asked Alec, insanely curious and wanting to touch Selene herself, but aware she might be overstepping if she did.

"She's…" Alec slid her hands over Selene's arms. "Warmer. Like sunshine on sand in the summer." Tears continued to slide down her face. "I'm glad you can't do that to me ever again."

A choked sound caught Meg's attention, and she turned around. "Oh gods. I completely forgot you were here."

Madison Ford stood with her cameraman. Both were covered in dust and soot, and Madison's hair looked like she'd stuck her finger in a socket. Her eyes were wide as she stared at Alec and Selene. Her cameraman was clearly still filming, though he too looked stunned.

Meg grabbed Dani and pulled her in front of the camera. At Dani's confused look, she smiled sweetly and said, "It's time." She turned to the camera. "I'd like to reintroduce you to Dani Morana. Most of you know her as Death, the one in the big cloak who carries that beautiful scythe." Dani smiled nervously at the camera, and Meg continued. "But what you've just seen is how your souls are handled when it's your time to go."

"But not everyone comes back the way Selene did." Dani squeezed Meg's hand. "Souls go to different places depending on your belief system. The one thing you can be sure of is that every soul is handled with the same care. It's an honor for us to help you take the next step of your journey, and as you can see, there's nothing in that first step to be afraid of."

Madison moved to stand beside Meg and Dani. "Can you explain what happened here today?"

Dani moved aside and motioned for Meg to take the stage. Meg spread her wings out behind her, liking the way they looked in the reflection of the camera lens. "Today, the gods fought for you. There were some who wanted to take away your rights, who felt they had the right to dictate who you were able to believe in, and how much freedom you were allowed to have. Other gods, those standing behind me, believe in the human capability to make choices based on their own needs and beliefs." She lowered her left wing to show Selene. "As Selene has been saying for some time now, you have the right to your faith. And now that you know the gods exist, you know you have choices to make about who to believe in." She lowered both wings completely, to show the gathering of gods standing behind her. The drama of it was thrilling. "These gods fought for every human to have the right to choose their faith. The ones on the ground trussed up like turkeys are the ones who would have made you into mindless servants. The building might have come down, but a building is just a place. The beings are the ones you can count on. Don't lose sight of that."

The cameraman panned over the gods, clearly going in for a close-up on each of them. As the camera got to each god, they stood straighter, raised their chins, brightened their glow. Those on the ground looked away, trying to hide. And Meg saw that when the camera had passed, several of the victorious gods slumped, looking tired and crestfallen. They wouldn't let it show, but they'd just gone to war with other gods, some who had been friends. They'd done the right thing, but the cost had been high.

The camera returned to Madison and Meg, and Madison said, "What else do you want people to know, Megara?"

Meg looked around at the people she loved. Her family, her friends. She lingered on Dani, who was radiant. Her followers had seen her and had a face to put to their prayers. Her power was growing even as they stood there. She looked truly divine, and Meg's knees were weak with the emotion flooding through her. She looked back at the camera. "Choose who you want to believe in, but do it because you want what they offer, and what they have to offer makes you a better human. Beyond all of that, love. Every one of these gods has that as one of their primary rules. Love each other, and do no harm. Pretty simple, right? If you have questions, ask. Every god has an email address, and they really do hear your prayers. If you can't get hold of them with your questions, get hold of me." With those words, she realized she knew her place. Selene had been the bridge to save the worlds, and Tis had made the choice to stay part of the world she knew and bring in Kera, who'd helped with the transition. It was Meg's job to keep it going, to be a kind of liaison between the gods and humans and help them understand one another. It would get crazy. It would be complicated. And she'd love it.

CHAPTER TWENTY-FOUR

Dani, the furies, and Zed stood behind Dis on level five, and the seriousness of the moment was so thick in the air Dani felt like she could barely breathe. The three Fate sisters stood in front of Dis, who remained bound in chains. With the news constantly replaying footage of the War of the Gods, as it was unimaginatively being called, people's fears and confusion had already diminished exponentially. Without Dis there to fan the flames of distress and anger, humans were settling. They'd seen the gods fight for them, and they'd seen the destructive gods vanquished. The followers of those gods who had been beaten were confused and angry, but the sub gods and nearby gods were already in those locations, helping defuse the situations. The humans had listened to Meg explain what had happened and why. Life was right side up again, and even the fear of death had already begun to change into something else. Dani wasn't sure what that something was yet, but it was definitely different from what she'd felt for the last three thousand years.

As a result of the changes, Dis's power had faded, and it showed in her being. She stared at the wall behind them, mute, her face a mask devoid of emotion. Her eyes were dull, her skin sallow.

"Goddess of Chaos, keeper of the cosmos. You have served your purpose here, and you are no longer needed." Clotho, Atropos, and Lachesis spoke as one. Clotho stepped forward and waved her hand over the chain binding Dis, and it fell to pieces at her feet. "It is time for you to take your place among the stars once more."

The door to the cosmos opened behind Dis, but she didn't turn around. Swirling balls of multicolored gasses passed by the opening, backlighting her. "They'll call me back, one day." She glanced over her shoulder and straightened slightly before turning back to them. "The last time you furies took charge, when you began putting things in order, you forced me away. But now you see, you can't keep me away. Even you aren't that powerful." She stepped backward toward the open doorway. "One day, they'll forget you. They'll have no help, no gods left. And then..." She laughed, a deep, dark, echoing sound. "Then they'll have no one but me."

She turned and stood in the doorway, her arms raised and her head thrown back. "Oh. One more thing." She spun, her hands outstretched, and trails of red and blue streaks shot toward Meg.

Meg swore and jerked back, but the ropes of color wrapped around her arms and jerked her toward Dis and the doorway. Dis stepped out into space and floated there, pulling Meg toward her.

Dani grabbed Meg around the waist and pulled her back as the others shouted and moved forward. Dani thought of her scythe, and it was instantly in her hand. She flung it forward, and it sliced through Dis's arm before returning to Dani, the cosmic ropes shredded, Dis's outraged shrieks filling the air as Meg fell backward into Dani.

Atropos slammed the door shut, and they heard Dis's scream of defiance, but that too faded.

Meg sat cross-legged on the floor, her back against Dani's legs. "Well, that was unexpected."

Lachesis huffed. "Silly old bat. As though we'd let anything like that happen." She yawned. "I'm going home to bed."

"Just like that?" Alec pointed at the door. "She just tried to kill our sister, and you're going home to cuddle your cat?"

Clotho shrugged. "She can't open the door from her side. There was a time she could drop in whenever she wanted, but we rerouted things to make sure we knew when she was here or being called back. She's gone, and our machines are working again. You go do your thing now. We'll let you know if anything comes up that concerns you." She left, elegant and composed as always.

"Wait. You rerouted...space? Time?" Selene shook her head. "You're beings created by humans, on this planet. How can you have that kind of power?"

Atropos laughed and touched Selene's cheek in a surprisingly gentle gesture. "There are still many things you don't know, child of the moon." She walked away, whistling.

Lachesis followed but looked over her shoulder. "And we don't like cats."

Dani helped Meg to her feet.

"And off they go, like they didn't just send old demented assface into space." Kera ran her hands through her hair and looked at Tis. "Sometimes, I'm not convinced you aren't keeping me drugged somewhere."

Tis gave her a quick kiss on the cheek and linked her arm. "Who says I'm not?"

As a group, they made their way back to Zed's office. Dani held Meg's hand. After the battle, and after seeing the devastating pain Tis and Alec had suffered when the loves of their lives were dead and injured, she needed to be with Meg as much as possible. And after what Dis had just tried to do, she wanted physical contact more than ever. The thought that Meg could have been dragged into the cosmos and lost to her forever…the thought was beyond sickening.

When they were finally back in Zed's office, Meg pushed everyone aside to get to the pizza on the table. With her mouth full, she looked at Ama, who was smiling at her. "You're the best goddess ever."

Ama laughed. "Well, I figured you'd be starving, and it never hurts to have food when talking about how life should proceed."

Dani and the others grabbed some for themselves before they fanned out around the table.

"Next step?" Kera asked after she'd downed her second piece.

Tis put her half-eaten slice down and looked at Zed. "We follow the constitution."

He kept eating but looked at her contemplatively. "I'll need to convene the high council. The things we put in place…it will be up to the three of you to carry out the verdicts."

Meg raised her hand to speak. "Both councils. This affects everyone, and now isn't the time to piss anyone off. Satan and Hades fought beside us, not below us."

Zed sighed. "You're right. I need to stop thinking like it's the old days." He turned to Dani. "I assume you'll take your place at the table, now that you've achieved goddess status?"

Dani wasn't sure how to respond. She'd been so busy learning how to be a god, she hadn't thought about the politics of it all. "High council members, and low council, for that matter, are the oldest gods of the biggest religions. I don't factor into either of those."

Meg shook her head. "True, but not true. You run a department bigger than anyone else's, that actually includes every follower and non-follower on earth, and you have for three thousand years. That makes you more powerful in a lot of ways than some of the high council gods." She took a noisy slurp of Coke and continued. "Plus, now that you're rebranding and working with every department, your opinion on things is going to matter a lot."

Dani looked back at Zed, who simply grabbed another piece of pizza and nodded.

"Sure. Thank you. I'd be honored."

"Okay. I think we've had enough insanity for one century. I'm going to convene the councils at an emergency meeting tomorrow, and I'd like all of you there." He stood, and Ama stood with him. "We're going to go show how grateful we are to be on the winning side. I suggest you all do the same."

Meg turned to Dani. "My place?"

Dani stood and took Meg's hand. "You lead." Time alone with Meg was something she wouldn't have contemplated as possible only a few short months ago. Now she knew she'd gladly trade her soul for the time they spent together.

Meg snuggled closer to Dani and listened to her steady heartbeat. "Do you ever wonder why we have heartbeats? And why we have bodily functions? Why we swallow, and fart, and cry?"

Dani laughed. "I think I get what you mean, but go on."

Meg shivered as Dani traced gentle circles over her back and along the top edges of her wings. They'd barely made it through the door before they'd begun tearing each other's clothes off, and Meg was only halfway on the couch before Dani was on her knees with her mouth over Meg's clit. It had taken another hour and two more rooms before they'd made it to the bedroom. And when Meg had passed Dani the leather harness and dildo set, it had been another few hours before they'd finally collapsed, momentarily sated. "I mean, take you and me, for instance. We're immortal, right? We live, we don't age, we don't die. Why bother with the actual physical element of being?"

Dani kissed the top of Meg's head. "I wondered that a few centuries ago myself. But I never came up with an answer. Maybe it's because we're creations of the human world, to some extent, and they can't conceive of beings without physical properties. And the longer we've been among them, the more that's become true for ourselves as well."

Meg pinched Dani's thigh. "You sound like Selene." She pushed up onto one elbow and looked at Dani. "And that, by the way, was amazing."

Dani swallowed, her eyes glassy. "Her soul was warm, light. I guess I thought that as daughter of the moon and darkness, it would be cool, maybe even cold. But it was like handling spring sunshine dipped in poetry."

Meg sighed and dropped back onto the bed with her head on Dani's chest. "You say some of the most beautiful things." She paused, thinking about what Dani had said and all they'd been through. "Can I tell you something?"

Dani started to shift to look at her, but Meg put her hand on Dani's stomach and stopped her. "No, just listen, okay?"

"Is everything okay?"

Dani's tone was soft, and Meg heard the worry in it. "I think so. I hope so." She took a deep breath. *Don't be a chicken feather.* "All my life, I've lived like there might not be a tomorrow. I've concentrated on being in the moment, and I've enjoyed every second." Dani started to speak, and Meg stopped her again. "Wait. Let me get this out." Dani settled, and Meg could feel the tension in her hand as she stroked her back. "But I've never once let anyone get close to me. I had my sisters, and they were all I needed when it came to people really getting to know me. I've had a lot of sex." She giggled when Dani harrumphed. "And I've met a ton of amazing and not-amazing people." Finally, she dug up some courage and moved to look into Dani's beautiful eyes. "But now I think all these centuries, I was just waiting for you. No one could understand me, or want me, the way you do. No one else looks at me like I'm the only thing they ever want to look at again the way you do. And I like that. A lot." She stopped, not knowing exactly what to say next, but knowing there was so much more.

Dani sat up and turned to face her. "Megara, I've spent centuries loving you. I've waited in the background like the most socially awkward teenager in recorded history, thinking I'm not good enough for you, that I'm too boring for you. That I could never match your passion."

Meg let the tears roll down her cheeks and started to speak, but Dani squeezed her hands.

"My turn." She smiled and kissed the tears from Meg's lips. "But now, I think we're pretty damn good together. Your passion heats my soul and makes me want to do impossible things just to make you smile. I think you're an amazing woman, and the fact that you'd choose to spend time with me, for however long I can have you, makes me the luckiest being in any universe there is."

Meg threw her arms around Dani's neck and straddled her. She couldn't get close enough to show her what those words meant to her. "I love you too. And if you'll put up with me forever, then we'll take the rest of this ride together."

They held each other, and Meg sank into the feeling of rightness that enveloped her. When her stomach rumbled, they both laughed.

"Before I feed you again, I want you to know something else." Dani held Meg's face between her hands. "I don't want to change you in any way, and forever is a damn long time."

Meg frowned, certain there was a caveat coming.

"So when you get a hankering for a bit of Viking goddess, or a little taste of Indian Kama Sutra, you just let me know, and we'll play those games together." Dani's grin was delightfully dirty. "And trust me when I say I'd be happy to oblige."

Meg kissed Dani hard and deep. "See? You're damn well perfect." She moved Dani's hands to her breasts and started to rock back and forth on her lap. "When that day comes, I'll definitely let you know. But for the next decade or ten, I think I'll keep you to myself."

Dani pinched her nipple between her thumb and forefinger and tugged, just hard enough to make Meg moan. She slipped her other hand between Meg's legs and pushed her fingers into her. Meg cried out and pushed against her. "More. Gods, Dani, give me more."

Dani wrapped her arm around Meg's waist and lifted her off her lap, only to push her back onto the bed. She pushed another finger into her and pumped hard, fucking her deeply. Meg loved the concentration, the adoration, and the near desperation in Dani's expression as she made Meg come over and over again. After the third orgasm, Dani slowed and pulled out. Meg's head and half her wings hung off the edge of the bed, and she murmured appreciatively when Dani kissed along her collarbone. Her stomach growled again, and they laughed.

"Okay, my beautiful firebrand. Let's feed you."

Meg fought her way free of the sheet and stumbled from the bed. "I've got a craving for buttermilk biscuits. I'll make them, you pour drinks."

"Yes, ma'am." Dani went to the bar. "Vodka? Tequila?"

"With biscuits? Mimosa." Meg pulled the various ingredients out and set them on the counter. Dani brought over the drinks and set them on the breakfast bar, where she took a stool and sat to watch.

"Babe, can I ask you something?"

Meg looked up from the flour at the seriousness in Dani's tone. "Sure. What's wrong?"

"Tomorrow, Zed is going to call everyone together, and they're going to decide on what to do about the renegade gods. You and your sisters are going to have to deal with the outcome of that. Are you going to be okay?"

Meg kept kneading as she processed Dani's question. "I have to be, don't I? I mean, this is what I am. I couldn't walk away from delivering justice any more than you could walk away from helping souls get to where they need to be."

"I wasn't asking if you'd do your job. I was asking if you'd be okay. You, Meg-the-woman-I-love, not you, Meg-the-fury." Dani smiled slightly over her mimosa.

Meg cut the dough into two-inch circles and put them on the tray. "I'm both. Unlike my sisters, I haven't doubted myself as a fury. Those gods knew they were starting a war. They knew humans would get hurt, and they didn't care. One of my jobs has been to keep the gods in check, and if now isn't the time to do that, then I don't know when it would be."

Dani nodded and walked around behind Meg. She nuzzled her neck and said, "Yeah, I thought that would be your answer. But it doesn't hurt to ask."

Meg leaned into Dani and sighed. She'd felt alone for more years than she wanted to count. She'd pretended to be strong, to not care about anything, but in truth, she'd needed...this. To have someone hold her and care about her emotional state, as up and down as that could be. Dani knew her better than almost anyone, and she still loved her for exactly who, and what, she was. The world had gone to hell, and they'd taken it on together. Things could only be extraordinary from here.

CHAPTER TWENTY-FIVE

"Hey! Tall, dark, and terrifying. Can I have a minute?" Dani turned and waited for Kera to catch up to her in the hall. They were heading to the main hall where the emergency council had been called, and all the gods at Afterlife had shown up, whether they'd been invited or not. The building hummed with tension, and Dani wondered if Kera, the only human left among them, should be in the vicinity of stressed-out gods. Although Ama had healed the initial wound, she still limped slightly from the metal bar she'd taken in the leg in Rome, a reminder that of all of them, she was the most vulnerable.

"Thanks for waiting." Kera looked behind her and up ahead, as though to make certain they wouldn't be overheard. "I wanted to ask you for something."

"Oh?" Dani liked Kera immensely, but she was also aware that Kera had been in business with some shady characters before hooking up with Tis. "I'm not killing anyone or taking a soul, if that's what you're going to ask." She smiled to take the sting from it.

"Nah. The people I know who need that kind of thing will do it on their own. It's something else." She grinned. "I've got this problem. This mortality thing is really pissing me off. I mean, I've found a woman I want to be with until this planet literally implodes. But apparently, that card isn't on the table, and the other day when I was up on that rooftop with a bunch of people who are exceptionally hard to kill, but I was the one bleeding out, I think I figured out a way around it."

"You figured out a way around death?" Dani didn't want to laugh in her face, but it was hard not to.

"Kind of. I'm going to come live with you."

Dani tilted her head. "Nope. Not following."

"I'm one of the souls you've been talking about. I'm not a follower of any one religion, but I know full well you all exist. That means I won't have anywhere to go once I'm dead."

Dani nodded, starting to understand.

"So, here's the thing. When I go, I want to work for you. Well, not really for you. I'm the boss, right? But if you take my soul, then you could let it free, right? I could still run Afterlife with Zed but not get indigestion or migraines from working with him anymore. Right?"

"Um…" Dani hadn't a clue what to say. She'd never thought about souls living outside the Deadlands. Would it even work?

"Don't answer now. Just think about it, okay?" The building rumbled, and the lights flickered. "But if I die in some shit storm before you decide, just remember that I asked."

"Of course. You do know it would be better if you stayed out of the way for a while, though, right?" Dani moved out of the way to let one of the Hindu gods pass, his arms waving as he hurried to the main hall.

"Yeah, that's not going to happen. I can't do what I need to do if I'm hiding. Just think about it, okay?"

Dani nodded, and they headed for the main hall together. It was an interesting question, and she'd have to talk to Idona about it once things had settled down a little. Hopefully, Kera could stay out of harm's way until she was able to work it out. When they entered the main hall, they were met with a cacophony of noise.

"Order!" Zed's thunder shook the hall, and his lightning sparked along the ceiling. The room grew quiet.

Dani followed Kera down the side of the room to the stage where the others were waiting. She'd spent some time in the Deadlands doing paperwork and answering prayers after she'd pulled herself away from Meg's place in the early morning, and it had felt good to get back to doing some of what she loved. Now, though, she wouldn't be anywhere but at Meg's side.

"Thank you for coming. After the altercation in Rome," Zed paused for the quiet laughter at his downplaying of the war, "there are some decisions that must be made." He nodded at Tis, who stepped forward.

She held up a piece of paper. "Every head of department who

works at Afterlife signed this contract when we began reorganizing. These rules were agreed to by majority vote and signed in front of witnesses. The rule set in place for those who went against Afterlife policy and willfully hurt humans was clear. Excommunication. They will be stripped of their powers, and they can stay among the humans, or they can fade."

The room was silent, and Dani could feel the horror and sadness in the crowd. Many of the implicated gods were friends of those in the hall.

"The gods who sided with Chaos in the war at the Vatican will be subject to the rules set forth in this document." Meg and Alec moved to stand beside Tis. "As has been the case at terrible moments in the past, it's up to the three of us to deliver that punishment, and we'll do what we need to do when those gods are found."

Her statement was again met with silence, and Dani watched as Tis looked over the crowd of gods below her. Beside her, Meg looked like she was on full alert, but Dani knew the excitement and suspense of the moment was feeding her penchant for drama.

Zed took the stage again. "There will be no trials for the gods involved in the Vatican situation. If one of them was from your department, you'll be contacted when the issue has been dealt with." Zed looked down the row of people beside him. "Anything else?"

Dani stepped forward and addressed the crowd. "One last thing. As you may have heard, we're changing the way the Deadlands works, to some degree. Thanks to a new type of non-believer, we're going to be adding sections, and we're looking for people from other departments to assist in building and running a new section on a cooperative basis. If you're interested, please talk to myself or Idona about the new plans."

Meg smiled widely at her, and Dani's stomach flip-flopped the way it always did. She'd gladly spend the rest of her days trying to make Meg smile like that.

"That's all. Go be with your believers, and answer as many questions as you can as simply as you can. Remember the Fates' suggestion about being vague when necessary in order to keep from backing yourself into a corner. Help them understand what your system is truly about and give them things to ponder. Keep them focused and busy." Zed waved toward the door. "Talk to me if you have issues, and we'll be in touch about the other stuff."

The gods burst into noisy chatter as they filed from the main hall and the group onstage came together. Zed rested his huge hand on Meg's shoulder. "Well, let's go round up some naughty gods, shall we?"

"Not you." Tis shook her head when Kera went to protest. "Not just because you're human, although I'm extremely aware of that now."

"I'm fine—"

Meg took Kera's hand in her own. "You're more than fine, gorgeous." She winked, and the tension eased slightly. "This isn't about you being okay or even about you being human. This is about us doing what we do, and it's a private matter. Zed isn't going with us either."

Zed looked surprised but shrugged. "Meg's right. The furies are meant to handle this, and no one else can interfere. It's best the rest of us aren't there."

"I'm going," Dani said. "There could be gods there that decide to fade rather than live without power. I want to make sure they're truly gone. And if something goes wrong and humans are involved, I want to be there to deal with things right away."

Meg threw herself into Dani's arms. "You're so hot."

The others laughed. Zed said, "You'd better get going. Good luck with your search, and let me know if you need anything. Kera and I will take care of things here." He looked at Selene, whose glow had changed from sunlit to moonlit. "You?"

"My mom is here, and we're going shopping. It's a full moon, and she's a little more talkative." She gave Alec a lingering kiss. "Come home to me, hot stuff."

"Always." Alec turned to her sisters. "Ready? I want to get this over with."

Meg tugged Dani toward the exit. "Let's do it."

Dani followed them into the midday sun. She opened a road, and they got into her car. They'd travel where necessary to find the gods they needed to deal with, and they'd do it together. When Meg took her hand as they headed off, she felt renewed and ready to take on whatever the rebel gods had to throw at them.

❖

Meg dropped onto the grass and stared up at the sky. She was more exhausted than she could remember ever being. They'd found several of the secondary gods and given them the option—live powerless among the humans or fade. Although, when Meg thought about it, the wording was wrong. It was polite, like saying "no, thank you" instead of "that looks like dog poop" when someone offered gross food at a party. Fading was slow and sad. What she and her sisters did…that was neither. They held hands, focused their power and decision on the being, and the focus of their attention essentially exploded into atomic dust. Like this last one had.

Cloacina, ancient goddess of the sewers, had been a pre-fader who'd tried to make a run for the real thing when Dis made her offer. She was no longer subject to sewage of any kind. Now she was simply part of the atmosphere. Meg knew her sisters felt the weight of what they were doing. Killing or defrocking gods was no small thing. But Meg felt it on a more practical level. Those gods wouldn't have done the humans any good, and they would have messed things up between the gods as well. There weren't a lot of options, so they'd put to use the few they had. And that was good enough for Meg.

Tis and Alec sat in the grass beside Meg. Alec stretched and leaned back on her wings, while Tis pulled her knees to her chest and rested her cheek on them.

"What are we going to do about the ones we can't find? And the ones who didn't get involved but don't want to come back to Afterlife, like Vishnu?" Meg asked, staring at a cloud that looked a lot like a strangely shaped breast. Every inch of her was exhausted, and she knew her sisters felt the same way. Taking out gods took a lot of energy, and she was just about out.

"As I see it, we wait. As secondary gods, they were either pre-faders to begin with, or they'll fade away once they're out of the limelight. Either way, they won't have the powers they wanted while they're living among humans. And if they surface, we'll deal with them then. Vish and Yama are doing good things, so I say if they want to stay where they are, we wait and see what happens with that too." Alec closed her eyes and tilted her face toward the sun. "That feels good."

Tis didn't move from her curled-up position. "The bigger question is what to do about the primary gods. Horus, Iblis, Osiris, Shiva. They're not as easily dealt with as the secondary gods. With their believers in full swing, we can't just make them go away."

Dani came over and sat beside Meg, who moved to put her head on Dani's lap. "I made sure her dust has truly scattered."

Meg looked up at her and smiled. "You're doing that super glowy thing again."

Dani smiled down at her and moved a stray piece of hair out of her eyes. "Yeah, well, thanks to you, my followers know my face, and the faith is even stronger. Plus, Idona called to say emails are flooding in asking about the Deadlands and what Death is offering as an afterlife." She shook her head, looking slightly bewildered. "Crazy." She looked at Tis and Alec. "What were you talking about?"

"What to do with the naughty primary gods who threw in with Dis." Tis finally uncurled from her position and settled back on her elbows. "Any thoughts?"

"Horus signed the original contract, right?" Dani asked.

Tis nodded. "So did Osiris and Iblis. Shiva wasn't part of the council at that point."

"They knew the consequences. But the thing is, those consequences were for gods working at Afterlife, right? And they took up with Dis after they left Afterlife?"

Meg pinched Dani's leg. She hated the idea of someone getting away with killing a bunch of humans. "So they get out of punishment because of a loophole in the contract?"

Dani swatted Meg's hand away. "I don't know. You can't get rid of them like you have the secondary gods. You can't really let them loose on their own, because they could try something like this again."

"That's a dangerous precedent to set. Find a loophole, and don't worry about the rules." Tis frowned, clearly concerned.

"True." Meg let her instincts rise and tried to put words to the knowledge. "But what if there's a...leash or something? Like, in order to continue to exist, they not only have to come back to Afterlife, but there's some kind of monitor placed on them? Like an ankle bracelet for parolees."

"Gods on parole. Kera will love that." Tis smiled and sat up. "I think you're on to something, Meg. We could have the Fates draw something up to the effect that if the gods on parole misbehave, they'll be forced into public retirement and dropped into the cosmic void with Dis."

Meg punched the air. "Exactly! It can be made clear it's only because they're department heads that they haven't had their asses handed to them already. That way any lesser gods won't be that dumb. And once we send out the memo on the gods we busted down, that will make all of them think twice. Plus, a lot of them really miss the way things used to be. I think they'll be happy to have some order restored."

Alec swatted Meg's face with her wing. "When did you suddenly get so politically savvy? I'd have thought you and Dani were too busy doing the dirty to notice anything beyond the handcuffs."

Meg plucked at one of Alec's feathers, and she jerked her wing back. "Spending time in the various departments has made me see them differently, I guess. They've always just been coworkers and people to party with, but with all the changes, they've really opened up to me. I like seeing how they work and how I can help." The feeling of vulnerability was new, but since she was with her sisters and Dani, she didn't have to hide it.

"I think you've finally found your way, Sis." Tis smiled and got to her feet. "I think we've got a plan to take to Zed. I also think we let him deal with the primary gods directly. If there's a problem, we'll step in. But I want him to put his foot down and be seen for the leader he is, which means the ultimatum has to come from him."

Meg sighed and let Dani pull her to her feet. "I'm all for that. I'll be glad when the gods' egos are in check and humans are settled again."

They piled into Dani's car, and as she pulled onto the road, she said, "You know, Meg, I wonder if you've brought up a way to deal with the aftermath."

"I have?" Meg put her hand on Dani's leg and liked the way it twitched under her fingers.

"It seems to me we're at another crossroads, and we should deal with it quickly. Thanks to Madison Ford's coverage, people are seeing over and over again the fact that the gods fought for their freedom. Selene has been saying since they came out that it's up to people to choose, and the fact that the gods fought one another for that right will do all kinds of good. And the gods really stepped up and fought for their believers, which, I think, takes them into new territory. They've always been there for their believers, but now they've actively put themselves on the line for them. I say we take that momentum and air it far and wide."

Tis squeezed Dani's shoulder from behind. "You're starting to think like Meg."

Dani smiled at her in the rearview mirror. "We should be so lucky."

"I'll talk to Selene about her show. She can bring up the war and the reasoning behind it. Open discussion will help." Alec stretched and yawned as they pulled up to the gate at Afterlife. "I don't know about you guys, but I'm wiped out."

When they'd pulled up outside Meg's house, Tis got out and motioned toward the office. "You guys head home. I'll go let Zed and Kera know we're back and give a full report. Maybe we can actually put all this behind us and move forward."

Meg grabbed Dani's hand and was already heading toward her house by the time Tis stopped speaking. "Come over with Thai food tomorrow and tell us how it went." She could hear Tis and Alec laughing, and she smiled. She wanted more alone time with Dani. For the first time in centuries, she wanted to be with someone more than she wanted distraction, and although it was an unusual feeling, she found she liked it. Especially when she could close the door behind them and have Dani all to herself.

Meg grabbed another handful of popcorn as she watched Selene's show. Angie Hicks had her arm in a sling and a bandage on her head, but other than that, she looked like she'd fared pretty well in the war at the Vatican. But she looked worn down and almost resigned. Her role in the fall of the Vatican had a hell of a lot of people calling for her head, but Zed had stepped in and made a personal request that she be released to the custody of Afterlife. As head of Humanity First, she could make amends by helping people instead of becoming a martyr. The Vatican had reluctantly agreed, and Meg wondered if she might have preferred prison. Beside Angie, looking like the shiny god he was, sat Zed, who was there to speak on behalf of Afterlife. Meg felt unreasonably proud of her department head and friend.

"It's hard to argue that the gods don't care, or that they aren't

doing any good, given the news footage and interviews we've seen."
Angie spoke quietly, looking at the floor rather than at Selene. "I still
say, however, that the war was an indication that the gods are as prone
to ego and mistakes as humans are."

Selene looked at Zed, clearly expecting him to answer. Meg
leaned forward and pushed another handful of popcorn into her mouth.
Zed wasn't always good at public speaking. He was fine one-on-one,
but in the spotlight, he tended to bumble and look distinctly ungodlike.

"To suggest gods don't have egos would be ludicrous. Of course
we do. You would too, if thousands upon thousands of people thought
you were the best thing since chocolate milk."

Angie looked surprised at his admission, and Selene's eyebrows
went up.

"But that doesn't mean we aren't good at our jobs. We tell humans
to love each other and that we love them. There's absolute truth to those
things, and we stand by them. And when misled gods tried to mess
with those rules, we took care of things. We took care of humans. All
of them, whether they were our own believers or not, whether the gods
fighting us were involved in our territories or not. Because we believe
in humanity, no matter who humanity chooses to believe in."

Selene nodded thoughtfully and turned to Angie. "Big change
always requires an adjustment period. And the gods coming out was
a fairly massive change, which seems to have required an equally
massive adjustment period."

"That adjustment period cost a lot of people their lives." Angie
finally looked up, and Meg saw a bit of her spark return.

"It did. And it never should have come to that. We tried to save
everyone we could. Hopefully, now that people have seen the gods who
will fight for them, and know that even though there were some gods
who couldn't join us in Rome, they were with their people when it
counted, people will see that although we can't answer every prayer,
although there are things humans can't know until they've left this life,
we're here for them."

Selene turned to the camera. "We're going to take a break. Please
join us after the commercial to hear how Humanity First and GRADE
will be discussing a way forward, together."

Dani came in just as the commercial started and handed Meg her banana split. Meg scooted back against her pillows and moaned at the perfect amount of chocolate sauce over the mint ice cream.

"Did I miss anything?" Dani asked as she curled up next to Meg with her own ice cream. She was wearing the ridiculous Hawaiian shirt Meg had bought her as a joke, but it turned out color suited her.

"I think Angie is still pissed off, but she knows it's a losing battle now. And Zed said gods have egos. Like that's news?" Meg bit into a cherry and turned so Dani could kiss it from her mouth.

"I wonder if a merger type thing will work?"

"If anyone can figure out something this complicated, it's Kera. And Tis. They'll figure it out." Meg slurped down some whipped cream and licked it from her lips. "How are the renovations in the Deadlands going?"

Dani set her ice cream aside and stretched out on the bed. "Really well. The new soul area is ready to go, and we've got quite a few people living there already. Idona has set up a new area completely separate from the rest of the Deadlands for the souls that are heavy, souls that would usually go to a hell of some sort, but because they don't believe in something specific, they're with me. I've asked for a department manager from each section to help oversee that area, and we've already set up a rotating schedule of hell workers to manage the area." She licked the chocolate from Meg's lips when she leaned over her. "And how is the marketing strategy working, media guru?"

"I'm amazing, do you know that? I've got each of the gods scheduled to go on Selene's show to talk about what improvements they've made to their sections. That includes you, by the way."

Dani shook her head. "And?"

"And every department head has finished their primary texts. They're being rolled out next week, all over the globe. I've helped with the social marketing campaigns, and the printed materials will still go to the physical worshipping sites. We're also going to use libraries and coffee shops for open discussion nights, so people can pick up things on different religions without having to go to that belief system's offices." Meg was quite proud of the work she'd done, and she knew there was clarity and simplicity that most of the religions had never had before.

"You are truly amazing." Dani pulled her close and gave her a lingering kiss.

"Selene just said every change requires an adjustment period. I think the biggest cry for stability is over. Now we just have to move forward."

Dani nodded. "Deaths from wars and general crime are way down. There are still some here and there, but for the most part, the world is becoming a better place. Selene was right. The gods being out among the people will be a good thing, even if it hit some pretty major bumps along the way."

Meg sighed happily and lay next to Dani. The world had gone crazy for a while there, and they'd hardly had time to breathe. But in the aftermath, the world looked brighter, like someone had taken a power washer to it and scraped away all the grime. Death, beautiful, sweet, kind Death, lay beside her; she loved her for who she was, all of who she was, and Meg would never take that for granted. Gods weren't fading, humans weren't scared or dangerously confused anymore, and both her sisters were madly in love with women who loved them back.

"Hey, what did you decide about Kera's request?" Meg asked and started removing Dani's shirt.

"I told her yes. Idona and I talked about it, and we'll treat Kera like any other non-believer. The difference is that she'll work in the Afterlife office instead of in the Deadlands, and she won't have to eat or sleep anymore."

Meg laughed. "She'll love that." She slid Dani's shirt off and threw it aside. "Now I want some of what I love." She traced a line up Dani's stomach with her tongue and shivered when Dani moaned.

They made love well into the night, and by morning, Meg lay curled in Dani's arms. As she fell asleep, she took a moment to think about the new world they were getting to play in.

She'd love every minute of it, and with Dani at her side, she wondered if forever would be long enough.

About the Author

Brey Willows (http://www.breywillows.com) is a longtime editor and writer. When she's not running a social enterprise working with marginalized communities on writing projects, she's editing other people's writing or doing her own. She lives in the middle of England with her partner and fellow author and spends entirely too much time exploring castles and ancient ruins while bemoaning the rain.

Books Available From Bold Strokes Books

A Country Girl's Heart by Dena Blake. When Kat Jackson gets a second chance at love, following her heart will prove the hardest decision of all. (978-1-63555-134-1)

Dangerous Waters by Radclyffe. Life, death, and war on the home front. Two women join forces against a powerful opponent, nature itself. (978-1-63555-233-1)

Fury's Death by Brey Willows. When all we hold sacred fails, who will be there to save us? (978-1-63555-063-4)

It's Not a Date by Heather Blackmore. Kade's desire to keep things with Jen on a professional level is in Jen's best interest. Yet what's in Kade's best interest...is Jen. (978-1-63555-149-5)

Killer Winter by Kay Bigelow. Just when she thought things could get no worse, homicide Lieutenant Leah Samuels learns the woman she loves has betrayed her in devastating ways. (978-1-63555-177-8)

Score by MJ Williamz. Will an addiction to pain pills destroy Ronda's chance with the woman she loves, or will she come out on top and score a happily ever after? (978-1-62639-807-8)

Spring's Wake by Aurora Rey. When wanderer Willa Lange falls for Provincetown B&B owner Nora Calhoun, will past hurts and a fifteen-year age gap keep them from finding love? (978-1-63555-035-1)

The Northwoods by Jane Hoppen. When Evelyn Bauer, disguised as her dead husband, George, travels to a Northwoods logging camp to work, she and the camp cook Sarah Bell forge a friendship fraught with both tenderness and turmoil. (978-1-63555-143-3)

Truth or Dare by C. Spencer. For a group of six lesbian friends, life changes course after one long snow-filled weekend. (978-1-63555-148-8)

A Heart to Call Home by Jeannie Levig. When Jessie Weldon returns to her hometown after thirty years, can she and her childhood crush Dakota Scott heal the tragic past that links them? (978-1-63555-059-7)

Children of the Healer by Barbara Ann Wright. Life becomes desperate for ex-soldier Cordelia Ross when the indigenous aliens of her planet are drawn into a civil war and old enemies linger in the shadows. Book Three of the Godfall Series. (978-1-63555-031-3)

Hearts Like Hers by Melissa Brayden. Coffee shop owner Autumn Primm is ready to cut loose and live a little, but is the baggage that comes with out-of-towner Kate Carpenter too heavy for anything long term? (978-1-63555-014-6)

Love at Cooper's Creek by Missouri Vaun. Shaw Daily flees corporate life to find solace in the rural Blue Ridge Mountains, but escapism eludes her when her attentions are captured by small town beauty Kate Elkins. (978-1-62639-960-0)

Twice in a Lifetime by PJ Trebelhorn. Detective Callie Burke can't deny the growing attraction to her late friend's widow, Taylor Fletcher, who also happens to own the bar where Callie's sister works. (978-1-63555-033-7)

Undiscovered Affinity by Jane Hardee. Will a no-strings-attached affair be enough to break Olivia's control and convince Cardic that love does exist? (978-1-63555-061-0)

Between Sand and Stardust by Tina Michele. Are the lifelong bonds of love strong enough to conquer time, distance, and heartache when Haven Thorne and Willa Bennette are given another chance at forever? (978-1-62639-940-2)

Charming the Vicar by Jenny Frame. When magician and atheist Finn Kane seeks refuge in an English village after a spiritual crisis, can local vicar Bridget Claremont restore her faith in life and love? (978-1-63555-029-0)

Data Capture by Jesse J. Thoma. Lola Walker is undercover on the hunt for cybercriminals while trying not to notice the woman who might be perfectly wrong for her for all the right reasons. (978-1-62639-985-3)

Epicurean Delights by Renee Roman. Ariana Marks had no idea a leisure swim would lead to being rescued, in more ways than one, by the charismatic Hudson Frost. (978-1-63555-100-6)

Heart of the Devil by Ali Vali. We know most of Cain and Emma Casey's story, but Heart of the Devil will take you back to where it began one fateful night with a tray loaded with beer. (978-1-63555-045-0)

Known Threat by Kara A. McLeod. When Special Agent Ryan O'Connor reluctantly questions who protects the Secret Service, she learns courage truly is found in unlikely places. Agent O'Connor Series #3 (978-1-63555-132-7)

Seer and the Shield by D. Jackson Leigh. Time is running out for the Dragon Horse Army while two unlikely heroines struggle to put aside their attraction and find a way to stop a deadly cult. Dragon Horse War, Book 3 (978-1-63555-170-9)

The Universe Between Us by Jane C. Esther. Ana Mitchell must make the hardest choice of her life: the promise of new love Jolie Dann on Earth, or a humanity-saving mission to colonize Mars. (978-1-63555-106-8)

Touch by Kris Bryant. Can one touch heal a heart? (978-1-63555-084-9)

A More Perfect Union by Carsen Taite. Major Zoey Granger and DC fixer Rook Daniels risk their reputations for a chance at true love while dealing with a scandal that threatens to rock the military. (978-1-62639-754-5)

Arrival by Gun Brooke. The spaceship *Pathfinder* reaches its passengers' new homeworld where danger lurks in the shadows while Pamas Seclan disembarks and finds unexpected love in young science genius Darmiya Do Voy. (978-1-62639-859-7)

Captain's Choice by VK Powell. Architect Kerstin Anthony's life is going to plan until Bennett Carlyle, the first girl she ever kissed, is assigned to her latest and most important project, a police district substation. (978-1-62639-997-6)

Falling Into Her by Erin Zak. Pam Phillips, widow at the age of forty, meets Kathryn Hawthorne, local Chicago celebrity, and it changes her life forever—in ways she hadn't even considered possible. (978-1-63555-092-4)

Hookin' Up by MJ Williamz. Will Leah get what she needs from casual hookups or will she see the love she desires right in front of her? (978-1-63555-051-1)

King of Thieves by Shea Godfrey. When art thief Casey Marinos meets bounty hunter Finnegan Starkweather, the crimes of the past just might set the stage for a payoff worth more than she ever dreamed possible. (978-1-63555-007-8)

Lucy's Chance by Jackie D. As a serial killer haunts the streets, Lucy tries to stitch up old wounds with her first love in the wake of a small town's rapid descent into chaos. (978-1-63555-027-6)

Right Here, Right Now by Georgia Beers. When Alicia Wright moves into the office next door to Lacey Chamberlain's accounting firm, Lacey is about to find out that sometimes the last person you want is exactly the person you need. (978-1-63555-154-9)

Strictly Need to Know by MB Austin. Covert operator Maji Rios will do whatever she must to complete her mission, but saving a gorgeous stranger from Russian mobsters was not in her plans. (978-1-63555-114-3)

Tailor-Made by Yolanda Wallace. Tailor Grace Henderson doesn't date clients, but when she meets gender-bending model Dakota Lane, she's tempted to throw all the rules out the window. (978-1-63555-081-8)

Time Will Tell by M. Ullrich. With the ability to time travel, Eva Caldwell will have to decide between having it all and erasing it all. (978-1-63555-088-7)

Change in Time by Robyn Nyx. Working in the past is hell on your future. The Extractor series: Book Two. (978-1-62639-880-1)

Love After Hours by Radclyffe. When Gina Antonelli agrees to renovate Carrie Longmire's new house, she doesn't welcome Carrie's overtures at friendship or her own unexpected attraction. A Rivers Community Novel. (978-1-63555-090-0)

Nantucket Rose by CF Frizzell. Maggie Jordan can't wait to convert a historic Nantucket home into a B&B, but doesn't expect to fall for mariner Ellis Chilton, who has more claim to the house than Maggie realizes. (978-1-63555-056-6)

Picture Perfect by Lisa Moreau. Falling in love wasn't supposed to be part of the stakes for Olive and Gabby, rival photographers in the competition of a lifetime. (978-1-62639-975-4)

Set the Stage by Karis Walsh. Actress Emilie Danvers takes the stage again in Ashland, Oregon, little realizing that landscaper Arden Philips is about to offer her a very personal romantic lead role. (978-1-63555-087-0)

Strike a Match by Fiona Riley. When their attempts at matchmaking fizzle out, firefighter Sasha and reluctant millionairess Abby find themselves turning to each other to strike a perfect match. (978-1-62639-999-0)

The Price of Cash by Ashley Bartlett. Cash Braddock is doing her best to keep her business afloat, stay out of jail, and avoid Detective Kallen. It's not working. (978-1-62639-708-8)

Captured Soul by Laydin Michaels. Can Kadence Munroe save the woman she loves from a twisted killer, or will she lose her to a collector of souls? (978-1-62639-915-0)

Under Her Wing by Ronica Black. At Angel's Wings Rescue, dogs are usually the ones saved, but when quiet Kassandra Haden meets outspoken owner Jayden Beaumont, the two stubborn women just might end up saving each other. (978-1-63555-077-1)